Anita Shreve is the author of many acclaimed novels, including *Eden Close*, *The Weight of Water*, *The Last Time They Met*, *Light on Snow* and *Body Surfing*. She lives in Massachusetts.

'Anita Shreve is back on cracking form with *Testimony*. What is so fresh and resonant about this novel is the clever way in which the author unpacks the events with a series of separate narratives. Each voice contributes an additional layer of impasto to the picture; each layer, in turn, has to be mined carefully for its information and character and situation. Poised and absolutely steady-handed, this is a gripping piece of deconstruction'

Elizabeth Buchan, *Sunday Times*

'Anita Shreve is a phenomenon. As ever – and even though the novel is written from different points of view – the power of Shreve's writing lies in it relentless passivity. The prose is undemonstrative, yet insidiously accomplished . . . It is so unforgiving of a panoply of human frailty as to be misanthropic' Charlie Hill, *New Statesman*

'Her experience as a storyteller shows in the writing, which is deft, the multiples voices authentic and subtly characterized . . . A story of ordinary people and of the ripples that spread out from the decisions they make. It touches on questions of privilege, class, community, and where we lay the blame when things fall apart'

Kate Salter, *TLS*

'*Testimony* is a page-turner, its language cluttered and crisp'

Daily Telegraph

'A narrative structure and a sense of place and character as delicate as a spider's web . . . At every level, our sympathies are engaged or repelled by qualities of voice – querulous, self-serving, coolly appraising, sleazy, hurt, confused, and oddly rhapsodic'

Brian Morton, *Sunday Herald*

'One of her best. With her acute eye for behaviour and an exquisite ear for dialogue, Shreve explores the actions and reactions that will destroy a community through their all-too-human desires'

Daily Express

'If Zoë Heller hadn't already used the title *Notes on a Scandal*, it would have suited this novel . . . Shreve's prose is spare and powerful, and she excels in showing how two people might perceive and interpret the same event in a contrasting way. [An] elegant and addictive novel about the way our lives can be shaped forever'

Scotland on Sunday

'Shreve has delivered a novel that not only gets under the skin of its characters, but also under the reader's skin' *Sunday Business Post*

'As each account of those involved unfolds, she expertly draws us into this heartbreaking tale' *In Style*

'Told with pace and intensity, the novel shows how one mistake can cause a ripple effect' *Eve*

'The brilliant Anita Shreve returns with another emotionally charged story that will keep you hooked until the final page' *Bella*

Testimony

Anita Shreve

ABACUS

First published in Great Britain in 2008 by Little, Brown
This paperback edition published in 2009 by Abacus

First published in the United States of America in 2008 by
Little, Brown and Company

A CIP catalogue record for this book
is available from the British Library.

ISBN 978-0-349-11902-1

Printed and bound in Great Britain by
Clays Ltd, St Ives plc

Papers used by Abacus are natural, renewable and recyclable
products sourced from well-managed forests and certified
in accordance with the rules of the Forest Stewardship Council.

Mixed Sources
Product group from well-managed
forests and other controlled sources
www.fsc.org Cert no. SGS-COC-004081
© 1996 Forest Stewardship Council
FSC

Abacus
An imprint of
Little, Brown Book Group
100 Victoria Embankment
London EC4Y 0DY

An Hachette UK Company
www.hachette.co.uk

www.littlebrown.co.uk

for Michael Pietsch

Testimony

Mike

It was a small cassette, not much bigger than the palm of his hand, and when Mike thought about the terrible license and risk exhibited on the tape, as well as its resultant destructive power, it was as though the two-by-three plastic package had been radio-active. Which it may as well have been, since it had produced something very like radiation sickness throughout the school, reducing the value of an Avery education, destroying at least two marriages that he knew of, ruining the futures of three students, and, most horrifying of all, resulting in a death. After Kasia brought Mike the tape in a white letter envelope (as if he might be going to mail it to someone!), Mike walked home with it and watched it on his television—an enormously complicated and frustrating task since he first had to find his own movie camera that used similar tapes and figure out how to connect its various cables to the television so that the tape could play through the camera. Sometimes Mike wished he had just slipped the offensive tape into a pot of boiling water, or sent it out with the trash in a white plastic drawstring bag, or spooled it out with a pencil and wadded it into a big mess. Although he doubted he could have controlled the potential scandal, he might have been able to choreograph it differently, possibly limiting some of the damage.

3

Much appeared to have happened before the camera in the unseen hand focused on the quartet. One saw the girl (always *the girl* in Mike's eyes) turning (twirling, it seemed to be) away from a tall, slender boy who still had his jeans on, and toward a somewhat shorter, more solidly built naked young man, who caught the young girl and bent to suck on her right nipple. At that point in the tape, no faces were visible, doubtless a deliberate edit on the part of the person behind the camera. Also, at that moment in time, Mike, who was then headmaster of Avery Academy, did not recognize the setting as a dorm room, though he would soon do so. The shorter boy then turned her to face the first boy, who by then was unbuckling his belt, his jeans sliding off in one go, as if they were cartoon pants, too big for the boy's slender hips. The camera panned jerkily, instantly causing in Mike the beginnings of motion sickness, to a narrow dorm bed on which a third boy, entirely naked and appearing to be slightly older than the other two boys, lay stroking himself. And Mike remembered, among other images he wished he could excise from his brain, the truly impressive length of the young man's empurpled penis and the concentrated tautness of the muscles of the boy's chest and arms. The camera slid back to the center of the room, producing a second dip and rise in Mike's stomach, to the two standing boys and the now kneeling girl.

It was at this point in the tape that Mike realized there was sound attached, for he heard a kind of exaggerated groaning from the side of the room where the bed was, as well as hard-pounding music (though the latter seemed to be, for some reason, muted). Meanwhile, the tall boy with the slender shoulders was holding the blond head of the girl to his crotch. She appeared to know what to do — even to have, at some point prior to the

4

event, *practiced* what to do — for Mike couldn't help but notice a certain expertise, a way of drawing the standing boy's engorged penis toward her so that it seemed she might painfully stretch it before gently swooping forward and seeming to swallow it whole. The slender boy came with an explosive adolescent sound, as if taken by surprise. The cameraman or -woman (it was difficult to picture a girl behind the camera) swung the lens up to capture the boy's face, which, with a start, Mike Bordwin recognized. He had assumed, when Kasia had solemnly handed him the tape just an hour earlier, saying to him in an extremely sober tone, *I think you should take a look at this,* that the tape was simply confiscated pornography (not that the tape *wasn't* pornographic) — something a dorm parent might have dealt with. The idea that there would be recognizable people attached to the action — students he had seen in hallways, in the cafeteria, and on the basketball court — did not really occur to him until he saw the face of the boy, contorted as it was in a paroxysm of pleasure and therefore somewhat grotesque to the outside observer. He thought, *Rob,* and *It can't be.* The Rob he had known was a polite, hardworking student who also happened to be an outstanding forward on the basketball team. And was that how Mike had seen his students, he wondered then, even as he was observing the moment of coming on Rob's face, as *excellent student* or *promising actor* or *pretentious brownnoser* or *good arm?* Because it was perfectly apparent that such descriptive tags were entirely inadequate. The Rob whom Mike had known seemed to be but an embryo of the full-fledged sexual being on the tape. There was a kind of seizure then in Mike's chest as he suddenly, from different parts of his brain, received alarming and unwanted bits of information, not unlike an air traffic controller watching several blips on his radar

5

screen inexplicably about to collide. The girl hardly seemed to come up for air when she turned to the other standing boy, whose face had not been visible during the first pan but which now clearly was, jolting the headmaster and causing him to cry out the name of the boy—*Silas*—and to emit a groan of his own, entirely unsexual. Silas and the girl lay down on the floor with Silas on top and went at it in an old-fashioned though frenetic way, the girl's body thudding lightly onto what was clearly now a dormitory floor, dotted with a half-dozen beer cans. Mike closed his eyes, not wanting to watch this particular boy have his own paroxysmal seizure. When he opened them again, the camera was on the face of the girl, who was either experiencing the heights of pleasure or giving an excellent imitation of same. It was then that he saw the girl was very young—very, *very* young: the number *fourteen* floated through his brain—though he didn't at that time know her name. It was not unusual for the headmaster not to know all of the students by name, particularly the underclassmen who hadn't yet distinguished themselves, which Mike was pretty certain she had not. He suddenly wondered how many other persons—faculty or students—had watched this performance on the tape, this particular worry marking perhaps the worst moment of his life to date (though far worse was yet to come).

Groping for the camera, he found and pressed the *pause* button. He was on his knees in his empty house, his breath tight, causing him to put his hand to his chest as if an angina attack might be coming. That any number of people might already have seen the tape was creating in Mike what felt like a temporary heart stoppage but what was really a temporary brain stoppage, his neurons refusing to fire, or whatever they did — *connect* — because he couldn't process another thought, the last having been too awful to contemplate, with its attendant images segueing into the words *police* and *rape* and *alcohol* and *press,* none of which any headmaster wanted in any sequence in any sentence. It seemed important then to focus on the girl to determine how willing a participant she had been in this … this *thing* that he was witnessing. Since he didn't have the heart to rewind and review what had gone before, he poked *play,* wishing he could slow down the action, not so that he could enjoy it more — Lord, no — but so that his whole being could catch up to what was inevitably going to be a difficult future. To ease into it, so to speak.

The tape started again with what felt like a snap, once more zooming in on the girl's face. Mike saw, to his dismay, that no matter how experienced she had seemed earlier (and also seemed now, in her fairly convincing expression of ecstasy), she was, in fact, as he had suspected, very young indeed. A freshman, there could be no doubt about it. He thought he could almost retrieve the face and body in a uniform — field hockey? soccer? JV? thirds? — and he was certain that she was a boarder, not a day student like Silas, who seemed to have collapsed upon the girl, who was smiling now, actually smiling. *Is this good or bad?* Mike wondered.

There seemed to be a great deal of chaos. Perhaps the unseen hand had lowered the camera for a moment. Mike narrowed his eyes to keep the nausea at bay while the lens momentarily came to rest on the perfectly innocent corner of a desk leg, with a boy's dirty white sneaker, its laces untied, leaning against it. Mike felt an ache in his throat at the sheer innocence of that image, since it seemed to represent, at that moment, a universe

7

of loss. In the background, there were sounds—none of them very articulate. Mike was fairly certain he heard *Hey* and *Go for it* and *Your turn* (and not necessarily in that order), and then the lens, with a sudden, wild swoop, settled upon the body of the third boy. (*Boy,* Mike thought, *isn't at all accurate in this case.* There was a subtle moment in time when boys turned into men, and it had nothing to do with age or facial hair or voice timbre. It had to do, he had decided—and he had seen this happen hundreds of times over the course of nearly twenty years in a secondary-school setting—with musculature, the set of the jaw, the way the male held himself.) The young man was quite literally holding himself, masturbating over the supine body of the (Mike had to admit) heartbreakingly lovely girl, who appeared to be urging the young man on with rhythmic movements and even various contortions, doubtless learned from watching movies. The unseen person behind the camera had moved his or her vantage point, and one saw now, saw all too clearly in fact, the utter determination on the face of the young man, who was, Mike instantly recognized, a PG (postgraduate) brought to the school to take the basketball team to the play-offs. It was then that Mike quickly calculated and arrived at the number *nineteen* just before the PG, whom the other students called J. Dot (as in *J.Robles@Avery.edu*), came all over the chest and neck and chin of the girl who was *at least* four years younger, causing Mike to reach forward and push *stop,* the way he wished he could push a *stop* button on the future long enough to figure out what to do with this very unwanted piece of celluloid now poised to explode inside his camera.

He sat back against the sofa in the TV room. Mike had tried, in the early years of their residence in the impressive Georgian,

8

to refer to the room as a *library*, as befitted his position in life, but in fact Meg and he had spent more time there watching television and DVDs than they had reading, and so they had started calling it what it really was. Mike was panting slightly, his mouth dry. That there was probably more to the tape seemed unthinkable. (And, after all, hadn't all three boys come within minutes of one another? But then again, these were teenage boys.) He doubted that he could watch any more. He was both glad and sorry that Meg was not in the house, glad because he needed to think about what to do, and sorry because it was just conceivable she might have comforted him, though probably not. Would Meg have been as shocked as he? Was she closer to the kids? Did she understand them better?

Mike immediately wondered when the event had taken place and in what dorm. It seemed likely that the incident had followed a drinking binge, to judge from the number of beer cans on the floor. Perhaps there was a clue on a desk or a date marked on a calendar. It almost certainly had to have been on a Saturday night, because students had to be present for study hall in their dorms at eight p.m. weekday evenings as well as on the Friday night before a Class Saturday. There had been a school dance the previous weekend. Geoff Coggeshall, the dean of students, had mentioned that there had been the usual number of kids who had been caught drinking or who were suspected of it. The abuse of alcohol was impossible to stop and was at the top of the list of worries for nearly every headmaster or principal of every secondary school in the country. Though there had been many assemblies and seminars on the subject, it was Mike's opinion that the problem was more severe than it had been in previous years. He sometimes wondered if all the focus on alcoholism, meant to promote awareness of the dangers of drinking, had not, in fact, subtly brought it to the fore in a way it had not been so blatantly *important* before. Every generation of students had done its share of binge drinking, but it was pretty clear, from all the data he had seen, that the drinking was starting at an earlier age and was both more habitual and more intense than it had been just a decade earlier.

He lay his head back against the sofa and closed his eyes. The house was empty and quiet. He could hear the wind skidding against the windows and, from the kitchen, the sound of ice cubes tumbling in the Viking, recently installed. Tasks now needed to be accomplished, students queried, the Disciplinary Committee convened, and all of this conducted beneath the radar of the press, which would, if they got wind of the story, revel in a private-school scandal. In this, Mike thought that private schools had been unfairly singled out. He doubted that such a tape would have been of any interest to the press had it surfaced at the local regional high school, for example. The tape might have circulated underground, students might have been expelled, and meetings might have been held, yet it was likely that the incident would have been greeted with indifference not only by the local newspaper, the *Avery Crier* (its editor, Walter Myers, could be talked down from just about any story that might cause embarrassment to local kids and parents), but also by the regional and national press. Mike thought the national media would scoff at the idea that sex and alcohol, even sex and alcohol involving a fourteen-year-old girl in a public-high-school setting, was news of any sort; *whereas* if the same set of facts, but in a private-school setting, were to pass across the computer screen of a reporter at the *Rutland Herald* or the *Boston Globe*, it was entirely possible that the reporter would be dispatched to Avery to find out *what was going on*. In such a story, there was juice, there was heat, there was blood. There was also, if this tape had been copied in any way, *footage*. Was it because private schools were held to higher standards, according to which such an incident ought to be nearly unthinkable? Or was it because everyone loved to see the elite (even if that elite involved a local farmer's son on scholarship) brought down and ridiculed? A little of both, Mike guessed, with emphasis on the latter.

More troubling, however, was the thought of police involvement. Though Mike felt nothing but revulsion when he thought of the Silas and Rob he'd just seen on the tape (boys whom he had previously much respected and even, in Silas's case, been quite fond of), the idea of them being led away from the administration building in handcuffs was appalling. (Did police routinely handcuff boys suspected of sexual assault, which was what this particular crime, in the state of Vermont, was deemed?) *Police* in this case meant either Gary Quinney or Bernie Herrmann, neither of whom would find any satisfaction in the arrest; Gary was, after all, Silas's uncle. Would the boys then appear some months later in the dowager courthouse across the street from the gates of Avery, the building itself smug in its self-righteousness? Mike's job would be at risk, and any number of teachers who were supposed to be supervising either the dance or the dorm that evening might be fired, for one could not expect the trustees to view the incident and its attendant legal fuss lightly. Would the boys then go to jail, to the Vermont State Prison at Windsor, where almost certainly they would be raped in turn?

Mike reined in his thoughts. He was getting carried away. No, he had to get a grip and act quickly. Three boys were in trouble, and a girl...well, presumably, if it did turn out to be a case of sexual assault, the trouble had already occurred to the girl, though the fallout for her might be endless.

Mike got up off the floor and sat on the sofa while he loosened his tie and unbuttoned the top button of his shirt, as if increasing blood flow to the brain might help solve his problem. And it was then that the word *containment* entered his mind. And with that word, moral, ethical, and political choices were made, though Mike would realize the implications of these only later, when it occurred to him that he might have chosen at that moment another word, such as *revelation,* say, or *help.*

Ellen

You wait for the call in the night. You've waited for years. You've imagined the voice at the other end, officious and male, always male. You hear the words, but you can't form the sentences. It's bad luck to form the sentences, so you skip to the moment when you're standing by the phone and you've already heard the news and you wonder: *How will I behave?*

Will you scream? It seems unlikely. You are not a screamer. You can't remember the last time you screamed out loud. Will you collapse then, knees buckling, holding on to the wall as you go down? Or will you, as you suspect, simply freeze, the paralysis immediate and absolute, likely to last for hours, because to move is to have to make a life after the phone call, and you can't possibly imagine how you will do that.

But the call doesn't come in the middle of the night—it comes at ten thirty on a Wednesday morning. You're rushing out the door because you're headed to the dermatologist's for a routine appointment. You've taken a personal day off from work so that you can fit all of your doctors' appointments into one day. You have already been to the dentist, and after this next visit, you will head to the gynecologist. It takes thirty-five minutes to get to the dermatologist's office, the appointment is at eleven, and Dr. Carmichael is remarkably punctual. Your son is a million miles away from your thoughts just then, safely tucked away in a school in Vermont, cosseted by people for whom you have come to have enormous respect, with whom you have happily entrusted him. You have your keys in your hand, your coat is on, it's freezing outside, it has been for weeks, and the counter is a mess, but that's all right because you'll have time to put away the junk mail and the cereal bowl and the carton of orange juice when you get home, and so you think that maybe you should just let this one go, let the machine take it. But then you wonder, *What if it's Dr. Carmichael's office, and she's canceling, and I'll have driven all that way for nothing?* And so you pick up the phone.

At first when you hear the voice (yes, male; yes, officious), you think to yourself that you've gotten off lightly, that this was your phone call and your child didn't die on a highway, and perhaps your voice is a bit too ... *relieved.* But then there is an awkward pause at the other end of the line, after which you actually hear all the words that don't belong in your universe, words from which you have gone to great lengths to isolate yourself: "Your son has been involved in a major rule violation of a sexual nature." You say, "I don't ..." and "It's not possible ..." and "I don't understand."

The voice at the other end is patient, has perhaps been anticipating your confusion, almost certainly has anticipated your distress. The voice repeats the unwanted bulletin, and you sit, hard, on a bench just beneath the wall phone, a bench designed for this purpose, for talking on the phone, though surely no one ever had this particular conversation in mind. You want to ask, *Are you sure?* and *Isn't there some mistake?* and *Are you certain?*, but you know already it is useless to ask such questions because no one in his right mind would deliver this news to the wrong mother. In fact, you realize that you are probably the last to know, that others are better informed, that conversations have already been had and digested, that conclusions have been drawn. You could ask for details, but you understand that the story might be too...shameful...to be discussed over the telephone. It is then that it becomes very clear to you that the only purpose for the phone call, besides informing you of the "incident," is to get you into a car driving north and west as soon as possible.

For a few minutes, you sit on the bench, your keys in your hand, the paralysis having settled in. You stare at the kitchen cabinets, and you think, *Rob*. A series of pictures emerges one by one. An upturned face, the light glancing off his fat baby cheeks, two teeth visible above a glistening pink lip. A wet, naked toddler caught up in a football hold, your son fresh from the bath and giggling. A fragile face, surrounded by the fake fur of his snow-suit hood, standing next to a melting snow fort. Your love for your son feels unbearable. And then you know why these inno-cent images have come to you at this moment, for innocence is what is lost now. Now that you have gotten the phone call.

You wonder if you should call Arthur at work, but then you immediately reject that idea because you know it will take him almost an hour to get home, and you can't wait that long. The trip to the school will take nearly four hours, which is a kind of living hell all by itself. You also know that if you call Arthur, he might call Tommy, your lawyer, and you understand instinc-tively that that is the wrong thing to do now. You have to see your son alone first.

You stand up. What do you need? The answer is, very lit-tle. Just your coat and your purse, both of which you already have. There is nothing preventing you from getting into your car except a quick trip to the bathroom, during which you notice that your hands are shaking.

By the time you get to western Vermont, where will Rob be? Will he have been kept waiting in the headmaster's office all that time? Will he be in his room, under some kind of house arrest? Will the police have been brought into the matter? These are all questions you might have asked on the phone, had you had your wits about you, which you did not and still don't.

You get into your car and back out of your driveway and make the turn onto the street, and immediately a new set of pictures darts in front of you like small boys on bicycles. Rob in a helmet on a skateboard, his sleeves comically chopped short. A face, barely visible amid a nest of stuffed animals on the floor. A boy with a bad haircut holding up his Cub Scout handbook, his yellow neckerchief crooked, his smile achingly proud. Under normal circumstances, you crave these pictures, because you can't remember everything, no mother can remember absolutely everything, and sometimes you worry that if it weren't for the photo albums, you'd have no images at all. And how long before you won't even be sure in what year a photograph was taken? But now? Now, the pictures are confusing you, because you just need to think.

You remember that you have forgotten to call the dermatologist. You wonder briefly if she will charge you for the missed appointment. Your cell phone is in your purse, you could make the call now, but the thought of fishing out the phone, finding the number, all the while trying to drive, seems just too hard to do. And what exactly would you use for an excuse? *My son is in the worst trouble of his life?*

You drive northwest. You have an image of driving not to visit your son but simply to be driving away. To drive and then to stop. A motel. Another city. Anonymity. Freedom. It is a familiar fantasy, one that you have had since you were seventeen. You have never indulged it, never once gotten into a car and driven just to see where the road would take you, stopping when you felt like stopping, no destination, no time constraints. There have been moments in your life when such a thing might have been arranged. And yet you have never done it.

As you drive, you think about how you have only thirty dollars in your wallet, which means that you will have to stop at an ATM. You wonder how far apart the ATMs are in western Vermont. You wonder if your son is crying, if he has cried at any point during the incident. You think about how clean you are, about how you have scrubbed for your appointment with the dermatologist. You think about the little mole that has just popped out on your abdomen, the one you now won't be able to ask her about, and just your luck, it will turn out to be malignant. Your right knee aches, and you try to move it slightly, even though you still have to press the gas pedal. You think you might have to find a room for the night, that the meeting with the headmaster might take some time and there will be no thought of heading back. And then you wonder if your son will be staying the night with you, if he has already been expelled from the school. The word explodes in your brain — *expel, expelled, expulsion* — and something harsh rips through your chest.

If Rob has been expelled, someone will have to call Brown. You remember the day, early in the Christmas break, when the fat package arrived in the mail. You called to Rob, who was upstairs in his room. You handed him the envelope on the stairway, and he buckled at the news. You had never seen him so relieved and proud all at once. You grabbed the camera from the shelf in the kitchen and snapped a picture you knew even then you would treasure for the rest of your life. Rob, his head thrown back, laughing as he held on to the torn envelope.

You exit the highway and move on to Route 30. You realize you are driving too fast. The school was your idea, and Arthur will remind you of this. You had heard that the drinking in the public school was ubiquitous, epidemic, and it frightened you. You remember a dinner party at Julie's house. A conversation. A friend of a friend leaning toward you and saying, "Have you ever considered? For his junior and senior years?" An idea took shape and blossomed. Arthur was wary; Rob, slightly intrigued. You told yourself you wanted to save your son.

You all took a day off and visited the school in western Vermont. The landscape was exhilarating, the school seductive. You imagined yourself there, and you saw how a similar fantasy might begin to take shape inside your son. You stoked the fantasy: a superior education, a better chance of getting into a good college, home on weekends, not so far away, great skiing. Small moments caught your son's attention, and you noted them. A poster announcing the impending visit of a well-known writer. A girl with long, slim legs perched atop a stone wall. A gym with two basketball courts. Dorms that looked like those of a New England college. Arthur was impressed, though he was baffled by your willingness.

You wanted your son out of harm's way, you told him. It was that simple. Even if it meant having to give him up.

Was that all? Or did you see in front of you a series of endless negotiations, a constant need to be watchful, the fear that your son might become a stranger? Did you picture a night when your son would come home drunk and lie about the drinking? When he might make the mistake of thinking he could drink and drive? There was something in your son that you saw, something he may not even have recognized in himself: risk intrigued him, drew him.

Miles merge into hours. You have to use the bathroom, and so you stop at an inn. You are hungry, but you can't take the time to eat now. You walk briskly to the car.

You go up a mountain and down the other side. You think about how you rented a ski house last year and how Rob came on weekends with his friends. You remember where they slept, the meals you ate together. You imagined that even after your son went to college, you and Arthur would still rent the ski house. Rob and his new friends from Brown could come on weekends.

When you see the sign for Avery, anxiety tightens your chest. You make your way through the village — past the general store and the church and the courthouse — and turn in at the gates. You pass the playing fields, empty and sodden this time of year, and then the gym. You remember all the basketball games you have watched. You wonder if you have seen your son play his last game.

When you park your car on the quadrangle, your hands are shaking so badly that you can barely get the car keys into the zippered pocket of your coat. You walk steadily toward the granite building that holds the headmaster's office. Your eye instinctively goes to a window, and you wonder if you will see your son staring out, the small eyes waiting for you the way they used to when you had to leave him at the babysitter's.

You enter a gracious lobby that looks more like the living

room of a house than the administrative center of a school. The headmaster's office is in the far right-hand corner. You approach the receptionist, who knows you already and who says, before you have even opened your mouth, *Your son is in the conference room. He is waiting for you.* She gestures.

You walk across a Persian carpet, resisting the urge to run. You note the wood paneling, the portraits of past headmasters, the lovely windows through which you can see the mountains in the background. There are people in other rooms. There is an unnatural hush.

You arrive at a doorway. A boy is sitting in a chair in a corner. He looks up at you. You don't recognize the boy. It is always this way. He is always older than you have remembered. But this is different.

He is sitting with his elbows on his knees, his head bent. When he glances up at you, he does not immediately stand. There will be no crossing of the room, no brief hug, no smile. His collared polo shirt has come loose from his belt. His face is a slightly uneven landscape of pimples and patchy spots of facial hair. His eyebrows are thicker than you recall. His eyes look tired, and they are pink. You wonder if he has been crying.

You speak to him. You say his name.

Owen

Owen was selling the farm. It stuck in his craw selling the land to the school, so he was waiting. He wanted to sell it to some young couple like he and Anna had been once, but no one wanted the burden. God knew you couldn't make any money at farming anymore.

Once, he and Anna had had forty registered Romney sheep. Premium breeding stock. Scrapie-free, the fleeces were. Anna would send out the fleeces to be spun into yarn, and then she'd do the dyeing herself and sell the skeins at farmer's markets. Soft, prizewinning fleeces, they were.

One lamb each spring would be sacrificed for the table. Always a male. Owen and Anna made most of their money selling the other lambs for breeding. Those and the pigs. Everything had a place and a purpose on the farm, even the dogs.

It was beautiful country.

But the farm, it didn't look the way it used to.

It had been Anna's idea, Silas going to the school. Owen had thought—well, what did it matter now what he had thought then? He had thought the public high school would be just as good, but then they cut the music and the arts programs, and you couldn't even pay for them. There were no teachers to teach them. The public school did at least have sports, but Owen didn't want to think about basketball right now.

The farm had once been beautiful. The Green Mountains on one side, the Adirondacks on the other. Owen didn't know of a more beautiful piece of land anywhere. Silas had once loved the land. Owen's family had owned it for three generations. Anna's family came from up north, by Burlington.

Owen blamed himself. If he had said, when Anna was thinking about the school... But he didn't want to think about that, either.

Someday Owen and Anna would have to leave Avery, but it would hurt him to do so. In Avery, it was still the 1950s, or maybe even earlier. When Owen drove through the village and along any of the roads, he often felt like he'd got stuck in time. Sometimes you saw a satellite dish or a new pickup truck, but they seemed more like visitations from another planet than part of the town. There was Peet's grocery store, the library, the courthouse, the church. There was a gas station connected to Sally's Qwik Stop, where his sister made the best doughnuts in western Vermont. There was no bank, no ATM, no drugstore. For that, you drove across the state line into New York, but only when you absolutely had to.

Sometimes tourists would come through and check out the maple products and the Carhartt overalls and the woven place mats. But what they usually came for was a copy of the local real estate paper. They'd see a ten-room farmhouse on twenty acres for the price of the cramped one-bedroom they had in Manhattan, and an idea would get hold of them, usually only for as long as it took to cross the county border. Once in a while, though, a young couple would give in to the dream and buy and renovate one of the dilapidated farmhouses in the hills, only to discover, when the kids were in school, that a ten-hour weekend commute to a second home wasn't really what they'd had in mind. In another few years, a postage-stamp picture of the farmhouse, looking spiffier than it had a half decade earlier, would appear in the local real estate paper, the turnover good for Greason, the only real estate agent in town.

The church had a minister who lived in the parsonage next door. There were a few row houses, some of them occupied by teachers and staff from Avery Academy. The houses were a holdover from the days when Avery was a mill town, manufacturing chairs from the acres of forest that had once dominated the landscape. The chairs, which were a type of ladies' rocker, were called Avery chairs and were hard to find now.

Greason had a Cape Cod cottage where he had his business. Bobby Peet lived above his own store. Aaron Davidson, a clerk of the court, lived with Gerri Burton, a court stenographer, at the edge of town in an old Victorian. Vicki Thornton had three small kids. She cleaned for the school. Natalie Beck worked in the dining hall. Eric Hunt, who had an apartment in one of the row houses, did landscaping at the school. Ask any one of them, and they would tell you the same thing. Silas Quinney had been raised right.

Owen hated the school now, but most people in Avery couldn't hate it. If it hadn't come along just as the chair factory was moving south, there wouldn't be any Avery at all.

For Owen and Anna, though, Avery had never been its village. Avery was its land. Where else did you have a view of not one but two mountain ranges with a river valley in between? The soil was not rocky, like it was in New Hampshire, and it wasn't covered with dark and dense forest, like it was in Maine. Mostly the trees around Avery were yellow and red maple that let in the light in summer and turned pink and gold in autumn. Bobby Peet once allowed he made half his yearly income off the leaf-peepers during the first two weeks of October. Owen used to hike up the path out back of his own house, the setting sun spreading in a nearly blinding fan through the trees. On days like that, with the air clear and bracing, he felt healthy simply breathing. He could always smell in the air wood smoke mixed with leaf debris and something else—wax, maybe, or pumpkin.

Silas, he was a hard worker. One time, when Anna and Owen were up to Canada looking at a ewe for breeding, and Silas was alone, he had had to birth fourteen piglets all by himself. Anna and Owen had not expected the sow to go so soon, or else they'd never have left Silas on his own. It was freezing, and the sleet was coming down, and Silas called Owen and said, *What do I do?* and Owen told him just to catch the piglets and make sure that old sow didn't roll over and crush the babies. Owen pictured Silas on his knees trying to catch those slippery little buggers, and all the time the sow trying to bite him. The boy was only sixteen then. That sow, she was ornery, meaner when she was birthing. Silas saved twelve out of the fourteen that night, which was a good haul. When Owen and Anna got home, they found Silas in the barn, covered with muck and blood and a shit-eating grin. Owen knew the feeling.

Silas, he had Owen's looks, but they came out different on him. Owen and Anna had brought him up good. You could ask anyone in town, and they would tell you the same thing.

Owen didn't know for sure how it had happened, but he had

his theories. He didn't know as he could honestly blame the girl, but sometimes he was tempted to.

All this Owen told to a young researcher from the University of Vermont. She was a lithe woman with red hair and a respectful manner. She didn't pry. She waited for Owen to talk. He didn't know why he had agreed to meet with her. He felt he had something to say, and Anna, his wife, she wouldn't listen anymore.

Sienna

I'm, like, if anyone touches me, I'm going to kill them. I have no money left. Do you have a dollar? I need...There's nothing in here. Just a bunch of dimes and nickels. I changed my name. I thought it up myself. My name used to be something else, but I like Sienna better. I was traumatized. I had to be in therapy for ages. You can put your life behind you and get a new start. I haven't thought about what happened in Vermont in, like, I don't know. I was the victim. I think someday I'll write a book about it. I was fourteen. Almost fifteen. You got a pencil? I have to finish this math before class. A pencil with an eraser? You want to do this in town? There's a place I know. I had to take a year off. I hate this shirt. I hate purple. It's just, I don't know. I'm, like, fine now. My mom says to forget it ever happened, pretend it never happened. You're asking *why?* I don't think *why* is the right question to ask me. You ask *them* why. You like Starbucks? We could do this there. I'm seriously feeling uncomfortable here. If my roommate comes in and sees this, she'll be all over me. I don't feel I should have to answer questions, do you? They call this a second-chance school. There are a lot of kids here trying to forget the things they did. Like, you know, drugs and stuff. Seriously, I didn't have any lunch. I can't eat breakfast, and if I skip lunch or just eat a yogurt, then I can eat anything I want for dinner. I'm just so glad to be out of Vermont. When we flew into Houston that first time, I could see the ridges on the hills. They looked like they'd been folded up, like green velvet. I could see streets and playing fields and baseball diamonds and clouds floating down there. The creeks in between were milky-green. I thought to myself, *I'm going to start a new life. I can be, like, Sienna. I can be whoever I want.* And I could see these developments with these huge houses, and the roads were white cement and curved like S's, and everybody had swimming pools, and I was trying to see the school from the air, and I think I might have because I saw this thing like a church and all green around it, not brown like most of the land is here. Everybody here is pretty religious. At Avery, we had to go to chapel once a week, on Tuesday mornings for assembly. Here, they go every morning to pray and sing, but it's not complimental. I couldn't go back to school for five weeks, and when I did, for those couple of days, people just stared, and I got all those threats. Me. Like *I* deserved threats? I think this must be the most expensive private school in the country. You must have to pay more for a second-chance school. For our community service, we have to turn an old ranch into a camp for underprivileged kids. The kids from Katrina are supposed to end up living there. They've got gangs in Houston now. My parents are still together. They really bonded over this. It's really, like, ironical. My roommate is seriously lame. She thinks she's so...Her alarm goes off an hour before it has to—dit dit dit...dit dit dit...dit dit dit—just so she can pray. Have you ever tried to sleep in a room while someone is praying out loud?

27

Football is huge here. I just want—when I get out of here—I just want one of those houses like I flew over with the white cement and the swimming pool out back. Either that or I want to be a singer like J. Lo. I was thinking I could just go by the one name, Sienna.

Mike

The scandal, which occurred in January 2006, ruined a number of lives, Mike's included, if a life can be said to have been ruined at any given moment in time. Personally, Mike believed erosion of character to be a longer and slower process. A chance letter from a researcher at the University of Vermont wishing to interview Mike about the scandal for a cultural-studies research project on Alcohol and Adolescent Male Behaviors in the Secondary-School Setting—a letter that Mike intended to ignore—had nevertheless awakened in him a personal need to commit his own story to paper. He wanted to do this partly to clarify the incident, which was widely and wildly misreported by the media, and partly for reasons that weren't entirely known to him, though he did have flashes of insight not unlike the nearly unbearable brightness of the hallucinatory peaks and Vs of a migraine. Those insights suggested a need for further illumination, as if the peaks and Vs might open up to a color-saturated, wide-screen explanation of why each of the principals did what he or she did and, more important, in Mike's case, the reasons for his own actions.

Mike had returned to Vermont after an exile of twenty-two months, not to the town in which the school was still located, but rather to a village some forty miles south, which, while charming, had little character of its own. A mecca for tourists and vacationers, the town boasted appealing inns and excellent restaurants, a thriving bookstore, and, at a discreet distance, a neighborhood of high-end outlets, all of which afforded Mike a certain degree of anonymity, a state he now valued above all else. Had he settled in a more authentic village, he would have been known as an outsider almost at once and would have been as visible as if he had walked the streets with a sign on his back. In this tourist town, however, he could be anyone — a leaf-peeper from Baltimore, a retiree from Providence, a shopper from New York looking for a bargain at Armani. Here he could stroll the famed marble sidewalks (heavily salted in winter), occasionally admiring the nineteenth-century houses that lined the green, secure in the knowledge that no one was paying him the slightest bit of attention. There was always the possibility that he would be recognized, since he had been, in the aftermath of the scandal, interviewed several times on television. He had light-brown hair that had once been blond, he was of medium height and was myopic, but, on the plus side, he had deeply recessed blue eyes that were distinctive. Depending upon how he dressed, he could be taken for a Realtor down on his luck or the headmaster of a private school, which he had been for nearly a dozen years.

He had a room at the largest of the inns in the village, a three-story classic of the Federal period. It was painted white with green shutters and could have passed for one of the buildings at Dartmouth. On its top floor were two dormers with large windows on four sides, the rooms like glass boxes perched precariously on the slate roof. Purely by circumstance, Mike had arrived on a Monday when there had been many empty rooms, and he had been given this desirable aerie. He hadn't imagined it would take so long to get started on his story, but he had, in fact, a lot of trouble with the first sentence. A first sentence, he had discovered, dictated not only the tone of the tale but also the manner in which it would be parceled out, and he had found his first few false starts to be inhibiting. In the end, he had settled upon a factual tone that suggested a *before* and an *after,* and he had decided, in the interest of moving forward, that he would remain content with that decision.

Mike had met Silas Quinney and his family under unusual circumstances four years prior to the incident at the center of his story. Mike had been at Middlebury College for a conference for secondary-school heads. In hindsight, he should have driven home straightaway, for there was some talk of freezing rain and snow in the evening. But when the last seminar was dismissed, and he was free to roam the small town of Middlebury, with its cafés and wine bars and good restaurants, he couldn't bring himself to get into his maroon Volvo and head south. Instead, he walked into the village—not a very long walk—and ambled up and down the narrow streets, feeling a rare sensation of freedom that in his job he was seldom able to achieve. The life of a headmaster was hardly a private one. In addition to teaching two courses in the History Department—the French Resistance During World War II and the History of the Civil Rights Movement—and addressing assemblies and appearing at all— *all*—home games, no matter how humble the team (for one had to give encouragement to the underclassmen as well), and from time to time eating his lunch with the students in the cafeteria, he lived in a house that was located more or less in the middle of the campus, so that all his comings and goings were a public matter. In New England, Mike had discovered, there was a moral charge to keeping one's curtains open in the evenings, particularly on the first floor, so that any movement Meg and he made once it got dark and the lights were turned on was visible to anyone passing by. Mike wasn't sure why this custom had developed in the way it had—doubtless it was a holdover from seventeenth-century Calvinist rectitude—but it seemed endemic to New England in a way it was not, say, in New York. The flip side of this custom, of course, was that when walking of an evening, one got a wonderful peek into the lives of others. Indeed, one of Mike's favorite pastimes was to stroll through a village and look into the windows of the houses and imagine who the people were and what they were doing. Invariably, he had found, a home seemed more charming viewed from the outside in. He often had moments when he wished very much that the inhabitants of this or that stately home might invite him in for a glass of wine around the fire.

That evening, the evening he met the Quinneys, Mike had had his walk and then a meal (and a glass of a local brew) and then had set out in his car to go back to Avery, an hour south of Middlebury. Contrary to the forecaster's warnings, the roads looked fine. Occasionally there were snow squalls, but as the flakes seemed to be drying as soon as they hit the pavement, the brief flurries did not concern him. He was aware, however, of a phenomenon called *black ice,* familiar to all who lived in northern New England. Just its name could cause a little fillip to the heart of anyone who had ever encountered it, whether on foot or in a vehicle. The ice was called *black* because that was how it appeared; more accurately, it didn't appear at all. It looked like wet pavement with no visible icy patches, and it usually wasn't until one had put on the brakes or tried to make a tight corner that one realized how treacherous that unassuming surface was. A rumor of black ice could clear out a dinner party in minutes, and a daytime warning would send parents scurrying to the local schools to pick up their children an hour early to avoid it.

Once, when he and Meg had rented a condo on a hill for a ski weekend, he watched his wife back straight out of the driveway in the Volvo and then slide *sideways* all the way down to the foot of the hill. She had to abandon the car and walk up the slope where the snow was crusted just to get a foothold. Unfortunately, she had walked up the *other* side of the hill and could not cross the street to the condo without risking sliding all the way down again. She tried crawling, but this resulted only in a spin, which cost her about ten feet. Mike had gone back into the condo and had tried to find a piece of rope he could throw to his wife, but in the interim, she had walked to the foot of the hill, crossed the road where there was traction, and hiked up the other side. It was twenty-four hours before they'd been able to get the car towed back into the driveway.

On Mike's return from Middlebury, traveling at forty-five miles per hour down a steep hill into the environs of Avery, he saw a car stopped in front of him and slammed on his brakes. The Volvo skidded on the black ice, crossed the road, went straight up on its nose, tumbled over, and slid for some distance on its roof with Mike still strapped inside. And in this way, he first encountered the Quinney family.

Mike didn't remember much of that initial sighting. He was unconscious for a time, and the first thing he recalled when he came to was a kindly-faced woman lying on her stomach, reaching in and holding his arm and telling him help was on the way. By then, Mike was shaking very badly, and though he knew that he had to prop his weight off the seat belt to release it, he couldn't seem to manage that maneuver. There was no air bag—the Volvo was an old one—but the roll bars, in combination with the seat belt, had kept him alive. When help finally arrived in the form of two young EMTs, the technicians were able to unfasten the belt and drag Mike out and lay him on a stretcher. He was taken to Western Vermont Regional Hospital, where Meg met him and where his bumps and bruises were looked at and x-rayed. Remarkably, he had escaped with little injury. More remarkable was the fact that the car, when flipped right side over, was able to be driven to an auto-body shop, where various dents and scratches were attended to.

Several days after the accident, when he had sufficiently recovered from an overall stiffness that had kept him slightly immobile, Mike borrowed Meg's car and drove to the site of the accident. He didn't know the inhabitants of the farm he had crashed into, though he had seen its buildings often enough as he'd driven north from town. There was a main house with a peaked roof and a front porch very close to the road, a detached garage that looked as though it had been built before the advent of the SUV, a large barn, and acres of pasture that rolled back to the tree line. Surrounding the main house and the garage was a split-rail fence, the front of which Mike had demolished upon entry. He noted, as he pulled into the driveway, a deep gouge in the dirt where his car had skidded upside down. Near the broken fence, a jagged post was tilted at a severe angle. He had beheaded, so to speak, the Quinneys' mailbox.

Mike had come to apologize—though a skid on black ice was hardly anyone's fault—and to offer to pay for damages. This wasn't an entirely empty gesture, since it was possible that the inhabitants of the farm would take Mike up on his offer. The local farmers were in constant danger of going under.

His arrival detonated two sheepdogs that began barking even before they emerged at a dead run from behind the garage. Mike hesitated before opening the car door—the dogs seemed very *annoyed*—but then he surmised that they couldn't be as threatening as they appeared since no one ever would have been able to visit the Quinney family home. In this he was proved right. The dogs stopped their yapping as soon as he opened the door. He tried to make friends with the mutts—*Hey, boy; thatta boy*—as he slip-slid his way across the driveway, where he noted a basketball hoop fastened over the opening of the garage, a skateboard in a corner of the porch, and, covered with a blue tarp to one side of the house, an all-terrain vehicle. He thus deduced a teenage boy. He didn't meet Silas that day, but he did meet his mother, Anna, who appeared at the door. Mike recognized her at once as the woman who had held her arm out to him when he'd been hanging upside down.

"I've come to thank you," Mike said after he had introduced himself and stepped inside the small house. "And to offer to pay for the damage to your fence and mailbox."

She put a hand to the place where her oat-colored cardigan was fastened, and Mike's eyes followed. She gestured to the kitchen table. "Won't you sit down?" she asked. She immediately began to fill a kettle with water, at least as much to occupy herself, Mike guessed, as to provide refreshment for a guest.

"Thank you," he said again.

Mike slipped off his gloves, set them on the table next to a blue woven place mat, and unbuttoned his coat. He guessed that he had interrupted Anna Quinney, who had on a pair of jeans and the sweater, before she had had her shower, for her light-brown hair was somewhat flat on one side and a little wild on the other. She had wide hips and long legs that gave her good lines. Beneath the oat sweater, she had what appeared to be fine breasts. She wore no makeup that he could detect. He put her at about forty.

"Coffee or tea?" she asked.

Since Mike gathered from the kettle that the coffee would be powdered, he asked for tea. She leaned against the counter and crossed her arms over her chest, a gesture that seemed both defensive and habitual. "How are you?" she asked finally.

"Amazingly well," Mike said. "Fortunately, nothing was broken. I'm just a little banged up. But I'm fine. Fine," he repeated as though trying to prove a point.

She smiled with some relief as if she had been worried about possible lawsuits. "We called Gary," she said. Mike knew that Gary was Gary Quinney, the chief of police of Avery as well as the brother of Owen Quinney. "He said he thought you would be OK. We were here in the kitchen when it happened. It was so loud, we thought at first a plane had crashed."

Mike hadn't been aware of any sound when he had experienced the moment of tumbling end over end, but then again he had briefly lost consciousness, so it was entirely possible that the incident, heard from outside the car, was as frightening as Anna Quinney was making out.

"Silas thought it was an earthquake," she added.

"Really."

"Silas is our son. He's fourteen."

"Eighth grade? Ninth grade?"

"Eighth," she said, naming the local middle school. "Owen, my husband, is in the barn. He'll be over in a minute."

Good, Mike thought. He preferred to talk money with a man.

The kitchen was a small one. In its center was a round wooden table with four small cane chairs, one of which Mike was sitting on. There was a fireplace so close to him, he could have reached out his hand and touched it. But he gathered, from the basket of dried flowers on the hearth, that it didn't work. On its mantel were various folk-art items: a wooden Christmas tree, a painting of a primitive landscape that he would later learn Anna Quinney had done herself, and a tin lantern. The fridge, at arm's length the other way, was a mosaic of snapshots, news clippings, a calendar with events marked in pen, coupons, and magnets representing local businesses. The table hadn't been entirely cleared off, and near his arm lay a white plate with a crust of toast and a blob of red jelly at its edge. Despite the clutter, or perhaps because of it, the kitchen felt inviting.

When the kettle whistled, Owen Quinney walked in, as if he had been summoned. Mike stood and introduced himself.

"Oh, I know who you are," Quinney said, hanging a thick plaid jacket on a hook in the hallway. He rubbed his hands together in anticipation of a meal.

He had the body of a farmer. His legs and arms were strong, but there was a hint of softness around the belly. The skin of his face and hands had long ago reddened and cracked, but beneath that baked exterior lay a handsome man. He had a full head of dark-brown hair that any man might envy, and Mike liked his eyes at once. They were a smudged brown, surrounded by wrinkles that suggested a no-nonsense manner with perhaps a slight hint of the mischievous.

37

Owen Quinney pulled a chair away from the table and straddled it, crossing his arms over its back. Anna was spooning cocoa powder into one of three cups. Mike guessed the cocoa was for Owen.

"We thought you was a goner," he said, his smile revealing a slight gap between his two front teeth. He seemed about the same age as his wife and smelled like animal, cold air, and, oddly, bacon. "Silas and me, we run out, and you was lying there upside down, and we thought you was dead or as good as, and I said to Silas, you go in the house and call nine one one. And Gary, bless his heart, he come out in a flash and got you out of the car." He gave a slight whistle. "That was some car." He paused. "Nothin' worse than black ice. Nothin'. Now that you're OK, I can say this, it was a good lesson for Silas. Scared the bejesus out of him. In a year or two, he'll be getting his learner's permit, and you have to scare 'em good before they go off half-cocked and kill theirselves. Gary'll tell you. Two years ago, we lost five kids from the high school. They were up to Poultney, partying. Slid themselves all the way down the hill here and into a telephone pole. They found one of the kids, a girl, in a tree about a hundred feet away. You got to scare 'em. Best lesson there was, seeing you helpless in that car."

"I'm glad I could be of service," Mike said, wondering if he would have been a better lesson had he died on impact. But he agreed with Owen Quinney. At Avery, the staff worried about the day students—the only ones allowed cars—all the time.

"I'd like to pay for the damages," Mike said, getting to the point of his visit. "For the mailbox and the fence."

"Weren't your fault," Owen said.

"Well, yes and no," Mike said. "No fault in the usual sense, yet I did cause the damage."

"Silas'll fix it," Owen said, and there was finality in his statement. "I'll pay him a little for the work. He'll be happy to do it."

"Well," Mike said, "that's very kind. If you change your mind, however, here's my phone number." He slid a small white card across the table.

Owen picked it up, held it at arm's length, and studied it. "Yeah, Gary said you was at the school. Headmaster, is it?" There was neither disdain nor respect in his pronouncement. He might have been saying *milkman*. Owen set the card down with a snap and took a sip of the cocoa. Anna had put a dollop of whipped cream on top. Mike picked up his mug and sipped and immediately burned his tongue. There was a smell in the room that he'd been trying to identify since he had walked in — something nutty, with a hint of cinnamon. Anna Quinney bent over the oven, opened it, and checked a tray of what looked like granola. That it should be, of all things, granola struck Mike as almost comically perfect. He had a sudden and urgent craving for a cereal he rarely ate.

Anna stood. "I've been trying to get Silas to visit your school," she volunteered.

"Really?" Mike said, much surprised.

"He's good at art," she added.

Owen snorted. "He's good at *basketball*," he said, correcting her.

"They did away with all the art programs at the high school," Anna explained.

Anna seemed nervous, and Mike wondered at the source of her fear: Mike as headmaster? Owen as disapproving husband?

"And the music programs," she added. "Some schools, you

39

have to pay now for classes in the arts, but at the high school you can't even pay. They don't have any teachers."

"I'm sorry to hear that."

"I know you have a good arts program at Avery," Anna said. "I've heard your studios are among the best in the state." She gave a quick glance at Owen and stopped herself.

"He'll play varsity up at the high school next year as a freshman," Owen announced, as if he hadn't been listening. "Coach already called around to say so. Silas doesn't have much height, but he's fast. He can drive to the basket like no one you ever saw."

"I'd like to see him play," Mike said.

"They play Avery Academy," Anna offered.

"And beat the crap out of them every year," Owen said with a chuckle.

"I'll bet they do," Mike agreed.

"Anyway," Owen said, "your school is a great school. I just don't think it's right for Silas."

There was a long silence at the table that Anna finally broke. "I've personally always wanted to see the school," she said.

"You can come visit anytime," Mike said.

"Do you give scholarships?" she asked.

"Thirty-eight percent of our students are on scholarships of one sort or another," Mike said. His statistics weren't entirely true. In that figure, he had included a large number of students who had jobs on campus that provided them with modest pocket money, most of which went not toward tuition but toward pizza and cigarettes.

"You can lead a horse to water, but you can't make him drink," Owen said, slightly off point.

Mike wasn't as disinterested as he sounded. If Owen's son was as good as the father had said, Mike would have to have a talk with Vince Blount, Avery's varsity basketball coach. Perhaps Blount had scouted Silas already. But there was, too, a potential political payoff in having local students attend the academy. The more people in town who felt connected to Avery, the better the school's chances for land purchases or zoning proposals. There was, in fact, one such proposal in committee at that very moment: the school wanted to annex a portion of an abandoned park for a second baseball diamond. Having the nephew of Gary Quinney, chief of police, at the school might be no bad thing.

"Is Silas a good student?" Mike asked casually, daring a second sip of his tea. He'd been blowing on its surface since he'd burned his tongue.

Anna hesitated and glanced over at her husband, who was studying the floor. "He's good," she said in a soft voice.

"Well, let's do this," Mike suggested. "Talk to Silas, see if he has any interest in touring the school. I'll call in a couple of days. What we do is, we have students give the tours. Puts the kids at ease, and they're more likely to ask questions. Of course, you would come, too," Mike added. "It's essential that the parents see the school as well."

Mike already had the particular student and itinerary selected. The best guide would start by taking Silas over to the art studios, where Mike would make sure student work was being exhibited. Silas and his family would swing around by the sports complex, talk to Vince Blount, and then visit Orpin Hall, the most appealing of the various academic buildings. Mike would have the Quinneys meet not only with the dean of admissions, Sarah Grace, but also with Coggeshall, dean of students. The tour would finish with lunch in the dining hall—usually the most persuasive selling point for a fourteen-year-old boy. Avery's dining hall was set up much like a college cafeteria, with several stations and many options. Students could go back for seconds, thirds, and even fourths if they had the appetite. The promise of ribs and tacos and mac-and-cheese with six glasses of milk and four pieces of chocolate cake for dessert usually sealed the deal for any adolescent boy.

Owen glanced up at his wife and then looked away. Anna's face didn't change. Mike caught then a hint of struggle between husband and wife, a battle that had perhaps been waged for many months, this but a small part of a possibly larger marital struggle, or, rather, *the* marital struggle, the same for all couples, different only in its particulars. Seen from Anna Quinney's point of view, Mike's sudden skid across their front yard had been a stroke of unimaginable good fortune.

Silas

I didn't, I didn't want. But I did, I did want, it is the truth. For those minutes, it was, I wanted. I was drunk. The room was spinning, and there was music, and I can never, I can never. You are gone. You will be gone, and I have ruined. There were six of us and two left and why didn't I? Why didn't I say your name or think your name? Instead I just heard the music and the anger. There was you, there was always you, how did I let what you and I were? The best I ever felt. You are the one. We should have run away. And they were taping, and you will see the tape, and you will be so hurt, and that I can't stand. No, you can't ever see the tape. I will have to talk to you and you will have to promise me that you will never, but why would you promise me? I am to blame. I was there. I wanted. And now there is nothing I can ever say or do. And you will be so sad, and I can't stand it.

J. Dot

I'm not straight with this at all. Not at all. I just don't get it. This happens all the time, right? I mean, this happens *all* the time. Kids get drunk and do stupid things. To take the hit for it. It just...it just sucks, man. Sucks.

The crap thing is, I can't get into college now. I took a year off and now I'm doing the PG year all over again, and I feel like the fucking oldest man on earth. I was headed for Gonzaga. For basketball.

The basketball was sick, man. Sick.

For a long time, I couldn't talk about any of this.

I don't know if you should have your life ruined over just one little time. They called me the *ringleader* in the press. That's insane shit. If anyone was a *ringleader,* it was her. I know it sounds crazy to say that, and my lawyer wouldn't let me go near it, but the whole thing was her idea. Sure, we were older and should have known better, but we were drunk, and...shit... what's the point? Why am I even answering your fucking questions? To save the next guy? I got news for you. The next guy can't be saved.

And Coach being fired? That was pure insanity. None of this was his fault. Just because we all happened to be on the basketball team? Like there was some evil streak running through the team that he was responsible for? Jesus Christ, give me a break.

I just don't get it. You take all those other days of the year — 364 of them. And all that pressure to get into a good college. And three hours a night of homework, plus all those hours of practice and games and Saturday school.... So you take all those hours and you put them up against *one* hour of getting wasted and acting like a jerk, and *that one hour* defines your life? Forever?

My picture was everywhere — every newspaper, CNN, the local news. I can't go anywhere without people giving me a second glance. Sometimes, the men will shake their heads like they're sorry, and once in a while someone will come up to me and actually say, *Hey, sorry, man*. But the women? The women look at me like I'm scum. Pure scum.

You think that's fair?

I didn't even know her. That's the crap thing.

I understand you have to pay. I get that part. My question is this: For how long?

Matthew

The whole thing just frosted Matthew's ass. The whole charade had ruined his son's life. Had any good come of it? Was Avery Academy better off? From what Matthew had learned, the school was about to go under. Were the individual boys better off for having been singled out? No one in his right mind would say yes to that. One of them, from what Matthew had heard, couldn't get off the couch. Another one, his own son, was stuck in a hellish quagmire between secondary school and college.

James was twenty-one now. Before the fiasco, he'd been on his way to play basketball for Gonzaga University. He'd been recruited by a number of schools. The packages that were promised! Both Matthew and his wife worked for Middlebury College—Matthew was in advancement, and Michelle was a math professor—and, naturally, money was always tight. The prospect of such a bright future was a dream come true. That dream was over now. That opportunity had disappeared. Something outstanding that was going to happen to his son would never take place. Even normal things that should have happened for his boy—they would never take place now.

Matthew believed the event should have been adjudicated between the school and the boys. Quietly. There had been no need—never any need—to go public with it, and for that, Matthew blamed the girl. They said she changed her name and moved to a school in Houston. When he thought about her, he could just spit nails.

For James's PG year, Matthew and Michelle had decided to send their son to Avery because it was close to Middlebury, where they worked—only an hour's drive away. Previously, James had been at Easton, and though he'd done well athletically, he'd had trouble academically. Matthew and Michelle knew that James would still have to be a boarder at Avery, but they'd be able to see him on weekends. And they did. Christ, Matthew had rearranged his entire class schedule around being able to get to the Wednesday and Saturday afternoon basketball games. He'd barely missed a one. The whole incident had been extremely difficult on Matthew, and Michelle as well. Their reputations had been tarnished. No one would ever say so to their faces, but Matthew knew it to be true. Overnight, they'd become social question marks. Some of that had eased up, but Matthew knew there were people on campus who would not have them to their houses for dinner. That had been particularly hard on Michelle. People were eager to blame the mothers. As if they hadn't taught their sons the right values. Matthew had never known a better mother than Michelle.

Matthew believed the entire fiasco happened simply so the girl could do some star-fucking. She wanted to prove to herself and to others that she could get a star. Why else would the incident have been taped? In that environment, James was already a star. All three boys were.

The girl and the person behind the camera had a lot to answer for, as far as Matthew was concerned.

47

Matthew didn't know who had been behind the camera. James had never said, and Matthew respected him for that.

When Matthew thought about all the bullshit that had been written in the press—about how the whole thing was Shakespearean in nature—he wanted to puke. How was what happened at Avery Shakespearean? Rise to greatness, fatal flaw, blah, blah, blah?

Matthew and Michelle had known that James had experimented with drinking and drugs at Easton. It had been a bit of a problem there, and James had been expelled for selling marijuana. So he and Michelle had wanted their son closer to home. Avery had seemed perfect for James. They'd been advised that one more year would only better prepare James for Gonzaga—a plan that, had it not been hopelessly derailed, would have unfolded beautifully.

In Matthew's view, nineteen-year-old young men needed to blow off steam. One hoped it happened on the basketball court, but the pressures on these children were enormous, and one had to forgive them the occasional lapse. And after what Matthew had seen at the college level, the private-school incident seemed tame in comparison. No, it didn't make the boys candidates for sainthood, but Matthew believed it should have remained a private matter. James's lawyer made a good case for the boys' not even knowing the incident was being taped. That, in fact, they'd been set up. Did Matthew believe it? He didn't know.

The irony was that if a few kids had done something similar at the college, they'd be calling it an art film.

The girl wasn't like any fourteen-year-old Matthew had ever seen. The word *vixen* came to mind. That suggested a seductress, and Matthew didn't care who knew his feelings on this subject.

James and his friends had had nothing to prove. They'd already proved themselves on the basketball court.

James didn't touch basketballs anymore. It killed Matthew to see this. James had loved basketball. He'd lived for it.

Michelle had shown Matthew the letter from the researcher at the University of Vermont. He didn't know if they should talk to her or not. Matthew had a lot to say, and he was fed to the teeth with lawyers.

Michelle

If anything I say can help another mother, then some good will have come of this horrendous time in our lives.

I'd known for years that something bad was going to happen to James. I didn't imagine the Avery incident—who could have predicted that?—but afterward, I understood that I'd always been afraid.

Sometimes I think I could have stopped it. At other times, I know I could not have. Occasionally, I used to wonder, *Is something wrong with James?*

The thing was, James could lie. Even as early as thirteen or fourteen, he could lie brilliantly. He was sweet and charming and very funny, but he could lie so well that even I wouldn't be able to detect it until much later. I would sometimes suspect only because of the illogic of his statements. Young teenagers can't fake logic very well. But he was so good at lying, I often doubted my own perceptions and intelligence. My son would look me in the eye and make a statement that contradicted everything I knew to be true. I would doubt myself, and then I would have to let it go.

I often wonder now, *Should I have been more strict? Should I have been less strict?* It's hard to know in retrospect. *Should I have been with him every minute when he was a young child? Should I not have worked?*

I think about these things all the time now.

The lying started in the eighth grade. Possibly it had begun earlier, and I simply hadn't noticed. I remember clearly one specific day when we were in a store renting James a tuxedo for my older daughter's wedding. I had picked him up after school, and we were driving to the store, and he was, I remember, very talkative that day. I recall thinking to myself, *This is a good day, isn't it? James is talking to me in a normal voice, and we are going to rent the tuxedo for Julie's wedding.* But when we got to the store, Julie looked at her brother in a curious and knowing manner, so much so that James kept turning away from his sister. He would pretend to be distracted by a jacket or a pair of cuff links. Julie said, "What have you been smoking? Your eyes are a mess."

I looked at my son. His eyes were pink and slightly bulging. How had I not noticed this before? They seemed full of water, as if they might burst at any moment.

I thought, *Maybe James has conjunctivitis. Maybe he's been on the computer too long.* On the way home, I asked him outright what Julie had meant. He said he had no idea. I stopped the car, and I said, "Look at me." He did. Straight on. He seemed exasperated. "We saw a movie in class," he said, throwing his hands in the air. "I don't know. It went on for hours. Maybe that's why my eyes look terrible."

You had to hear James say that to understand that he was utterly convincing. I let it go. I never mentioned it again.

But after that day, I began to be more watchful.

First there were the stories from the middle-school mothers. Seventh graders were drinking, they said. Eighth graders were smoking pot. I thought it couldn't be true. We live in a small town, though we do have the college, and I suppose because of that, pot and alcohol might be readily available, even to middle schoolers. I noted, though, that no mother believed it possible of her own child. I certainly did not believe it possible of James.

Within the family, we had established rules. James had a curfew. He had to be home by eleven. He had to call me on his cell phone if he went anywhere other than the place he had told us he was going. I quickly realized, however, that I could never be certain where he was. I started checking on him, calling the parents at the houses he would say he was visiting. Once, I called and the mother said she had not seen him all evening. I could hear the surprise and the slight pity in her voice, and I knew exactly what she was thinking: *Michelle has a son she cannot trust.*

When James got home, I asked him where he had been. He said he had been where he said he'd been. I told him that wasn't possible, that I'd just spoken with the mother. He said he had been in the basement playing video games. There had been a crowd of boys, eight or nine maybe. The mother simply hadn't known he was one of them. I knew this couldn't possibly be true. What mother did not know who was in her house? But to hear James say these words was to believe him. To look into his eyes and to hear his tone of voice was to believe him. I hesitated, and he saw. At the moment of my hesitation, my son became indignant. Other mothers didn't call parents. Why did I? Didn't I trust him?

After that, it seemed, James began to lie even more. Yes, he had read the book for English. I knew better; he had not. Yes, he had done his homework. I wondered when. I could no longer demand that he do his assignments in the kitchen; my son insisted that he be allowed to study in his room. I was to knock before I entered. I would knock and enter quickly, and I would

52

see him on the computer, instant-messaging his friends. I would have glimpses of words within the little boxes. James would look at me and lie. He would say he was doing research. Or he was checking what the homework assignment was. There was no open book on his desk.

Occasionally, I attempted humor. Sometimes I was stern. I would be an ally, I thought, or I would lay down the law. I would change the rules or I would adapt. I would pick my battles.

I talked to my husband and told him what I thought. James was lying, and he was drinking. It's a phase, my husband said. Sons need to break away from their mothers. I was overprotective, and I nagged too much. Let go of the burden of his responsibilities, my husband said, and he will pick them up for himself.

It seemed a reasonable proposition.

Our son is a good kid, my husband added. Has a teacher ever called? Has the principal ever called? Has any parent ever suggested...?

We decided in the spring to send James to Easton Academy in northeastern Connecticut. We had talked for some time about sending him away for high school, since the school in our town was not very good. But when we suggested the idea to James, he rebelled. He wouldn't go, he said. How could parents want to send their child away?

I nearly relented; I didn't want him to go. I loved him and wanted him near me. Away from me, I thought, he wouldn't study. I might not know what he was doing on a weekend night. But then again, I thought, wouldn't he be better off at Easton, subject to stricter rules? Hadn't I lost control already? Mightn't it be easier on everyone if he went off and found himself?

Reluctantly, James went to Easton, and immediately he

set out to prove our decision wrong. His grades suffered. The reports that were sent home spoke of a lack of organization, of having an innate intelligence but not trying. There was a suggestion of making excuses for missed work. We talked to James, and we visited the school. We had conferences with his teachers and with his adviser. Our son had accumulated demerits for skipping classes, for dress-code violations, and for smoking. I didn't know that our son had ever smoked a cigarette. When I confronted him, James said he had tried it just once. I wanted to believe him.

James said he didn't care about the school, and he didn't like the teachers. He thought his adviser was lame. He hated his history teacher.

Only his basketball coach sent home good reports.

James grew six inches his sophomore year. Another two his junior year. He was exceptional at basketball. One in a hundred. One in a thousand, his coach said. One of the best players ever to go through Easton. Though James had always played basketball in town leagues, we hadn't realized he had such talent. I thought to myself, *This is it. This is the thing that will turn our son around. This is the thing that will save him.*

James would come home, for a weekend or for a vacation, and for a few hours he would seem to be another person, a nice boy, a good boy. More mature, less volatile. He would talk to us, share his ideas and his plans. We would chat about basketball, about which games we'd be able to make. I would be so happy then. I would think, *We did the right thing. Sending James to a private school was the correct decision after all. James is growing up and taking on responsibility. The basketball has changed him. He believes in himself.*

But later, James would go to his room and shut the door. He would come down for meals and then go out with his friends. The lying started again, and this time I discovered that our son was a pro. He had logic now, and I could never be sure if he was telling the truth. I could never seem to catch him out. I would make discreet calls, inventing pretexts. He would ask, *Why are you calling people?* He demanded a later curfew and then a later one. I would ask, *What can you possibly do in this town after midnight?*

I worried constantly. I felt that my son was chipping away at me. This small thing and then that small thing.

One night, over Christmas break during his junior year, James came home drunk. I had waited up and was sitting in the kitchen in my bathrobe. I confronted him, told him he was drunk. I could smell it, and he was slurring his words. He became belligerent and denied that he'd been drinking.

I woke my husband and told him to come down and see for himself. Matthew told my son to go to bed. We would talk in the morning.

In the morning, James was painfully hungover. When we said that we were grounding him, he said that he was unhappy, that we had ruined his life. He hated Easton and was miserable there.

I see now that planting the idea that we had ruined his life was a brilliant tactic on James's part.

In January of his junior year, a scout from Gonzaga University traveled from Washington State to Easton to take a look at James. The basketball team that year was winning every game they played. My son scored twenty, thirty points a game. He was a "phenom," we were told.

Taking James out of Easton was no longer even a possibility. If he could get into Gonzaga on a full scholarship, did the grades matter all that much?

The academic reports continued to be poor. James showed tremendous promise, but he didn't do the work. I thought that maybe he had had an organizational problem all along, and that I should have had him diagnosed when he was younger.

I could have done more for him, I thought. I might have helped him.

In the fall of his senior year, my son was recruited for Gonzaga. The offer they made him was stunningly complete. We celebrated at home. My husband and I drank champagne. My husband offered my son a glass.

In April, James was expelled from Easton for selling marijuana on school grounds. He did not deny the charge. He told me it was just the one time, that he was doing it for a friend because the friend desperately needed money. I told him I did not believe him. I was furious, and my husband was heartsick. Our son had thrown his future away.

Perhaps not, the recruiter said when he called our house after hearing of the expulsion. If James could make up the credits in the summer and then go on to a postgraduate year somewhere else, the college would still hold open the offer.

We scrambled to find a private school for our son. It was late in the year, too late for the normal application process. We wanted him close to home so we could keep an eye on him.

We visited Avery, and they accepted James within the week. They made a show of caring about the expulsion and of making James take the entrance exams, but you could see how happy they were to have a basketball player of James's caliber.

We made our son go to a therapist. James thought he was smarter than the therapist. He was cynical about all therapy, he said. He didn't believe in it, and if he didn't believe in it, it wouldn't work. By July, he had started to skip appointments.

Let it go, my husband said. You can't make an eighteen-year-old boy do something he doesn't want to.

In the summer, James went to a succession of basketball camps in preparation for what we hoped would be a stellar and redemptive year.

In the fall, we drove him down to Avery. By then, I hardly recognized my son. He was large and muscular and had grown a beard. He towered over me, a fact that only served to emphasize how little influence I now had over him. Before we left, I sat him down and told him I loved him. I said to him that as long as he lived in our house, I would never give up on him. I said to him, "You reap what you sow."

I could see a small smile playing about his mouth. I thought, *He's laughing at me.*

In the fall, we drove to Avery, and I lost my son.

What do I want to say to mothers of sons? Something hurts these boys, and I don't know what it is. Take away the alcohol. If you suspect a problem, there is a problem. Don't let them get away with even the very first lie. Be vigilant.

Natalie

You see them come in, these big lumpin' boys, can't get in the dining hall fast enough. Somethin' in them frees up inside when they come in here. They're animals wanting their feed. They'll take four, five hamburgers and ask for extra fries and then take half a dozen pieces of cake. You can eat as much as you want at Avery. I've seen the boys down six, seven glasses of milk. I hardly know a one that eats a vegetable. I don't know why we bother with vegetables. The food is good here. We have the salad bar, the frozen yogurt machine, the grill. You can get whatever sandwich you want. We have "Italian Night," "Mexican Night." They'll eat seven, eight tacos at a sitting. I've known these boys since they were freshmen. Except J. Dot. He came in as a PG.

Her, I didn't know as well. The girls don't eat. Or if they do, they do it in secret. They go straight for the salad bar. I'm behind the counter with the entrées. I'll tell you, though, we got a dress code, but these girls, they dress like tramps, with their tiny tank tops and the skirts that show a lot of leg. I don't know how the boys—or the male teachers, for that matter—can keep their pricks in their pants. It's like *The OC* in there.

I knew Silas and his family real well. We all went to the same church. They were a good Catholic family. Owen's people have been here in Avery, oh, three generations, anyway. Anna, she was a fine mother. I always knew if I sent my kids over there to play, they'd be looked after. You never had to worry like you did with some mothers in town — the ones who drank, I mean. There's always some of those.

I liked Rob. He used to say thank you. No one ever says thank you. J. Dot, though, he was always looking to get a laugh. Center of attention. If you heard guffawing and you looked up, it would always be the table where J. Dot was sitting.

You pick a boy in the whole school who was raised with the right values, though, it would be Silas.

I don't blame the girl. I blame the reporters. I could kill some of those reporters for what they did to those boys.

Mike

In April, Silas Quinney was accepted to Avery Academy for entrance the following fall. By then, Mike had progressed from the Quinneys' kitchen to the dining room, as he had taken it upon himself to expedite the application and financial aid processes personally, bringing the forms to Anna and Owen to sign. In the interim, Mike had gotten to know Silas reasonably well, having met him several times and having attended one of his middle-school basketball games. Predictably, Coach Blount was wildly enthusiastic about Silas as a prospect, and Mike was beginning to feel that he had done Avery as well as the Quinneys an enormous service, more than compensating for the property damage that his Volvo, in concert with Mother Nature, had caused.

Mike regarded Silas as a quiet, thoughtful boy with more than his share of what Mike liked to call *character*, a trait that seemed to have been traded, in recent years, for *achievement*. Whether this was a consequence of the boy's religious upbringing—the Quinneys were devout Catholics—Mike couldn't say. The boy took after his father in looks, though he hadn't developed anything like the potential for a mischievous smile around the eyes. One doubted that he ever would. Silas seemed to take life, if not necessarily himself, seriously, and so made an ideal student as well as varsity basketball player (one of only two freshmen admitted to the team).

One advantage private schools held over public was that they kept their students *busy*. School started at eight in the morning, and though classes were over by two o'clock, sports were mandatory for all students. Also mandatory was an enforced study hall for two hours in the evening for boarders. Though Silas was not a boarder (unlike Rob, J. Dot, and the girl), he was busy until six thirty most days and could be counted on to have at least three hours of homework of an evening, if not more. The teachers tended to pile it on freshman year to indoctrinate the students. Many was the time, when visiting the freshman dorms, Mike had looked into the open rooms between the hours of eight and ten p.m. and had seen the new students, heads bent to their desks not in sleep but in despair, some of them actually weeping. Mike liked to think that Avery students were exceptionally well prepared for college, and, indeed, new alumni often reported that because their academic training at Avery had been rigorous, college seemed easier to them than high school.

Silas, on a varsity team, often had to travel long distances to at least half the games. In addition, Saturday school was mandatory every other week. These rules had grown out of a need to leave boarding students with little time to get into trouble, but they applied to day students as well. Anna complained laughingly that she hardly ever saw her son anymore, though she seemed happy enough that he was at Avery. She had become at first a tentative and then a tireless volunteer for the parent-teacher association. Owen, not one to hold a grudge, though Mike sensed he was willing to snatch his son from Avery at the least sign of trouble, took pride in his son's success at basketball

61

and tried to get to every home game. Each time Owen entered the gym and made his way over to the home bleachers, Mike would manage, at some point, to stand or sit next to him and ask after Anna and, if Owen had missed a quarter or a half, fill him in on the team's progress, Silas's in particular. Owen never boasted about his son, and when someone complimented Silas, he would give a slight nod in acknowledgment. One could see, however, in Owen's eyes, that beam of pride that only a father possessed. Mike envied him, for as much as he could cheer and celebrate when Avery had a winning or even a championship team, Mike never had that intimate jolt of joy that Owen Quinney had access to.

Owen always came to games in worn overalls and the thick plaid jacket that smelled of sheep. He showed not the slightest discomfort about being either underdressed or a local. Indeed, if questioned, Owen probably would have admitted to a feeling of superiority over his fellow parents—some of whom had traveled great distances to attend the games—because, well, that was just how Vermonters were. Occasionally, after a game, Owen and Anna would invite Meg and Mike to come for a meal, but, oddly, in all the time Mike knew them, Meg had never accompanied Mike to the Quinney house. Mostly this was circumstantial—his wife often had meetings or practices that ran through the dinner hour—but some of it was simply her sense that the Quinneys were Mike's deal, part of his job, and Meg did not consider his job her job. They had separate spheres of influence, separate universes of responsibility.

Anna Quinney was a superior cook of the Vermont farmhouse variety. Mike remembered her buttered biscuits especially, and he doubted he would ever taste anything as good again.

She made a lemon meringue cake worth dreaming about, and she could roast a chicken to perfection, the meat tender, juicy, and flavorful. The dining room was small, but because there was only the one son, there was always an extra chair or two for guests. Anna, Mike thought, liked to show off a bit, though one had to guess at that: she was modest almost to a fault. The table was underlaid with a blue woven cloth, similar to the place mats in the kitchen. The dining room and the linens reminded Mike of childhood meals at his grandmother's house, and he often had the sense, when visiting the Quinneys, of having stepped back in time. He worried always about spilling gravy over the side of his plate, but the linens were spotless whenever he dined there. *Dined* was not really the correct word, he thought. *Had supper* would be more appropriate. There was never any wine; the food, however good, was not gourmet; no one dressed for the meal. Owen would be at one end of the table, Anna at the other. Silas and Mike would sit across from each other, Silas often looking slightly pink from his exertions on the court.

Mike seldom visited in the fall or spring, since there were fewer occasions then for him to run into Owen, but he might eat there twice a month during the winter. There was a single window in the room, a large clock that chimed the quarter hour, a shelf of knickknacks that must have held some special significance for Anna. On another shelf was a series of colored photographs, many of Silas as a baby and as a child. Owen was a raconteur and could hold forth on any number of topics. Certain issues in particular would set him off. The man in the White House made him eloquent with rage. The war in Iraq rendered him apoplectic. Owen was a pacifist, he announced, and would encourage his son, if ever drafted, to make his way north to Canada rather than serve. Tourists gave him a chuckle, and he had an endless store of anecdotes about clueless visitors from out of state that tickled him no matter how many times he told a particular story. Such tales might encourage Mike to tell stories of his own about visiting parents and prospective students—not the most politic of conversations for a headmaster, but in that dining room he felt safe. It was, doubtless, the combination of the exquisite comfort food, the evocative tablecloth, and the small space that in other circumstances might have made him feel claustrophobic. He thought, on balance, that Silas, though an only child, had been lucky in his family.

Owen had not been bragging when he had said no one could drive to the basket like his son. Though the boy was short in stature, he more than made up for it in speed. He was gifted in his footwork as well, and it was a joy to watch him outwit opponents twice his size. When he missed a shot he should have made—particularly a three-pointer—or his team lost a game, Silas took it hard, often hanging his head to one side as if he expected to be taken out to the woodshed. Mike didn't think either Owen or Anna had ever raised a hand to Silas, yet he seemed to have access, at times, to a deep well of shame. Failure was not acceptable, and Silas appeared not to be able to shrug it off in the way the other boys often did.

Sometimes, when Mike encountered Silas crossing the campus, they stopped and chatted for a moment, Mike asking the questions and Silas answering. How were his folks? How did it look for the game on Saturday? How were his studies going? During Silas's sophomore year, Anna and Owen held the annual dinner for the basketball team at their home; Mike was invited as well, and on that occasion, he progressed from the dining room into the living room. And once, during Silas's junior year, the boy and he had had a real conversation.

Oddly enough (and sadly), it was a circumstance that involved sex. Two boys, juniors, had been caught after school hours in the day-student parking lot smoking marijuana in a gray Honda Civic *at the same time* that one of the boys was being fellated by a sophomore girl. That a teacher had stayed late and happened to jog by the Civic on the way to his own car was simply bad luck for the trio, who were at once brought to the headmaster's office. Mike spoke first to the boys, one of whom he had never liked and both of whom he had no trouble suspending from school pending further action by the Disciplinary Committee. As for the girl, whose name Mike could not remember, she sat across from his desk as he questioned her gently. He had wrongly assumed that she had been taken advantage of by the boys, that some sort of transaction might be involved. He was therefore somewhat shocked (though after nearly two decades with adolescents, little should have shocked him) when she freely admitted that she had followed the boys to the parking lot and had asked for a ride. Once in the car, she had begged to be allowed to perform the sex act on one of them. That the boys happened to be smoking a joint really had little to do with anything as far as she was concerned. Mike then asked her—perhaps out of annoyance that she could so blithely and casually perform what ought to have been an intimate sexual act, thus demeaning herself—if she routinely followed boys into cars and had sex, and she said, somewhat wistfully, he thought, "A couple of times." When Mike asked her whom she had followed, she named a half-dozen boys, among them Silas Quinney. Mike was so taken aback that he had her repeat the name. "But it kind of didn't work out," she said, with apparently no sense whatsoever of female pride. "He didn't really want to."

The girl was suspended for four days and readmitted, and then, if memory served, went on to Bowdoin. Mike then asked Silas to come to his office, and it was there that they had their first conversation of more than three sentences in a room not in the boy's own house.

Mike watched Silas walk across the office, his book bag slung over one shoulder. He settled himself into the chair in front of Mike's desk, the chair the girl had so recently occupied. He seemed confused and perhaps a little wary. He didn't know why Mike had called him in, but on the other hand, being summoned to the headmaster's office was seldom a *good* thing. He was taller than when Mike had first met him and had filled out considerably. He had thick hair like his dad, and one could already see a dark growth of beard even though Mike guessed he had shaved that morning or the previous night. He wore a blue Shetland wool sweater that Mike had seen on him often, the sort of sweater one could buy at Wal-Mart. Like most boys his age, he had on jeans, though Mike was happy to see they did not hang below his hip bones, exposing inches of boxers.

"How are your folks?" Mike asked.

"Good," Silas said, and then, perhaps out of politeness, he added a bit more—in the way children are taught to write additional sentences in a thank-you note. "My mom is talking about going back to school," he said.

"That's great. Where?"

Silas named a local junior college. "She wants to get a business associate's degree and then start a bakery."

66

"Well, she's the right person for that," Mike said with enthusiasm. "We could use a good bakery around here."

Silas nodded, at a loss for more news.

"Well, you're probably wondering why you're here," Mike said. "There's been an incident."

Mike named the girl and told Silas the reason he had been summoned. The blood left Silas's head, and the skin of his face turned the color of the cream trim at the windows.

"Silas?" Mike asked.

Silas gave his head a slight shake.

"Silas, you're not in trouble."

The silence was so prolonged that Mike had time to register Kasia's voice in the anteroom, a worrying ping of rain against the window (there was a varsity soccer game he was scheduled to attend later that day), the smell of coffee brewing in the lobby. "All I'm doing, really," he explained, "is trying to confirm the truth of what the girl said."

Mike shifted in his chair. Silas's gaze was fixed on the lip of the desk. Mike didn't know what the boy was seeing in his mind's eye: His mother's reaction to the news? The girl groping him? A future at the public high school?

"Silas, look at me."

Reluctantly, Silas raised his eyes to meet the headmaster's. Mike noted that the boy's foot was jiggling furiously against the leg of the desk.

"You are not in trouble," Mike explained. "You are not accused of a crime. If anything, you might reasonably have accused the girl of..." — he couldn't exactly say the word *harassing;* it seemed too extreme — "*bothering* you," he finished. "She has admitted to asking you for a ride and…" He hesitated again. "*Groping,* I think, is the appropriate word here."

Silas shook his head.

"That's not the way it happened?" Mike asked.

"It did," Silas said quietly. "It kind of did."

"Well, I'm sorry," Mike said. "She's been suspended for four days."

The boy shook his head again, violently this time. "She shouldn't be," he protested.

"Well, that's my decision, isn't it?"

"It wasn't anything," he said.

Mike leaned back in his chair and tapped his pencil against the desk. "Sometimes," he said, "a student needs, for lack of a better description, a time-out. A wake-up call. There have been a number of other incidents. We can't let that kind of behavior continue."

"It was just…" Silas said, opening his palms.

"I have a pretty good idea of what went on," Mike said. He was beginning to regret his decision to have Silas come into the office at all. The color still hadn't returned to the boy's face.

"So, listen," Mike said, hitching himself forward. He was developing a sudden desire for a cup of coffee. "We're fine here. I just needed verification, and you've given it to me. If it weren't true, and the girl was simply naming you, well then, we'd have had to take some other course of action. Get her help of some kind. Not that she doesn't need help as it is." The boy shook his head. Mike noted that his foot was still jiggling.

"I won't tell your parents about this," the headmaster said. "There's no need."

Silas's head snapped up. "You think that's all I care about?"

Mike was taken aback by the strength of the emotion behind the question.

"What my parents will say?" Silas added in case Mike hadn't understood.

"Well, no…" Mike began.

"I *let* it happen," Silas said. "I was in my car when she tapped on my window. I was a little surprised she was asking for a ride, since I didn't know her. Before we were out of the parking lot, she put her hand on my fly. I just stopped the car, and for a moment I let her."

"Silas," Mike said, "you're a sixteen-year-old boy."

"Seventeen."

"You were undoubtedly stunned. A little paralyzed. Any boy would be, in that situation."

"I could have…"

"Could have what?" Mike asked. "Acted a split-second faster?"

"I think you should suspend me, too," Silas said earnestly.

"Silas, I can't suspend you. I have no cause."

"It doesn't seem right. She didn't know what she was doing."

"I think she did know what she was doing," Mike said calmly. "She may not know why she did it, and I am hoping she will be a little shocked at her behavior and that this…time-out…will give her time to think, so that she won't want to do it again, but I do, Silas, I do think she knew exactly what she was doing."

The boy took a long breath and let it out. Mike noted, with tremendous relief, that the color was returning to Silas's face.

"It's not that I'm a masochist or anything," the boy said. "I'm not trying to get myself in trouble." He paused. "If I got suspended, my dad would kill me, and I wouldn't be able to play

69

basketball." Another pause. "It's just that I think I did hesitate too long, that I could have stopped her, that I could have asked her to get out of the car a little faster. Instead, I just froze."

"Silas, it wasn't your *fault,*" Mike said, a little more sternly than he might have otherwise. He didn't want Silas to obsess about this. More important, he didn't want it to get in the way of what he had to do in life, which was to continue to be a decent student, a good kid, and a sensational basketball player.

Surprised by the sudden change in Mike's tone, Silas sat up straight and put his hand on his book bag.

"Where are you headed now?" Mike asked casually.

"Chemistry," Silas said.

"You need a note?"

"No, I'm good," he said, standing.

Mike stood as well. "Thanks for coming in," he said, as if they'd been chatting about a course change.

Silas nodded.

"And say hello to your folks."

Mike watched him walk to the door. Silas had an odd hitch in his walk that reminded Mike of the boy's father. At the threshold, Silas turned and seemed about to speak. Then he shrugged and left, and after a minute, Mike walked into the lobby. He poured himself a cup of brutally strong coffee.

In the days that followed, Mike wondered why he'd called Silas in. Had it simply been for the purpose of verifying the girl's account? Had that really been necessary? Or was there another reason: a father's need to convince the son that he knows and sees everything? Mike was perfectly aware that he was not Silas's father, but if there had been, despite the girl's testimony to the contrary, some illicit participation on Silas's part, mightn't Mike have subtly wanted the boy to know that he knew it?

After their "conversation," there was a change in Silas's attitude toward the headmaster. Whereas before, if Mike had visited the Quinney home and found the boy lounging in front of the television, Silas would have stood and walked over to Mike and shook his hand and said hello, now the hand wasn't as ready and the eyes weren't as willing to meet Mike's. It was as if each time they saw each other, they were both reminded of the talk in the office and therefore had to imagine or remember—whether they wanted to or not—the incident in Silas's car, knowing full well that the other was doing this, too, so that the picture of the girl with her hand on Silas's fly functioned as a thin curtain between them. And in that way, Mike became a little more reluctant to just pop over to Anna and Owen's house to say hello or to greet them in Silas's presence when they came to the games. Mike was aware, however, in the spring of Silas's junior year, that the boy now had a girlfriend, a lovely violinist named Noelle who Mike hoped was headed for Juilliard. Avery seldom had such outstanding and accomplished students (*trophy students,* they were called in the business because the school could easily point to them as bona fide successes, thus enticing prospective students as well as alumni donations; such students were nearly worth their weight in checks), and Mike had been following Noelle's progress with growing enthusiasm. Just that September, she had given a concert in the chapel that had brought both teachers and students to their feet. Many had been weeping. It had been an extraordinary moment.

Noelle was slender, with long dark hair, and she moved like a dancer. She had a winning smile. Had Mike been Silas's age, he might have fallen in love with her, too. The headmaster thought Silas very lucky to have captured her attentions. On the other hand, Mike liked Silas tremendously and thought Noelle had chosen well herself. When he saw the pair of them, shoulder to shoulder, walking across campus, talking earnestly or laughing, he was suffused with a sense of the rightness of things. Occasionally, it did work, he would think to himself. There were teens who studied hard and had character, who didn't routinely drink or take drugs, who had instead demonstrated exceptional promise in their chosen fields. Avery had harnessed their energies and had guided them along the correct path. Such successes briefly made one recklessly sanguine about the future of the human race.

Noelle

We are sitting on Silas's bed. The house is still and quiet. His room is cramped, tucked under the eaves, with a window that looks out to the woods. The trees have just begun to bud, with clusters of red among the healthy green. I think it is a child's painting. We are sitting side by side, almost touching but not quite. His parents are up across the Canadian border, looking at a sheep. I try to imagine what it means to drive all the way to Canada to look at a sheep. Though Silas hasn't said so, I am guessing that his parents wouldn't be happy to find me in the house in the middle of the school day. We are away from school when we shouldn't be.

Silas wants to show me things. He shows me his baseball-card collection and his CD collection. He shows me his trains, which he keeps under the bed, and tells me they are the N Series. I don't know what the N Series is, but I like it that he used to like trains. There's a picture of him shearing a sheep and another of him birthing a lamb. I study the second picture for a long time, having never seen a birth before. He tells me what it is like. He and his father have to wear beepers for a month in case a ewe should go into labor. One person cannot birth a sheep; his mother, who never leaves the house during lambing, can't do it alone. Someone needs to hold the animal while the other puts his hands in. The ewe could give birth by herself, Silas explains, but the livestock is too valuable to allow for any kind of mistake or accident. This is how his parents make their living—by producing undamaged, quality lambs. Silas has been beeped in math class, while he was playing Wiffle ball with friends, and during a test. The teachers understand. They think it's cool, he says, the way something can be more important than school. Silas says he loves the birthing but doesn't want to inherit the farm. He and his father have never directly discussed it, though Silas knows this is his father's wish. His mother and Silas have other plans. Silas says he might apply to the University of Vermont and to Middlebury College. Middlebury is a reach, he says.

I tell him I want to go to Juilliard, but there are other schools I am probably more likely to get into.

Silas shows me a portfolio of drawings of animals that he has been working on for three years in different art classes. I think they are amazing. There are sheep and dogs and hedgehogs and deer and horses, and it almost feels as though I can hear them or smell them. I tell Silas he should be an artist, and he shrugs.

I can feel his nervousness all along the side of my body. The bed ripples each time he stands to show me something. When one of the dogs barks, Silas hops up and walks across the hall to look out the window. I can see the relief in his spine. Just the mailman, he says when he walks back in. I can hear the cars coming down off the hill into Avery, the steady whoosh of traffic. Even in the country, there are always cars.

■

"So," Silas says.

Silas is not tall for a basketball player, but he has broad shoulders and he is strong. I have seen this when he plays. He dribbles the ball as if pummeling it. For two weeks now, Silas and I have been finding each other in places where we never noticed the other before. In a hallway after a class. Hovering by the door to the dining hall. In assembly or in the distance when he is walking with friends and I know that somehow he has spotted me, too, though he gives no sign of it. It is in his body and his posture. A sudden sense of being alert.

Silas has smudged brown eyes and hair that won't lie down. He wears a baseball cap except when he is actually in a school building during school hours, which is the rule. When he takes his cap off, his hair is not flat like it is with most boys: it stands up with a life of its own, and that is how I think of Silas, as someone with a life of his own.

He looks over at me and then away. There is the question of what we will do now, with the free half hour that we have, here in his bedroom.

I want it, and I don't.

He wants it, and he doesn't.

He asks — surprising me — if I play Boggle.

I laugh. We have not even kissed.

I am in a practice room at the school. The acoustics are terrible, and I don't understand how this came to be a practice room.

The ceilings are high, the windows are tall, and the walls are wood paneled, as if this might once have been a library. When I practice, you can hear what I am playing outside in the hallway, but I don't care. When I practice, I go someplace else, and time moves at a different pace than it does when I am in math class. When I practice, I think about nothing except the music.

I pack up my violin and open the door. Silas is standing across the hallway, leaning against the wall. He isn't pretending to look at the canvases of student art that have been displayed, and he doesn't look away.

"Hey," I say.

"Hey," he says.

He reaches forward and takes my case. I hoist my book bag over my shoulder. It's a short walk to the dining hall, and I didn't bring a jacket. I pick my hair up with both hands and let it fall onto my back. We both know this is a nervous gesture. Silas looks too strong to be carrying such a small case. He walks with an odd gait, his legs slightly apart. He has blemishes beneath the stubble on his chin. He still smells of Neutrogena shampoo.

When we reach the dining hall, he stays with me in line. We sit by ourselves at a small table, and I know without even looking that his friends are watching us and making comments. I don't really care about that, but still, I can't eat. When we stood in line, I let them put Salisbury steak and mashed potatoes on my plate, even though I never order from the entrée counter. I don't even like meat. When I get up for a glass of milk, my hands are shaking. I take a deep breath and close my eyes.

This is going to be different, and I'm excited.

■

We are standing against a brick wall outside the gym. I waited for Silas outside the double doors. He didn't know I would be there, and when he saw me, he smiled. He is wet from his shower. We are kissing for the first time.

We move along the wall until we turn a corner and are out of sight. I have been waiting for this for what seems like forever. He puts his hands at the sides of my face, and I can smell the shampoo and his soap. His breath tastes like popcorn. Our feet get in the way, and I'm not sure at first which way to bend. Silas is taller than me, but not by much. He throws his arms around me, and I am surprised by his strength. He pulls back and laughs. We are both nervous now.

Silas laughs and kisses me again, hard this time, because we have to go and he wants me to remember the kissing.

We break apart and make our way to the parking lot. I stand at the side of his car while he fiddles with the key. His car is old and rusted and has many dents. The upholstery smells like dogs. We don't make any plans because we know that we have tomorrow and the day after that.

"See you," he says as he slips into his car.

"See you," I say.

Instead of driving away, Silas gets out of the car. He comes right at me and kisses me again, in the parking lot outside the gym. There are students getting into cars, parents waiting for their kids. A coach whose name I don't know walks by and stares at us. He has his hands in his pockets and is hunched over, but I see him smile to himself as he hurries on. I pull away for breath.

77

Silas leans against his car. He wants to say something but doesn't know how. I think that he is wondering if this is too soon. I want to tell him it is not too soon.

"Noelle," he says.

I wait.

He laughs at himself and turns around. He lightly punches the side of his car.

I smile. It's all so easy, so uncomplicated.

He turns and puts his arms over my shoulders and draws me to him. He is like a furnace, burning. He doesn't kiss me this time, just holds me.

"See you," he says. He gets into his car and stays there. I watch as he backs his car out, makes the turn, and leaves the parking lot. I wait for the wave. He bends down so that he can see me through the passenger-side window. I smile and wave back at him.

I run to the dining hall, trying to decide if I will tell my friends or if I will keep this new thing to myself for a little while so that I can savor it.

Before I reach the top of the hill, Silas calls. I fumble for my cell phone.

"Hey," he says to me.

Daryl

So, who told you it was me? They kept that out of the papers. I was glad for that. But, fuck, you tell me you're not the press, I have to believe you. I don't think anyone would be too interested now anyway, do you?

Yeah, I sell the booze to the kids. So what? I got eight guys who want my job. Some kids have their own IDs and don't need me. They buy the fakes from this guy in town, you don't need to know his name. He gets two hundred bucks apiece. These kids, they got money comin' out their assholes. They tell their parents they need two hundred bucks for cleats, and they got the money that afternoon. Me? That'd be my paycheck for a week.

The kids come swaggering over to my truck like they're not the little fags they are. Everybody knows who I am and what I do, and the kids are trying to be so street, like it's nothing, buyin' a case, and when I give it to them, you can see this, I don't know, this *look* on their faces. Like they just scored their first pussy or something. So, yeah, I like that.

I didn't know any of the kids. I don't ask names. Why would I do that? Ruin business. I don't care who they are. It could be the fucking president's daughter, for all I care. I sell a product. I mark it up. These kids, they're so fucking eager to score, they pay double what you would in a package store.

79

Rite of passage, buying their first case.

I don't see girls buying too much. It's mostly the guys. I know the girls are drinking it, though, because I see some of them at the parties in the woods. Shit-faced. Truthfully, nothing worse than a shit-faced girl. A shit-faced guy? That can be funny. Nothing funny about a girl falling down and puking her guts out, getting it in her hair. That's the worst, a real turnoff, when the girl gets it in her hair.

I do a sideline in cigarettes. Don't touch the drugs. There's other guys you go to for that. You get caught selling booze in this town, it's a slap on the wrist. You get caught selling drugs, town doesn't have anything to do with it. You got to go to the county courthouse. You're fucked.

I been doing this five, six years now. I'm living with my dad, saving on expenses. Putting some serious money in the bank. I got some guys down in Florida want to go in together on a condo. I need eight thou for the down payment, another eight to meet expenses for the first six months or so. Get myself set up down there.

I don't think what I do is immoral. What's morality got to do with it? If they didn't get it from me, they'd just get it from someone else.

Silas

Your smile is sweet. I remember it the first time we met. You don't remember, but I do. I saw you coming across the quad. It was in the spring, there were red buds still on the trees and no one was wearing a coat. I saw you coming on the diagonal across the quad. You had no idea anyone was watching you. I saw you lift your arms, ever so slowly, like a dancer warming up. I think I was already in love with you, with the way your arms moved just ever so slightly. And then, later, I fell in love with your mouth and your smile and that little laugh you always had, a little laugh, but so real. There was never anything fake about you, you never pretended.

If I could go back, I would erase that day, that night. I would stay home in my room and lock the door until the anger was through with me and then I could come out, and you would have been worried, I know you were already worried because I didn't call you or answer your messages, and I'm sorry about that, too, and my mother would have been knocking on the door and the coach would have wondered where I was, but it would have been so much better than what I did, which was to start drinking even before I went to the game. It was in the fridge, the beer, and I drank it for breakfast before the game. I threw the ball into the stands. It hit that woman, and then I was gone, and then all I could think was to get as drunk as possible. And none of this is an excuse, there is no excuse, and I am so sorry that I didn't lock myself in my room. Because you will never understand, because I cannot understand, even though I was there. I was there. I did it. But I don't want to remember that. No, I want to cut it away from my brain. I want to go back in time, want to stop time and cut the day away. Cut the night away. Just cut it from my brain, and if only there wasn't a tape. If only I had left. If only I hadn't been so drunk. If only I hadn't been so angry.

It will hurt you, and that I can't stand. It is that, of everything, that I can't stand. And I can never look at you again. I can never face you. I can never see your face again.

You moved your arms just ever so slightly, as if you might dance or twirl with the spring inside you, and I felt it, too, and I fell in love with you that day, and you never even knew.

Mike

Mike had first encountered Avery Academy on an afternoon when a snowstorm had lightly dusted the frozen grasses and bare trees that bordered the long drive into the campus. The clouds overhead were dispersing, and the school and its grounds were lit with that miraculous clarity that accompanies a sudden occurrence of sunshine on a gray day. It would have taken an insensitive man, Mike thought, not to be awed by the sparkle on those granite buildings, and it was difficult to regard the spectacle as anything but a good omen. As if on cue, the doors to several of the four-story edifices opened, and pods of students, wrapping their scarves around their necks but not zipping their jackets, spilled onto the lawn, amazed by their own footprints in the shallow dusting. A few attempted snowballs, and there were many chases and squeals. It was the first of a number of such scenes Mike would witness that would remind him that secondary-school students were as much children as they were adults, and that therein lay the dilemma of how to educate and parent them simultaneously. Mike was cheered by the general ebullience and by the homogeneous campus, architecturally speaking. A dozen imposing buildings were evenly spaced around a large quadrangle that was neatly crisscrossed with paved pathways. Some of the more formidable buildings had white columns set atop

83

granite steps, while others, which he took to be dormitories, had shutters, suggesting large New England houses. Beyond the quadrangle, treed lawns sloped away from the center of campus, and through the thinning foliage, one glimpsed other similar buildings and several good houses, one of which Mike was hoping would be given to him.

He parked his car in front of the central administration building, wondering if he should have taken the trouble to find a parking lot, since his was the only vehicle on the pristine quadrangle. He stepped briskly to the front door, wishing already to make a good impression on the trustees, who had hastily been assembled for his interview. The previous headmaster, much beloved, had recently been diagnosed with pancreatic cancer and had very little time left to live, none of it available to the school. He had, in fact, already left the campus to live with his sister in Boston. It was only after the headmaster had gone that the fact that he, a tolerant man of fifty-five, was gay was openly discussed. This information was seen to be largely irrelevant by an equally tolerant faculty, though it may have induced the trustees to view Mike favorably since he had a wife and had been married for half a decade. (The phrase *married for half a decade,* with its suggestion of stability and harmony, hardly described the tempestuous and fragile union Meg and he had forged, but the trustees did not know that.) Mike was, if the board approved, to be hired as interim headmaster while a formal search was conducted. It was no secret that a number of the deans, Geoff Coggeshall among them, were angling for the spot—Mike had been told this over the phone—but he hoped to remain above the fray and simply do what was needed, which was to hold a slightly grieving campus together until June and to graduate as many students from the senior class as possible, given, for some, an impressive number of *units,* or demerits, that threatened to send them home. In addition, he was also to raise money for a campaign that had been started the year before with the goal of building a new field house and an arts complex.

Mike had been called to the interview because he was then the dean of students at a lesser institution in Hartford, Connecticut, and it was known among some of his peers that he was unhappy with the job of policing an extremely diverse student body, most of whom were day students, in a city with one of the highest crime rates in the nation. At the school in Hartford, the gates were locked, students had to pass through metal detectors to enter buildings, and there had already been one stabbing during a rancorous soccer game with a school across town. Mike's was a high-stress job in a high-stress school that had more in common with the public schools of New York City than it did with the collegiate atmosphere of the private schools to which he had aspired. The salaries of the faculty and deans were pitiful by most standards, forcing Meg and him to live in a neighborhood that only added to the strain. (Meg, however, thrived at the school and was one of its more popular teachers, owing to an ability to clarify even the most abstruse math for well-intentioned pupils as well as to a remarkably deft touch with students who were not.) So it was with a somewhat selfishly light step that Mike opened the door on that briefly sparkling afternoon, buoyed by the chatter of seemingly happy students and excited by the prospect of a headmastership at a bona fide private school more in keeping with his academic dreams than the one he had just left.

First impressions are enduring ones, but Mike found that

the longer they lingered, the more at odds they later seemed with the reality of the setting or the people in it. He was, for example, very taken with the reception room that was the hub for the various administrative offices that surrounded it — those of the deans, the development officers, the admissions people, and the headmaster and his assistant. The lobby resembled a living room, with a herringbone-patterned floor (once again, those peaks and Vs), fresh white paint, and a number of portraits on the walls. There were several Persian carpets and, to one side, an attractive area where a visitor might make himself a cup of coffee and select an apple or a cookie for refreshment. The effect was calculated to impress parents and potential donors, but Mike found that it impressed him as well, since the administrative offices at the school that he, feigning illness, had left earlier that day had iron webbing across their windows to protect them from vandals.

However, even at Avery, where Mike initially felt cosseted, he would discover over time that the carpets were not true Persians but rather cheap reproductions; that they were, in addi-tion, stained with blots of spilled coffee and something that could only have been axle grease; that the cookies — the same as were mass-produced by the dining hall chefs — often lingered untouched on their plates for days, causing Mike to wonder if they oughtn't be dusted; and that the portraits on the walls, which had at first seemed so venerable, were in fact of benefactors and not of headmasters. (In years to come, Mike would develop a sharp, unyielding antipathy to a chinless man depicted in one of those oils, a financier and trustee of the school for most of his term who spoke to Mike, even in front of his colleagues, as he might to one of his many underlings at his Wall Street firm.

Mike particularly disliked the phrase *Do it now,* which the man seemed to think he had coined and trademarked.)

Mike's first impression of Mrs. Gorzynski (shortly to become Kasia to him) proved his point. She glanced up at Mike as he crossed the wide expanse of polished floor, and even as he was trying to impress her, he was thinking, *Glasses, thick in the waist, permed hair.* He then formed the image *matronly,* when in fact nothing could have been farther from the truth. Mrs. Gorzynski, Mike was to discover, had been married three times and was possessed of an earthy wit and throaty laugh that suggested a varied and rich sexual history. Sarah Grace, Mike's colleague in admissions, could speak volumes on the issue of deceptive first impressions and often did, recounting how the most promising and clear-eyed of young men might turn out to be the one procuring alcohol for younger students or how the sweetest-seeming girl might become the one who was downloading term papers at a considerable profit to herself.

Mrs. Gorzynski asked Mike to sit a minute. She offered him coffee and cookies, all of which he declined, since nibbling on a cookie while he shook hands with trustees could hardly be viewed favorably. He was nervous, but he was something of a fatalist as well, and he knew that even if he didn't get the position, he would have enjoyed the excursion to an especially beautiful sector of Vermont and that he'd at least have had a day off from a job he both feared and loathed. In addition, the few minutes of first impressions would have fed his imagination and produced a new gloss on an old fantasy. Perhaps it would spur him to actively seek another post.

He was met by Geoff Coggeshall. Mike was aware of a moment or two of mutual assessment, much in the way of two actors auditioning for the same part sizing each other up. Coggeshall guided Mike to a conference room in a corner. When Mike entered, five trustees (all the school could manage to assemble on such short notice) were sitting around an oval walnut table. They nodded in his direction and did not get up.

The position was described to Mike, and he was questioned at great length. He was told at least three times that the job was for an *interim candidate only* (surely any person worth the post, Mike thought, might be expected to have absorbed this information the first time). He listened carefully, he answered all questions, he was alert to nuances. He smiled, he laughed, he made assurances. He nodded politely, he asked a few good questions himself, and before he had returned to Hartford later that evening, he had been given the job. He was to start as soon as he possibly could, according to a message he heard on the answering machine shortly after he walked in the door of their apartment, Meg standing not five feet away from the telephone with an expression on her face that could only be described as curious and furious together.

Mike had a great deal of hasty explaining to do to his wife, in whom he had not confided the fact of the interview. *Why* was perfectly obvious: Meg would have argued strenuously that she could not be uprooted in the middle of the academic year, that she had no thought of leaving the school at which she was now quite happy, and, furthermore, how could Mike even think of not fulfilling his own responsibilities to a school that needed him far more than any elite academy did? Had Mike known that Avery would respond so quickly—and by phone—he'd have given Mrs. Gorzynski his office number only and then would have begun a campaign of persuasion that might have convinced his wife of the benefit to herself of his taking the job at Avery.

After three hideous days of acrimony, it was decided that Mike would accept the interim job in Vermont, but Meg would finish out the year in Hartford. In June, if Mike was offered an extension of the post, they would reassess the situation. He was to commute back and forth to Hartford on alternate weekends, and vice versa, actually quite a difficult enterprise at private schools because of the necessity to be present for Saturday games. Mike thought at the time that each welcomed the separation. Meg would have to weather the storm his departure would create, but she could come home to an apartment empty of tension. For Mike's part, he would have a shot at fulfilling a long-held academic fantasy, one that would require all his attention and time.

Mike and Meg had met in Hanover, New Hampshire, at a pre-Thanksgiving dinner party given by a fellow graduate student in the Master of Liberal Arts program at Dartmouth. Those enrolled in the program were a motley crew — many (of which Meg was one) former high-school teachers hoping to better their lot and their salaries, others (like Mike) unable to commit to a doctoral program. As a result, there was a great deal of fluidity in the course offerings and one might find oneself taking seminars in developmental psychology as well as creative writing. Since Mike did not then know how to cook, he had brought wine to the party. Meg had brought a pumpkin eggnog flan, a nontraditional dish that at first puzzled the partygoers and then pleased them so much it became the most popular offering at the table. She had made it, she said, from a recipe handed down from her grandmother in Ohio, and though it contained nearly lethal amounts of sour cream and eggnog, it was always a hit. She sat across the makeshift plywood table from Mike, slightly too far away in the noisy conviviality either to hear or to speak to him, but he spent much of the meal too obviously observing her. He was awed by something both feisty and warm in her, suggesting a sexual appetite that might hold many surprises. At one point during the dinner, Meg returned Mike's stare, opening her eyes wide and smiling, as if to say, *Well now,* and after the meal, when he sought her out, she appeared to enjoy his attention. He learned her name, her course of study, her hobby (volleyball), and her profession (she had taught for three years in a public high school in Lewiston, Maine). He also learned, by touching her on the upper arm to move her out of the way of an oncoming pumpkin pie, that she was tautly muscled. Because of that first touch, he was never able to shake the notion that she was tightly wound, high-strung.

Later that night, both before and after he learned that his instincts about her sexuality were correct, he also came to understand that she was slovenly beyond belief. It was something of a small miracle, actually, that she was so presentable and seemingly well-groomed in public—her chestnut hair neatly trimmed to fall just below her ears, her face always fresh-scrubbed and gleaming. She shared with another woman an apartment that seemed tidy enough until Meg opened the door to her own room, where Mike discovered there was not one inch of uncovered floor space between the door and her bed. Her entire wardrobe, as well as bits of odd wiring leading to various electronics, and loose-leaf notebooks with pages spilling out, made a kind of carpet. This squalor only partly registered at the time, for by then Meg was raising her sweater up over her long white back as she walked toward the bed. A few hours later, however, the chaos hit Mike with a shock when he discovered that the tub in her bathroom was filled with grayish water that clearly hadn't drained in days, if not weeks, since it appeared to contain the scummy residue of a number of baths, and that her sink was so encrusted with dried toothpaste and makeup and bits of tissue that he nearly gagged when he caught sight of it.

"I've got a drain problem," she called to Mike from the bed in a not-very-worried voice. "Had it for weeks."

After Mike had used the toilet, trying not to touch anything in the room, he asked her how she was managing to shower. She answered, "Oh, it always goes down a little bit each day," clearly demonstrating an enforced frugality with the earth's resources that even Al Gore might have envied. Disgusted, but by now thoroughly besotted by Meg's dark nipples, the slight hollow in the curve of her hip, and the feel of her silky pubic hair on his cheek, he offered to do what any smitten suitor might. He would return, he said, with a snake and a bottle of Drāno.

The task was odious and revolting. Any sane man, Mike thought, might reasonably have come to the conclusion that Meg's sloth was an unnegotiable flaw. Surely that man would not then have proposed marriage six months later, having taken on the task of keeping Meg's quarters more or less sanitary even if they were never tidy. That Mike did, he thought, was a tribute either to Meg's nerveless charms or to his own belief that marriage to him would reform his beloved.

(Mike had loved Meg from the first moment he'd seen her across the plywood table. Exactly when Meg had discovered she loved Mike was less clear. It seemed to him that she had *consented* to marriage, and in that verb lay the very heart of the union, with its innate imbalance. Mike asked. Meg sometimes consented. Sometimes, she didn't. That Meg had more power in the marriage than he didn't surprise or even displease Mike.

That Meg had the power to *withhold* was what bothered him most.)

In due course, Mike was given the post of headmaster of Avery Academy (nothing interim about it now). Meg reluctantly joined him in the headmaster's house, a very good reproduction of a brick Georgian that came with a maid and access to the various chefs in the dining halls, thus nipping a great many housekeeping disasters in the bud. Mike grew into his post in a way he felt few before him had ever done, the fantasy and reality of being headmaster of Avery Academy fusing into a passion and loyalty to a job he considered himself extraordinarily fortunate to have. His early success was largely due to an exceptionally generous gift to the school during his *interim-tenure-only* months as headmaster, a gift in excess of four million dollars that he was instrumental in quickly shepherding through the previously archaic bureaucracy. Though it was understood that the part he had played was rather small in relation to the size of the gift, there was nevertheless an aura of luck briefly associated with him that few wished to ignore. (The serious, not to say *stern,* demeanor of the trustees was dispelled some four months after his interview at a dinner following a long day of meetings in New York City and the announcement of the spectacular donation to the school, the news causing Mike's chinless nemesis to order a dozen bottles of champagne, which predictably loosened tongues and produced much laughter as well as some memorably foolish behavior.)

At first Meg had held fast to her desire to stay in Hartford, but she proved herself only human—and female at that—when she visited the campus during a particularly lovely stretch of mild summer weather. She was drawn outside the Georgian reproduction that was causing in her the first stirrings of appreciation, and wandered the vast lawns of the campus for long walks and picnics and occasional visits to the playing fields, where summer soccer and field hockey camps were being conducted. From certain hillocks, one had views of both the Green Mountains to the east and the Adirondacks to the west, as well as of the snug valley that lay between these two ranges, and something in the landscape, those rolling hills perhaps, briefly softened the feisty bit of Meg's nature so that she was able to convince herself that adolescents requiring both parenting and an education have more similarities than differences, and that this particular age group was ferociously needy on all fronts. The fact that she would be permitted to teach Advanced Placement Calculus as well as to coach girls' varsity volleyball sealed the deal.

In August, Meg moved in with Mike for good. Mike viewed this move as a success, though he shortly came to understand that Meg was there on sufferance, an attitude that expressed itself occasionally as irritation, dismissiveness, or a ready cynical smile when presented with anything that might be construed as elitist.

Back in his den, Mike stood up from the couch, intending to retrieve the small cassette from the movie camera and then to summon Arlene and Kasia to his office so that he could question them about the provenance of the tape. He heard the front door open. Mike panicked slightly, not wishing to be caught with the apparatus—with the *evidence*—on the floor. He unplugged the camera, unhooked the cables, and pushed the mess under the sofa. By then, Meg was in the kitchen, where he went to meet her.

"What are *you* doing here?" she asked, setting down on the

kitchen table both a small bag of groceries and her bulging brown leather briefcase. He could see that she'd been counting on having the house to herself and now was annoyed. The briefcase had a zip top, the zipper long broken, and Mike could see from across the room the bunches of student papers that had been stuffed into the bag, Meg's disorganization extending into the classroom, where it didn't belong. His wife was forever losing pens and lesson plans and calculators and, once, a set of student exams. Invariably, Meg was the last teacher to turn in her grades. Many of the faculty would try to get their grades done immediately after the last exams so that the students could head home for the holidays or the summer break with some idea of what their report cards would look like. None of Meg's students had ever had that luxury, and it was not uncommon for her to receive, well into the break, calls from distraught students who still didn't know if they had passed the class or, if the callers were top-shelf candidates to various colleges, if they had gotten their all-important A for the term. Mike dreaded hearing that a promising student had asked Meg for a college recommendation, since she was unlikely to get the appropriate forms in by the deadlines. Mike could only hope that no student had been turned away from a university because of his wife's negligence. She was, he kept reminding himself, a superb teacher.

Mike was not in the habit of being in the house midday, and though his wife's question was a reasonable one, he stumbled over his answer, which was as good as admitting he was telling half-truths. "I left a list here," he said. "You didn't come across it? A list of donors' names for the annual bulletin?"

Meg removed the first of a dozen fat-free yogurt cartons from the bag. She narrowed her eyes.

94

"Also," Mike said, "there's been a tape. There is a tape."

"Of what?"

Meg shrugged off her jacket and let it fall onto the seat of a kitchen chair. It wouldn't occur to her to hang it up.

"There's been an incident," Mike said. "A potentially serious incident."

Meg peeled back the lid of a small yogurt container and examined its contents as though she suspected she had been cheated.

"I think you'd better come see this," Mike said. "It's important."

"If you say so," she said.

As they walked together down the hallway, he was already regretting having slipped the camera under the sofa. He explained himself as he retrieved it. "I didn't know who might be at the door," he said.

"People regularly walk into our home without knocking at noon on Tuesdays?" Meg asked.

Mike connected the various cables and wires. "This is going to be rough," he said.

"What's it of?"

"Some kids," Mike said. "They're having..." He paused, stopping at a word that ought to have been easy to say to his wife but was not, and he wasn't sure if it was the situation itself that was inhibiting him or simply its boldness. "They're having sex."

"Avery kids?" Meg asked. "Where did you get this?"

"Kasia gave it to me. She got it from Arlene." Mike watched Meg mold the yogurt on her spoon with her upper lip, producing an erotic sculpture, though at that moment Mike was immune to eroticism of any sort. Meg ate five small meals a day and one large one (dinner), and the yogurt was, he calculated, meal number three. It consisted of a sixty-calorie carton of fat-free peach, and she liked to make it last.

"Here goes," Mike said.

He had rewound the tape to the beginning so that it started precisely as he had seen it begin: with *the girl* twirling between the tall boy who was still clothed to the sturdy boy who was naked. Mike noted, on the second viewing—no easier than the first—that one could not see any of the faces. The boys were cut off at the shoulders, at least in the beginning.

"Oh my God," Meg said, lowering her spoon. It was not an utterly shocked *Oh my God* but rather said quietly, as one might say, also quietly, *Yikes,* and Mike realized that being told about the tape was no preparation for the real thing.

"Oh my God," she said again after several seconds.

The naked boy had bent to kiss the girl's nipple, and the slender boy was now allowing his jeans to fall off in one go. The girl began to kneel at the crotch of the taller boy. Meg covered her mouth.

"I'll stop it," Mike said, bending forward.

"No, wait," she said.

Again, Mike looked for clues as to when the incident had taken place—for a calendar on the wall, a school diary open on a desk—but the camera panned so quickly and so inexpertly between the participants that it was difficult to make out much of anything, and, once again, he had to ward off incipient nausea.

They listened to the moans of the boy on the bed as they watched the girl perform. "This is *awful,*" Meg said.

"She's young, isn't she?" Mike asked.

"A freshman. She's on thirds soccer."

"How old?"

"Fourteen, fifteen?"

"You know her name?"

"No."

By now Meg was perched at the edge of the couch. She had bent forward so that her arms rested on her knees. It was both a rapt and a defensive posture. Where normally there was a Wolf Blitzer or a Jim Lehrer, the intense visage on their television screen was that of Silas Quinney.

Meg turned and stared at her husband. "You've got yourself a hell of a mess here," she said.

Laura

When my parents dropped me off that first day of orientation our freshman year, they weren't impressed with my roommate. She was acting weird with them—kind of all over them but fake, if you know what I mean. I think that was her way of trying to impress, of trying to be charming, of saying *look at me*. It didn't work *at all* with my parents, and I know they later tried to get my room changed. The freshman class was a big one, though, and the administration couldn't do anything about the situation.

When I got to Avery, I knew that I was going to have to get along with lots of students I didn't have much in common with, so I was pretty much, like, prepared for anything, and looking forward to it, too. I wasn't prepared for her, though.

That first day of school, she got there before I did. She took the best bed and the best desk. That was OK, I expected that. Though if it were me, and I had arrived first, I would have left the best desk and the best bed for her. But that's just me. When we got there, she had a couple of purses and maybe a dozen pairs of shoes strewed all over her bed, which had an incredible down comforter on it already. I don't know designer pocketbooks from knockoffs, but you could tell that the leather and the quality were good. My mother, later on the phone, referred to them as *designer*.

No one at Avery has purses, never mind designer ones. We all just use backpacks. My roommate's closet was so full of clothes, she had nowhere to put the purses and shoes, so she ended up stuffing them under the bed, where she kept her candy.

We all keep candy under the beds. If it's out on your desk, it's understood that anyone can eat it. If it's under the bed, it's your own private stash.

That first day, I was a little shaky since I'd never been away from home except for camp. Right off, she offered me a joint. I remember being stunned. I'd never had a joint before. Never even held one. I was fourteen then. I said no. She lit up right there in the room, and I thought, *Oh my God, we're going to get expelled before my parents even get home.* I didn't know what to do, so I just got up and went for a walk until I thought it was safe to go back.

The next morning, when I woke up, she seemed to be in a panic over what to wear. She kept trying clothes on and ripping them off. I thought she looked great in everything. She was really beautiful. She had long blond hair and wide green eyes and a perfect nose. She was slender, not skinny, but slender. She looked great in a tank top.

I would have to say that she dressed kind of sexy. Some girls did without even trying, but you could see that she was trying. I would watch her get dressed, and see how she changed her underwear or picked a shorter skirt or put a lace tank top on under her white shirt. She kept to the dress code but pushed it right to the edge. I know you shouldn't judge a person by how she dresses, but it seems to me that she was asking to be judged by her clothes. By how she put them together. If you're asking to be judged like that, then I think you're trying to send a message.

She drank a lot for a freshman girl. I think that came out in the newspapers. It was a badge of honor with her, how much liquor she could hold. She was kind of wild. She had no interest in the freshman or sophomore boys. There are girls at the school who will immediately go for the PGs, and that's what she did. Sought them out. That's what she was doing with J. Dot. That's James Robles, who was involved.

She liked to come across as a dumb blonde. She was always talking about her "blonde moments." But, actually, I thought she was pretty smart.

I went to Avery Academy because it was the best school I could get into. My parents are from New Hampshire, and they believe in the value of a private-school education, since both of them went to private school. I was very resistant at first, and I cried a lot that September. But then I got used to it, and when I go back home now and I look at our public school, how it's only the one building, and I hear from my friends how big the classes are and how the teachers can't even assign the books they want because there isn't any money anymore, I think I am lucky to be where I am. I know that I will, like, have a better chance at college from here than I would have had from my public school, and I have had some wonderful teachers who you can see really care about the students. And I have had some terrific opportunities, too. Right away, that first September, I made the varsity soccer team. I would never in a million years have made the varsity soccer team at my public school my freshman year because my school was huge, and they already had more good players than they could use. Probably not even my junior year. So that's an opportunity that I never would have had. I think the soccer will help me get into a better college.

My roommate was at Avery for what is actually a common reason. Her parents were rich and they traveled, and they just couldn't put in the time to be with her. She'd been left on her own a lot, and I think that got to be a bit of a problem. Some kids are here because their parents are getting divorced or the kids have gotten into trouble and the parents don't know what to do. She said her parents didn't get along very well, that they were always fighting. I met them only once, when they came for parents' weekend. They seemed nice enough to me.

The night the tape was made, there was a dance. A lot of freshmen went to the dances, and sophomores, too. Less juniors and seniors, who thought the dances were lame. I wish our class now had more spirit and would go to the dances, but we hardly ever do. Back then, they were kind of a big deal. I was surprised to discover how prevalent alcohol was. I guess I had just been living in a bubble, because it was all new to me. Some of the guys would have gotten ahold of it and it would be outside at the back of the gym, and you could buy a can and drink it right there. What happened was, it made you drink very fast, because you were always scared you were going to get caught. So you'd dance a bit or hang out inside, and then you might run out and have a quick one and run back inside. And you could see, as the night progressed, that kids were getting more and more hammered. I'm talking about freshmen and sophomores here. There are always initiatives about stopping the drinking. Each class, I think, tries to take that on. Or at least some kids in the class do. But it never seems to go anywhere. They keep trying to crack down, but it's amazing how smart some kids are. How they manage to get it.

That night, she was drinking even before the dance, while we were all getting dressed. I don't know where she got it. She had it under the bed with the pocketbooks and the candy. She was drinking from those little bottles that you get in hotel rooms. Scotch and vodka and whatever. She once gave me champagne in one of those little bottles, and I drank it, but it was warm and gave me a headache. I can't say how many of those bottles she had to drink before she went out, but she was definitely feeling good. I'm trying to think now of who might have drunk more than she did that year, and I can't think of anyone.

She didn't own a movie camera. I'm pretty sure I would have known if she did, because she'd have been making movies of herself all the time.

When she went out, she had her 7 jeans on, the ones that made her butt look great. She was wearing a blue halter top. She had light tanned skin, and it shone. She wasn't very toned, but it didn't seem to hurt her any. She had on a narrow white cotton jacket, like a blazer, and even though it was January and completely freezing, she wouldn't put another, warmer jacket over that. She had these fabulous hippie silver earrings, really big and dangling. She had on a pair of silver stilettos. When she left, she looked kind of amazing.

Jonathan

Oddly, what I remember most about Rob Leicht is the paper he wrote on Faulkner. The class assignment was to pick a passage in *As I Lay Dying* and develop a thesis that might explicate either a character or a theme in the book. In the beginning, I recall asking Rob repeatedly for his outline, for his ideas about the book, for any hint at all as to what he was planning. He gave me very little response in return, and I had the distinct impression then that he hadn't even read the book. But as the due date got closer, I could see that he was bearing down on the project. A number of questions he asked me in the final days struck me as remarkably perceptive. Truthfully, I'm not sure I've known a better reader/thinker ever to go through Avery. I've been here nearly fifteen years, and I can speak only about the students I've personally taught, but I think Rob was generally recognized by all of the faculty to be brilliant.

The problem with Rob was that he was inconsistent. If challenged academically—and I think he would have responded to Brown as a tremendous challenge—he would rise to the occasion and produce excellent, even outstanding, work. If he thought a class was easy, however, or if he had taken a dislike to a teacher—which occasionally happened—he would tune out and produce work of a barely passable nature. He was exceptionally good in class discussions, and I think that carried him through a number of courses in which he'd done less than outstanding work. I should probably state for the record here that I was Rob's adviser as well as his AP English teacher his junior year.

As for the Faulkner paper, Rob had taken the most difficult passage in the book: the one time that the matriarch—Addie Bundren—speaks. The meaning of the passage is not immediately clear, and one must dig to understand this woman who is at once so unnatural and yet so central to the novel. Rob turned in a paper that I won't soon forget. I seriously doubt most college juniors could have written a work that so well understood the concept of "death in life." It was as if Rob *knew* Addie Bundren. I was flat-out blown away. I checked all the obvious sources to see if he might have plagiarized the piece, but it was pretty clear the work was his own. He was certainly capable of it; that, I didn't doubt. There was a witty side to Rob, but also a profound—even dark—side, and I think the character of Addie Bundren spoke to that side.

The paper won the Junior Class Writing Prize. None of the other contestants even came close.

I wrote one of Rob's recommendations for Brown. I was not in the least surprised when he was accepted "early decision."

But there was about Rob, as I say, this dark side. I've met his parents, who seemed perfectly ordinary to me, so I can't say it was a result of his home life. Who knows why one person is the way he is? I don't mean *dark* in the sense that Rob was going to pick up a shotgun one day and spray bullets all over the library. No, I mean it in the sense that he had access to a kind of nihilism that you don't ordinarily see in sixteen-, seventeen-year-olds. He skipped a few classes toward the end of his junior year, and that pattern was continuing in the fall of his senior year. I tried to talk to him about this, but I don't recall getting very far. He'd been clipboarded once, but he stopped short of having to appear in front of the Disciplinary Committee.

I enjoyed the Rob I knew a great deal. You've probably seen his picture. He was a tall, skinny kid with thick dark hair. Not a handsome face, but a nice face. I used to look forward to our conferences. He appreciated being addressed on an adult level, and he would even bristle a little if he thought he was being talked down to. One quickly learned not to do that with him. Some kids never reach that level of maturity.

He was excited about Brown. He must have called me within minutes of getting the news because his voice was still breathless. I was thrilled for him. It's one of the reasons the entire episode was so terrible to watch. You hate to see the best and the brightest self-destruct like that.

I have very little insight as to why Rob did what he did. I don't see him in that scenario at all. It's hard for me to imagine that at some point he wouldn't have said, either to himself or to the others, *This is insane.* I try often to recall what it felt like to be that age. I try to put myself in his position.

I attempted to get in touch with Rob about a month after the incident became public, just to lend my support. I called him at his house. I could hear his mother trying to get him to come to the phone to speak with me, but he wouldn't. Perhaps I had called too soon.

Sienna

So this is better. I love Starbucks. I'd die if they didn't have one close by the campus. I always get a grande decaf skim latte. I could eat a sandwich. You want to split a sandwich? I like the panini things. With the ham. But let's, like, get this over with. So what else do you want to know? They got me drunk. I don't like to talk about this. It's embarrassing. It's cold in here. If I'd gone to the hospital right after, which I should have, they probably could have found one of those things in my blood that you put in a drink to make the girl pass out. Rofatol or something. I think that's what they must have done to me, because I would never. Well, look at me. Do I look like the type that would do that? Be honest. I never drink now. Because I know the dangers. I was thinking that if the college thing doesn't work out, I could go on the road on the lecture circuit and give talks about how girls can get taken advantage of, but I know my parents would kill me if I ever did that. They just want it all to go away. So, like, maybe we could get the sandwich now. It's not like I'm starving or anything. It's just that I think I should keep my blood-sugar levels up. If you order it at the counter, they'll bring it to the table. They do that here. I would have kept my mouth shut, I really would have, except I got called into the headmaster's office on, like, the Wednesday morning after it happened. God, it was so early, I was hardly awake, and I couldn't really understand Mr. Bordwin's questions. He said he had a tape, and I said, *What tape?* And he was, like, *It's a tape of you in a room in the boys' dorm having "relations,"* as he called it, *with a number of boys.* And I was, like, *What the fuck are you talking about?* Though I'm pretty sure I didn't say *fuck.* And he said he would play the tape for me if I wanted, and I said I didn't need to see any tape, and he said this was a serious offense, that I wasn't in trouble yet but that the boys were, and anything I could remember about what happened would be good. Mr. Bordwin, he was just so lame. If it had been a different headmaster, I'm sure this whole thing might have been handled another way. That's what my dad says. And I said, *Well, maybe I had gone to a party on Saturday, I go to a lot of parties, and sometimes, you know, maybe someone tries to get me to drink, and maybe I had one beer, but maybe I didn't, I didn't remember much about Saturday night, because, like, maybe someone put something in my drink? Which was why I couldn't remember?* Mr. Bordwin, he had these deep blue eyes, and it was hard to look at him straight on, so I said I really wasn't feeling good, I had to go, and he said I should go back to my dorm and think about what we had just talked about, especially about how what happened last Saturday night could be very serious, and when I was ready to talk about it some more, I should call him. And I was, like, out of there so fast, you can't believe it. So I went back to my dorm, and I was, like, scared shitless, because if there was a tape, then, oh God, it would be embarrassing, right? And the night sort of started to come back to me, it took a few hours to get these, like, strange memories. And then I realized I had to call my parents. Because if I didn't, Mr. Bordwin was probably going to, and truthfully, I was kind of amazed he hadn't done it already. So I called. My father, he was, like, *Oh my God, you have to call the police.* And I'm going, *I'm not gonna call the police.* And my father said I had to do this, because it was rape and I was a victim and this was wrong, and no school should get away with this, and so he called the police, and when they came to my room I was so freaked out, because it was so weird and so surreal, and I knew everyone would hate me for this. But they said I had to go to the hospital, it was the law, and then I knew that my father was right, this was big, and I had to do the right thing, so I went and told them everything I knew, which wasn't much because I was, like, completely out of it the entire time. I don't remember anything about that night. I know they found alcohol in my blood when I went to the hospital, but my lawyer got that thrown out because it was four days later, and what difference did it make that I had an alcohol level of, like, whatever? I was self-medicating. I had to. It was very traumatic for me, being the center of attention like that. The other day I was watching *Oprah,* and I was thinking I could go on *Oprah* with some other girls my age and we could talk about this and bring it out into the open about how guys can get you drunk and get you to do stuff you would never do, and how you're not even conscious so you're not responsible. And here's the thing I wonder about all the time: If I wasn't conscious, not really, I mean, except that maybe I was, a little bit, then it's as if it never happened, right? I think this ham is a little slimy. I'm going to eat only half of my half and bring back the other quarter for tonight. So that's not too many calories today. The food in the dining hall here sucks, really sucks, though they have a salad bar and soup and frozen yogurt, so I can do that. It gets really hot here in the spring, you could die if you didn't have air-conditioning, which they do. It was disgusting being examined by the doctors. It's, like, you're the victim twice because you have to go through this humiliation afterward, and I've read a lot about it, I think I could be an avocate for kids, in college or whatever. I hate this shirt. I hate purple. I think I'm going to give it away to the homeless. I told you about that community-service project we did with the homeless. That's going to look really good on my application. But if the college thing doesn't work out, I think, like I said, I might do the recording industry. My grades have kind of tanked as a result of all this. I had to leave school, so I missed those credits, and I'm not being completely successful in getting all this behind me, so I think it interferes with my studying. They say they understand, but then they still give me the Ds, so what's up with that? But, you know, seriously, I could do a killer college essay on all this. I really could. My college counselor is driving me crazy. It's all the time, read about this school and read about that one, and it's just more homework as far as I'm concerned. And I know they help you get into college and everything, but that's their job, right, so I don't understand why I have to be supernice to them, like my mother says I should. She says if your college counselor doesn't like you, you're screwed. The one good thing is that it's never going to be on my record that I was expelled or anything, because, first of all, I wasn't, I resigned, and second of all, they'll just say I needed a change of scenery, or my allergies were acting up, or something like that to explain why I came to Houston. Because, really, my grades weren't all that bad when I was at Avery before all this happened. That first semester, I got mostly C+s and B−s, which is average, right? I would have brought those up, but then the whole thing happened, and, you know, it was really traumatic. I have post-traumatic stress disorder. So I think that will help, too. On my college application.

Noelle

I wait for Silas after basketball practice. I stand out in the white tiled hallway with the blue painted floor and watch through the chicken wire in the rectangle of glass. Most of the practices are over for the day, and I can smell the sweat on all the athletic clothes left in the Cage. I am hoping that Silas will come out soon so that I won't miss dinner in the dining hall.

There are younger boys on the court, and Silas is with them. He moves around the floor like an animal—something graceful and quick. The boys are freshmen or maybe sophomores, having a pickup game. Silas gives instructions and shouts out encouragement, and I can see on the boys' faces that they like Silas. They do everything he asks of them. He makes one boy who has missed a shot take it over, and then over again, until he gets it right, until it puts a smile on his face. I can see that Silas might be a good teacher. He makes the boys better at what they are doing. I stand on the other side of the chicken-wire glass and imagine Silas years from now as the basketball coach at a high school or even at a private school. I can see how the boys will respect him, how he will shout at them when necessary, encourage them when they need it. The girl students will all fall in love with him, but I will be the only one Silas loves. I will be his wife, and he will be a wonderful father. I can see this—all of this—already.

I do not go home for Easter break, because it is too short a time to go so far. Silas's family invites me to Easter dinner at his house. I have met Silas's father at basketball games, but I have never seen his mother. Silas comes to the school to pick me up, and he is dressed in a shirt and tie. He tells me he has been to church with his family. I want to touch his shirt and his tie. I have on a dress that, when I sit in the front seat of Silas's smelly car, I realize is too short. It rides up high on my thighs, and I know it is a dress that Silas's mother will hate. For a moment, I think about running back into my dorm room and putting on a pair of pants and a top, but Silas is already making the turn out of campus and toward his house.

My legs are cold in the car, because even though it is Easter, it is not spring. There is still snow on the ground, and I don't even own a pair of panty hose. My dress is cotton and light blue. I thought it would be appropriate for Easter, but it is not. Silas reaches over and puts his hand on my bare leg just above my knee. I don't know what he is saying with that gesture. Does he mean to make me feel better about the dress? Or does he just want to touch my skin?

Maybe I'm wrong about the dress, because his mother is nice to me and talks to me in the kitchen. I think it is funny that within minutes after Silas and I arrive at the house, I am in the kitchen with the women, and Silas is in the living room with the men. They are watching a golf championship on television. Mrs. Quinney is baking hot cross buns. I have never known anyone who baked hot cross buns. She has made an Easter basket for me and hands it to me. I don't know what to say. In my family, Easter has never been an important holiday. I haven't gotten an Easter basket since I was eight years old. In the basket, tucked inside all the yellow plastic straw, are colored chocolate eggs that look like real robin's eggs, even with the speckle. There are jelly beans and cookies that have been decorated to look like Easter eggs. I don't know what to say. I give Mrs. Quinney a quick hug. Just like that. I didn't plan it. Mrs. Quinney seems surprised, and then she smiles. After that, I am not nervous.

Silas and I sit across from each other at the dinner table. I can see him over the centerpiece, which is a sparkly bunny with a hole cut in its back for flowers. I think Silas and I were not seated side by side because no one wants to say officially that we are a couple. I try to keep up with the conversation, but Silas catches my eye. Every time he does that, I forget what we are talking about. Every once in a while, Mr. Quinney looks at me and then at Silas, as if he is trying to puzzle out a clue to a mystery.

After dinner, Silas announces that he and I are going for a walk. We put our coats on, and he takes my hand right in front of his parents and his aunt and uncle. He holds my hand all the way across the back lawn, which still has some snow on it, and onto a path in the woods. I am wearing a pair of Mrs. Quinney's winter boots, which are slightly too big for me. They slip up and down against my heel. My bare legs are cold. I think about Mrs. Quinney wearing the boots, about how they must have walked into the barn where the sheep are kept hundreds of times.

We slip and climb along the sloped path, Silas leading the way. From time to time, he looks back at the house. I can just make out Silas's car through the bare branches. I think Silas is worried that someone is following us, but then I realize he is just trying to figure out the exact moment when we are out of sight.

He stops on the path and waits for me to catch up to him. I am panting slightly. He laughs at me and tells me I'm out of shape. Silas hooks his arm around my shoulder and pulls me close. He kisses me. At first, the kisses are hard and a little frantic, and then they slow down and feel warm and hungry. I am hungry, too. I touch Silas on the chest, on his nice white shirt. He slides his arms inside my coat, and I can sense the heat of his palms through the thin cloth of my dress. We kiss for a long time, and when finally Silas breaks away, it's as though he has taken a thin layer of my skin with him. I bend toward him and then have to rise up on my toes to keep from falling over.

When we return to the house, I go immediately into the bathroom off the kitchen. In the mirror, my mouth is raw and swollen. The edges of my lips are blurred. I run the water until it is cold, and then I wash my face. I splash the cold water on my mouth again and again, and then I dry it with a towel. I look in the mirror. My mouth is still swollen, and it is perfectly obvious what Silas and I have been doing. But I have to leave the bathroom or people will wonder if I'm sick.

When I enter the kitchen, Mrs. Quinney has her back to me, just finishing up the dishes. I realize I should have offered to help, but I didn't. I say that to her, that I'm sorry we went off and I didn't help her with the dishes. She turns around, about to say something easy, but the words get stopped up in her mouth. I can see that she is staring at my face. I think that she should not be too surprised—what does a mother imagine will happen when a teenage boy and girl go off together?—but it seems momentous just the same. Momentous. Mrs. Quinney did not imagine this. I can hardly breathe.

"Silas is in the other room," she says.

Geoff

As headmaster of Avery Academy, I believe the matter was handled in a manner that exacerbated the difficulties for the school. I have tried, over the past two years, to repair the considerable damage that was done, but this has been an uphill battle. The maelstrom of media attention, plus the various ongoing lawsuits, have made this nearly impossible to put behind us. When January 21 rolls around in about a month's time, there will be a phalanx of media trucks parked on the quad, and reporters will be interviewing every student willing to talk to them. I can tell you right now how those stories will begin. "On the second anniversary of the Avery Academy sexual-assault case…" Contributions to the school are down, applications are down, and our yields are way down. Had Mike Bordwin not attempted a cover-up and not forced the boys' confessions without benefit of parental or legal counsel, and had we handed the boys over to the police immediately, we would not be in this mess. Well, there would have been a mess, but it wouldn't be of this magnitude. Before, one could point to the behavior of one or two students. By the time Bordwin was done, there were questions of integrity from the top down.

Although we didn't know it at the time, portions of the footage had been posted on the Internet as early as Monday. The quality of that footage was very poor, for which I have to be a bit thankful, but I have no doubt now that a number of students had seen excerpts. One might have expected someone of Silas's or Rob's integrity to have come forward with this information, but who knows how one will react when confronted with such humiliating evidence?

I spoke to Kasia Gorzynski on the afternoon of January 24. She told me she had been asked by Bordwin not to reveal the existence of the tape, and that he had locked it in his safe. I was told that the tape had been confiscated by Arlene Rodrigues, a dorm parent, who had walked into a room where three boys were viewing the original on a television screen. When I spoke to her later that same afternoon, she informed me that Bordwin had extracted the same promise of silence from her. We spoke a bit about the impossibility of containing such a story, and we determined together that I would speak to Bordwin myself, which I did immediately after hockey practice. At that time, I coached the varsity hockey team.

Unable to find Bordwin at his office, I walked round to his house. He answered the door.

"Geoff," he said, looking not at all happy to see me. Or possibly he was simply exhausted. "Come in, come in," he said. "Have a seat. Meg is at a meeting. Can I get you a drink?"

I declined. This didn't seem a conversation one should have while drinking.

He led me into a sitting room I had been in often. He took the wing chair, and I sat on the couch. "I'll cut to the chase," I said. "I understand you have a tape in your possession."

"I do," he said, shifting his position in the chair. "It's locked in the office safe."

"It's my impression that a number of people, students and teachers alike, know about or have actually seen footage culled from the tape," I said. "Bits of it, I think, are already on the Internet."

Bordwin blanched. "I was afraid of that," he said.

"I think we need to address this straightaway," I said.

Bordwin was silent a moment. "I'll have the three boys come to my office first thing in the morning," he announced finally. He paused. "I'll confront them with the evidence and inform them that they'll likely be expelled pending a hearing on Friday."

The Disciplinary Committee was scheduled to meet on Friday afternoon, which it does every week to review school infractions. "We might be on thin ice here," I said, hitching myself forward. "Not informing the police could be construed as conspiracy to cover up the incident."

"I firmly believe that this should remain an internal affair," Bordwin said, having regained his color. "We owe it to the boys to hear from them first before we inform the police, if we do so at all. Once this becomes public knowledge, we'll be hounded by the press. We haven't had enough time to properly assess the situation."

"But don't you think, given the number of students who may know about the tape, that it's already public?" I asked.

"Public within the school is not the same as *public*," he argued.

"Have you talked to the parents of the girl?" I asked.

"I intend to speak to the girl first thing in the morning."

"You want me to take care of it?"

"I can handle it," he said.

I didn't know at the time that Bordwin planned to extract

118

written confessions from the boys. I can't positively say that he did, either.

We talked for a bit about how astonishing it was to discover Silas Quinney and Rob Leicht on the tape, that one would never have guessed they would behave in such a manner.

"*You* were at the dance, weren't you, Geoff?" he said.

I nodded.

"You mentioned excessive drinking, as I recall."

"Did I use that word?" I asked. *"Excessive?"*

"I believe you did. In fact, if I'm not mistaken, I made a notation of that in my files. I could print out a copy for you tomorrow if you'd like."

I wondered if it was Bordwin's intention to pin the blame for this fiasco on me. "Although I am dean of students," I reminded him, "I was not responsible for that specific dance myself. If you recall, Asa Troy was in charge that night."

"Wouldn't you agree that the dance was the responsibility of all of us?" he asked, employing a smug tone I had seldom heard him use.

I stood. "I think we've said all we need to say about this matter." Bordwin nodded, and I left the house.

I never really warmed up to Bordwin during his tenure at Avery. I will admit that he was a good fund-raiser—he had exceptional skills in this arena—but I always felt that he failed to set a high moral standard at the school. He was not a natural leader, he was not an enthusiast, he did not actively seek to bring out the best in the students. I always felt that he was a little too comfortable with the status quo. The school needed someone to set challenges for both the students and the faculty, but Mike Bordwin was not that man. I have always thought that the board acted too hastily in giving him the permanent post, but as I was also in competition for the position, I could not really complain. After the legal and media chaos that followed the arrest of the boys for sexual assault as well as Bordwin's resignation, it was felt by the board that I was the best person to handle the school, and I was offered the job of headmaster. A number of the members of the board said that giving me this post was long overdue.

Mike

The interview with the young woman, whose name he had learned from a quick perusal of the student directory, had been harrowing. In the flesh, across from his desk, she had looked extremely small and confused. At first, she didn't seem to know what he was talking about. Then she admitted to having been in the room. She may or may not have had a drink. She appeared to know nothing of any compromising tape and was shocked to hear of its existence. She wept. And yet all the time she sat across from him, Mike felt that something in her was tightly coiled beneath the surface. He wasn't certain he trusted that observation, however, because he had not, during the entire interview, been able to erase the images from the tape, which kept superimposing themselves upon her small frame. He had his own level of confusion. She altered her story so often that Mike thought he had lost his way within her labyrinthine tale. In the end, all he could do was send her back to her dorm and ask her to think about the night in question prior to their speaking again in a few hours. He thought she understood that he and she would together call her parents.

Frazzled and with a sense of dread, Mike waited for the boys, whom Kasia had summoned. Silas's mother—Anna—would find the tape scarcely credible. He could not imagine her sitting in front of a television, watching the sexual offenses involving her son, without being heartbroken. He knew he should make an effort to call her about the incident and the fact that he had summoned Silas to his office. He would beg her not to watch the tape. Kasia interrupted his thoughts by poking her head inside the door and reporting that Rob and J. Dot were on their way but that Silas could not be found. Mike tried to hide his enormous relief. "Keep looking," he instructed her.

Almost immediately there was a tentative knock on his door. Rob entered the room but wouldn't meet Mike's eyes. Nor did he ask the headmaster what the matter was, all of which convinced Mike that Rob had guessed the agenda. Mike noted that the boy was nicely dressed in a royal-blue polo shirt, smartly tucked into his chinos, which were belted. He had his baseball cap in his hand.

"We'll wait for J. Dot," Mike said, employing the nickname that he knew the students used for the basketball player. Rob briefly closed his eyes. "We haven't been able to locate Silas as yet," Mike added.

Rob nodded. It was all Mike could do to keep himself from blurting out the questions he personally wanted answered. *Why? What were you thinking?* He wondered if Rob knew he had seen the tape. He wondered if Rob himself had seen the tape. Mike thought it would be unimaginably difficult to watch oneself in a sexual encounter with others in the room.

Because the door was open, J. Dot strode right in. J. Dot, who pushed the dress code to the limit with his shirt tucked behind only his belt, the rest hanging sloppily over his pants, the pants themselves riding a good inch or two lower than Rob's. The two boys did not speak to each other, nor did they make any kind of eye contact. J. Dot took the chair beside Rob's.

Mike saw no reason to delay getting right to the point. He did not want this meeting to last one second longer than it had to. He told the boys he had seen the tape. Rob winced and bent his head. J. Dot had the gall to ask, "What tape?" Rob shook his head at the question.

"The tape in which the two of you are having sex with an underage girl," Mike said.

"I'm not aware of any such tape," J. Dot said.

"I have the tape locked in my safe," Mike said. "I'd be happy to have a TV brought in so that we could all view it together."

"That won't be necessary," Rob said quickly, as he shot J. Dot a sharp glance.

"What the hell were you doing?" Mike asked, his anger seeping out at last. "Do you know the age of the girl you all had sex with? She is fourteen. Fourteen. Are you aware that in this state, sex with a minor is called *sexual assault,* a crime that can lead to a jail sentence?"

Rob still would not look at the headmaster. J. Dot leaned back in his chair in what struck Mike as an inappropriately casual pose. "It was her idea," the boy said. "You ask her. She'll tell you. She came right for us."

"And you did what?" Mike asked. "Did you gently steer her away? Did you make sure she got back to her dorm safely? No, it would appear that you took full advantage of a girl too young to know any better."

"She knew better," J. Dot said.

"And how do you figure that?" Mike asked.

"You've seen the tape," J. Dot said, acknowledging the very thing he had just denied knowing about. "What do you think?"

"I think you're both in a lot of trouble."

The boys did not turn to each other.

"And another thing," Mike said. "I want to know the identity of the person behind the camera."

Again, there was silence in the room.

"OK," Mike said. "We'll do this the hard way."

He pulled two sheets of lined paper and two pens from his top drawer. "I want signed confessions," he said, "unless you want the tape shown at Friday's Disciplinary Committee meeting. I want details, I want names, I want times, I want specific amounts you had to drink. I want it all, and I want it now. No one will leave this room until I have two full confessions in my hand."

"Are you going to call my parents?" J. Dot asked.

"Yes," Mike said.

J. Dot's body hit the back of the chair hard, as if he were outraged. "What do my parents have to do with it?" he asked.

"I would think that they would want to know their son has been expelled from school."

"But I'm my own person now. I'm nineteen."

"Precisely the problem. I want you to write down everything you can remember about that night and then sign the document. I will put the confessions in the safe with the tape. On Friday, I will present only the documents to the members of the DC. You should both be in attendance, in case there are any questions."

"What about Silas?" J. Dot asked, looking around the room. "Where is he?"

"We're looking for him," Mike said. "He, too, will be asked to write out a confession."

"What about the girl?"

"I've already spoken to her," Mike said.

"And so...?" J. Dot asked.

"And so what?" Mike asked in return.

"And so did she tell you it was her idea?"

"The conversation she and I had is privileged," Mike said. "For the moment." He felt on shaky legal ground here.

"No one else will see the confessions?" J. Dot asked.

"No one else will see them," Mike said. "And I would rather that you kept this whole fiasco to yourselves for several days. I see no need for this incident to come to the attention of anyone outside the walls of Avery. After viewing the tape and thinking about it, I believe that this matter can be handled internally."

Mike slid the paper and pens across the table. Rob looked at them as if he were being asked to sign his own death warrant. J. Dot picked up the pen and began to flip it back and forth so that it made a beat upon the desk.

"None of us will leave this room until I have those signed confessions," Mike repeated. "I will be sitting here the entire time you write. What you did was an unspeakable act, with the most serious of consequences."

J. Dot squared the sheet of lined paper in front of him. Rob still hadn't moved or said a word.

"And here's what I would personally like to know," Mike said, hitching himself forward. *"Why?"*

J. Dot curved his shoulders in an exaggerated shrug. Rob— the boy whom Mike had once greatly respected—slowly bent his forehead to the polished mahogany desk.

Mike's nerves were still frayed, even though it had been more than an hour since he had locked the confessions in the safe. He had read the documents first. J. Dot's had been defensive, emphasizing once again that the entire episode had been the girl's idea, that she had come after them, that she was drunk when she first spoke to J. Dot at the dance. At no point in his confession had J. Dot taken any blame upon himself.

Rob's confession had also been brief but not at all defensive. It read like a police report. He named the specific amounts he had had to drink and where, the time they had all left the dance, approximately how long they had remained in the room, and precisely how he had had sex with the girl. There was no attempt to blame the girl or anyone else. He had signed his document *Robert Leicht, '06*. Mike was certain the signature had simply been a reflexive gesture, not a defiant one, for surely Rob would have known that he would not now graduate with his class.

After Mike had locked the documents in the safe, he had sat for a time. Though he had quite justifiably allowed his anger to rise to the surface, inside he had felt nothing but panic. J. Dot, he could care less about. The sooner the boy left the school, the better. But Rob, prior to the incident, had done nothing but contribute to the school academically and athletically. He had raised the school's profile by getting into Brown early. Mike didn't know Rob well, but what little he did know, he'd admired. Rob would be expelled and his acceptance to Brown withdrawn, and what would the boy do then? Such promise destroyed in an hour of dangerous foolishness. And for what?

And Silas... Mike could hardly bear to think about Silas. He so wanted Silas not to be on the tape. If only the cameraman or -woman had not shown his face. But Silas *had* been there. He was culpable. The loss to him would be considerable. He, too, would be expelled. His relationship with Noelle, assuming it had survived that Saturday night, would be in tatters. And Mike could not imagine how Silas would be able to remain in that house with Anna and Owen. Again, Mike thought that he must call Anna, and soon.

Mike turned in his desk chair and looked out the window. He thought of the years he had been at Avery, of all the students he had watched graduate. He had had to deal with dozens of disciplinary problems, but nothing quite like this. He thought of Silas and Rob and J. Dot. He thought of Anna and Meg and Owen. Mike had not written out a confession, but he knew that he was culpable. Indirectly to blame, but to blame nevertheless.

Laura

On Wednesday morning, my roommate left the room early. When she returned, she was in a state. She shut the door to our room, but she didn't ask me to leave. I was studying. Honest to God, sometimes I think she didn't even know I was there.

The first call was to a friend. I really don't remember a lot about this conversation, because my roommate often did that, made calls while I was in the room, clearly trying to study. But that was just her. I think I first began to pay attention when I heard her say, "But how did the tape get out?" I thought she was talking about music, except that her voice was a little frantic, and then she said, "Oh my God, my parents are going to kill me!" I turned around to look at her, and I swear she looked right at me, but I know she wasn't even seeing me, she was just seeing the person at the other end of the line, or else she was picturing how mad her parents were going to be. I couldn't figure out what she was talking about, but now I was paying attention. I heard her say, after that, "What am I going to do?" and "You think?"

She talked for about ten minutes. Mostly she was just listening to what the other person had to say. Once in a while, she would say, "Oh God, do you think so?" I also remember her saying, "What's the name of that drug anyway?" and "If this doesn't work, I'm dead."

I couldn't imagine what was going on. When she clicked her cell phone shut, I turned around. "Are you OK?" I asked. She opened her cell phone and dialed a number. "What?" she asked me. I asked her if something was wrong. But by then the person at the other end had answered the phone. My roommate immediately started to cry. I was shocked. She really was crying. Or, if it was an act, it was amazing. She could hardly get her words out. Crying and hiccuping and everything. She bent over the phone as if she had stomach pains. "Mom," she got out between sobs, "I've been raped."

I was stunned. This was the first I'd heard of any rape. I know I was sitting there with my mouth open. Someone knocked at the door to our room, and my roommate made a frantic motion with her arm to get rid of whoever it was. I went to the door and told my friend Katie that I was on the phone with my mother and that I'd come over when I was done. I went back and sat on my bed. I just stared at my roommate.

I heard her say there were three boys, two seniors and one postgrad. That it had happened on Saturday night. That she hadn't said anything to anyone because she was scared. She hadn't been to a doctor. It wasn't important. She wasn't going to go to one, either. No, she didn't know the boys. They all ganged up on her. And there was something else. There might be a tape.

I could hear her mother screeching from across the room.

"I didn't know it was being filmed!" my roommate wailed. "I was drugged." Then she cried. She didn't want to tell anybody. No, no, no, she wasn't going to tell the RA on duty. She was just letting her mother know, just in case she heard something about it. No, she wasn't hurt physically. At least, she didn't think so. And all this time, she's sobbing and crying and snot's coming out of her nose, and she's pleading with her parents to come get her. She hates the school, she says. She just wants to go home.

Finally, she hung up the phone. I handed her a tissue. "Are you all right?" I asked.

She sniffed. She blew her nose. She got up to look in the mirror and dabbed under her eyes.

"I'm fine," she said.

I swear to God, that's what she said.

Noelle

It is May, just before dark. For the first time in weeks, the air isn't chilled at the edges. All day, the students have been playing Frisbee on the quad. Silas has to play baseball for his third sport, but he is not good at it and doesn't take it seriously. Sometimes he gets to start at second base, but mostly he sits on the bench. He has a good arm and is a natural athlete, but he can't hit the ball very well. He could take extra batting practice, but Silas doesn't really care about baseball. Silas loves basketball. He would play basketball every season if he could. After practice and after supper in the dining hall, we sit outside on the lawn until it starts to grow dark. The windows are open in the dorms, and from time to time we can hear voices and music, and sometimes a shout.

We sit close together, with our legs stretched out in front of us. I lie back on the grass. All spring, Silas and I have been looking for places to go so that we can be alone. We don't say that's what we are doing, but it is. Most of the time, we sit in Silas's car. In the good weather, we lie on the grass. All day I have been thinking about the fact that my roommate has gone home for the weekend and won't be back until Sunday night. I have never committed a major rule violation, and I'm wondering if I have the nerve.

The backs of my shorts and T-shirt are growing wet from the dew, and the temperature is dropping fast. Even in early May, nights in Vermont stay cold.

I stand and hold out my hand.

When we round the corner of my dorm, Silas must guess where I am headed, but he doesn't say a word. Would we both be suspended? I tell him to wait by the door while I go inside and check out the student lounge. No one is in there, and the television isn't on. Everyone wants to be somewhere else tonight. I open the door and beckon Silas to follow me. He takes off his shoes, and my eyes widen. Maybe he does this at home all the time when he arrives later than he told his parents he would. I remember his room at the top of the stairs. I lead Silas up my own dorm stairs, making as little noise as I possibly can. Silas puts his hand on the small of my back, and I sway from lack of balance or excitement.

When we reach the next stairwell, I motion for him to wait. I run ahead to my room, unlock my door, and leave it open a crack. Then I signal through the glass-and-wire windows of the stairwell door for him to come. He runs along the hallway and slides inside my room like a soldier on a mission. We both start to laugh, though we are trying not to make any sound.

There is only one reason I have brought him to my room, and we both know what it is. Silas pulls me to him and kisses me hard. We have never made love, and I am a little bit afraid of it.

I am a virgin. I don't know about Silas. He once asked me if I had ever been with anyone. I said no, and I could see relief on his face.

I lead him to the bed and pull down the covers. The room is only slightly messy, because my roommate cleaned her side before she left. I lie down on the bed. I don't know how to do this. I have watched a thousand people pretend to make love on television and in the movies, but I think that in real life, it doesn't happen like it does on the screen. I still have all my clothes on. Silas stands over me and takes his cell phone and his wallet out of his pockets and puts them on my bedside table. He starts to unbuckle his belt, but then he stops, as if he thinks I might mind. He slides into the bed beside me, and he has to cradle me in his arms, because there's really room for only one person.

We lie motionless for minutes. I wonder if he is waiting for me to give him permission, but I am afraid to say anything. Maybe this is all he wants to do: just hold me in my bed. Maybe he is a virgin, too, and doesn't know what to do next. In the TV shows and movies, the girl always swings on top of the boy, her hair falling at the sides of her face, and takes off her shirt or his, but I am pretty sure I could not do that right now.

Silas finds my mouth and kisses me. He slides his hand under my T-shirt. I can feel him trying to undo my bra with one hand at my back, and I can tell he is having trouble. I wait for a minute, and then I raise myself up and unhook my bra myself. He

133

helps me with my shirt and my bra, and then he unbuckles his belt. He pulls it through the loops in one tug and then unzips his jeans. He slips them off so that now he has on only his shirt and his boxers. I am wondering if I remembered to lock my door.

I discover that making love is not one moment or two. It is a hundred moments, a hundred doors that open, doors to rooms you have never been inside before. The first time Silas touches me between the legs is a door. The first time I touch his nipples is a door. All the open doors seem momentous and important, and they all feel good. None of the doors seems any less important than the final door, which really isn't the final door at all, because there is always the door after that, and the one after that. How Silas looks at me, for example. How Silas covers me. Even the soreness is a door, one I have never been through before. That, more than anything that happens that night, makes me feel like a woman. I lie in Silas's arms, feeling the soreness, and I think that I have crossed over into being a woman.

Silas does not talk when he makes love, and I am glad for this. I am glad that he doesn't tell me that he loves me. It would feel like payment, like something I had earned. I would rather that Silas said it to me on the trail up the mountain, or on the grass of the quad, or on the way to physics class.

When we have gone through almost all the doors, and I am lying in his arms and feeling sore and thinking I am a woman for the first time in my life, Silas's cell phone buzzes. The buzzing is shocking in the silence, and for a moment, I think we have been discovered. But in the next moment, I know exactly what the buzzing is for. Even before Silas opens his phone, I know what the message will say.

Come home.

A lamb needs birthing.

Silas

The last time I took you up this path, it was just before the summer break, and I let you walk in front of me, and I watched the way you walked, and you asked me if I ever hunted, and I knew I couldn't lie to you and so I said I did, and you were upset, and you asked me what it felt like to kill a bird and watch it fall from the sky or to kill an animal running on the ground, and I couldn't answer you, and then you asked me if I had ever killed a deer, and I was ashamed even though I hadn't ever been really ashamed about that before, and I told you I had, and I could see you shudder a little in front of me, and I remember that afternoon, you moved slightly away from me when we were sitting on the rock so that we weren't touching, and I knew that I should not try to touch you that afternoon because you had to get the deer out of your system, and I told you how I felt, that I didn't want to do it again, and it was the truth, but I am not sure if you believed me. And the day was so fine, and I could see the house and the car, and I wanted to hold you and tell you that I loved you, but I knew that you would always associate whatever I said with the deer, and so I didn't, even though the words were bursting inside me and I wanted to. I knew it, and I wanted you to know it. I was afraid that something might happen, something might come between us, and I might never get to tell you. I was afraid of that for a long time.

But I did tell you and I am glad of that, I am glad that you knew how much I loved you.

And now this thing has come between us, and there will never be a day when it is not there, and no matter what I say, there will be the picture of me on the tape doing things to that girl, and I know that you will never be able to get the images out of your mind, they will be there forever, every time I touch you, every time I kiss you, even when I am just sitting in a room and I look over at you, any time you could be picturing the thing that happened on the tape and it will be like something harsh and ugly is always in the room with us, is always in your mind, and nothing could ever be any good between us again, and that is the hardest part. I could go to jail, I could stand the humiliation, I could even let my father hit me if he wanted to, but I couldn't bear to look into your eyes and see the tape running, I just couldn't.

Mike

In September, four months before the scandal broke, Mike had knocked on Anna Quinney's door. In his arms, he had a half-dozen bottles of very good wine that he was delivering, because that evening Anna was hosting the first meeting of the parent-teacher association. At that time, Mike considered himself something of a wine connoisseur, and he prided himself on having on hand for any school-occasioned social event only the best. He doubted that many of the parent volunteers would know the difference between a good red or white versus a poor one, since most, by geographical necessity, were parents of day students and therefore tended toward the lower strata of the economic spectrum. Anna smiled at Mike when she opened the door. She exclaimed over the bounty, and there was some discussion then of where to put the box, which bottles to take out first, and which bottles to put in the fridge. When Mike had set the bottles where she wanted them, he stood in the middle of her clean and tidy kitchen, empty cardboard box in hand, wondering if he should leave. He hesitated, however, and Anna, perceiving his hesitation, asked if he would like a cup of tea. Never having confessed to Anna his dislike of tea, Mike developed on the spot an urgent thirst. He said that was precisely the thing he was wanting at that particular moment. He set the box on the floor, shrugged off his jacket and draped it over the back of a kitchen chair. He sat down while Anna put the kettle on.

He watched her as she fetched the cups, the sugar, and the creamer. She had on a scoop-neck blouse, belted over a gray skirt. He thought she must have dressed for her meeting ahead of time to accommodate his visit. Through the fabric, he could see a white slip with lace on its bodice. He hadn't before realized she had so trim a waist. She usually wore sweaters or overblouses that hid her figure. Or possibly it was only that he had not seen her in some time, since he seldom had any reason to visit the families of the students in the summer. He and Meg, during their monthlong break before administrative duties resumed, had gone to the south of France and rented a villa. It had been a remarkable time-out between them and had filled Mike with optimism. He had hoped that when they returned, the tension and the bickering that had characterized the last six or seven years of their marriage (indeed, had characterized most of the marriage) would get their own time-out. That fond hope, alas, had not survived the long layover at Charles de Gaulle. He wondered if Anna and Owen ever took a vacation and, if so, how the animals were cared for. Clearly Anna had been baking, since the dining table was arrayed with platters of appetizers, and he could see on the counter, waiting their turn, plates of brownies and lemon bars and tarts with berries. Mike wouldn't have minded one of those lemon bars, but he would not ask Anna to undo her careful wrapping.

Anna leaned against the counter in her usual posture. Her arms were crossed beneath her breasts, as if supporting them. The lace of her slip was in full view.

"Normally, Owen would be home by now," Anna said.

"He's away?"

"He's down to Bennington."

"Business?"

"Always."

Waiting for a tea whistle, Mike thought, promoted a tense and stilted conversation. It was as if one had to wait for the signal and the delivery of the tea before speaking freely. For a time, he and Anna avoided each other's eyes, until—and it did seem forever—the kettle announced itself and they were allowed to get on with it. Which, Mike thought, was possibly the reason he had never really liked tea all that much.

Anna sat across from Mike and unwrapped the plate of lemon bars. "I saw you eyeing these," she said.

"I'm that transparent?"

"Occasionally." She smiled.

"Thank you. For some reason, I'm starving."

"Silas always points out to me, when I use that expression, that I'm not actually *starving*. I am merely hungry."

"And Silas would be right about that," Mike said. "What did he do this summer?"

"He worked as a counselor at a camp up near Burlington."

"Live-in counselor?"

"Yes, it was good for him. To get away. He missed his girl-friend, though."

"Noelle."

"Yes."

"Bodes well for going away to college," Mike said. "Has he thought about where he would like to apply?"

"He says Middlebury, but I worry that he'll disappoint himself."

"I don't know," Mike said. "With the basketball, he'll have a leg up. And you know I'll write him a strong recommendation. I write only three or four a year, so they tend to have some weight."

"Thank you," Anna said with feeling.

"Sometimes I'm asked to do these things and I have to because the parents have given money to the school or are friends of a trustee, and I just hate writing them. This one, however, would be a pleasure."

Anna smiled again.

Mike fussed with the tea bag and looked around for a place to put it. Another thing about tea that annoyed him to no end. If you put the tea bag on the plate, it ruined the pastry, and you couldn't very well just put it on the tablecloth. If you put it in the saucer, the bottom of the cup became wet, and that in itself was irritating. "What's Silas doing for a fall sport?"

"Soccer. He hates it." Anna took a sip of tea. "He always starts off the year a little slow, but then he buckles down. You can almost time it. Somewhere between October fifth and tenth, he seems to get it."

"Who's his college counselor?"

"Richard Austin."

Mike made a mental note to speak to Richard in the morning to ascertain Silas's chances of being accepted to Middlebury. He finished off a lemon bar and reached for a napkin. "You look nice," he said.

Her face flushed with color. "I got dressed early because when Silas gets home, I like to be around for him. Not rushing, trying to get ready for something else."

It seemed a thin reason—did she and Owen often go out

in the evenings?—but Mike simply nodded. It then occurred to him that though he had eaten perhaps a half-dozen or more meals at the Quinney residence, they had never been invited to the headmaster's residence. He vowed to rectify that soon. Meg would just have to suffer through the meal. Mike had, over the years, learned to cook a few dishes for such occasions.

"Where are you from?" Anna asked suddenly. "I realized the other day that we always talk about Silas or things having to do with the school, but you never talk about yourself."

Mike seldom talked about himself for a good reason: his origins were humble and working-class and, here and there, a bit ugly—a background that didn't at all befit the headmaster of a private secondary school. Despite the fact that it was 2005, the assumption often was that the headmaster had come from an educated if not actually an upper-class background.

"My father was a mechanic at Logan," Mike said. "He was a good man, though I think he was disappointed in me. I've never had any aptitude for anything mechanical. I turned to books at an early age, mostly because of my mother, who had wanted to go to college and didn't."

"Why not?"

"She got pregnant with my older sister, and she and my father married. She was only nineteen at the time. The marriage didn't last. After the divorce, my mother married a teacher. I was nine."

"Oh," Anna said, folding her hands under her chin. "That must have been hard for you."

"It was," Mike said honestly. "I didn't like the man my mother had married, and I was very angry with her. My sister and father raised me. But, really, I know most of what I know

142

about life through books. It's one of the reasons I was drawn to academia."

"Do you want to open one of those bottles of red wine?" Anna asked suddenly. "Don't they have to breathe properly?"

"Absolutely," Mike said, relieved to no longer have to talk about his past.

Anna produced a corkscrew. Mike, in turn, picked out the best of the reds he had brought. Altogether too good for the parent-teacher association, but perfect for a spur-of-the-moment glass in the late afternoon, an occasion that was beginning to feel European in flavor. There was the business with the corkscrew, a cheap version that caused him to worry he might break the cork. Mike poured the wine into two mismatched goblets Anna had brought to the table.

They raised their glasses simultaneously. "To . . . ?" she asked.

"To involved parents and excellent students," he said.

"No, to you," she said, and clinked Mike's glass.

He accepted and took a sip. There was a certain incongruity in drinking a good wine in such a modest kitchen, but Mike had largely come to think of the Quinney kitchen as a backdrop for Anna only, and so was able to convince himself, at odd moments, that they were at a café in the south of France in early September, drinking a very good red at an outdoor table, watching the light hit the tops of the trees. That this view was echoed at the edge of the Quinney property aided his fantasy.

"Owen would kill me," she said.

"For drinking wine at four o'clock in the afternoon?"

"Pretty much."

"He drinks," Mike said, remembering the dozens of beers the man had put away in his presence alone.

"He wouldn't like this," she said.

The word *this* seemed freighted with meaning, and Mike was surprised that Anna had said it. He couldn't remember what it was he was supposed to be doing at that hour, but it certainly hadn't included a glass of wine with Anna Quinney.

"You've done so much for Silas," Anna said. "He's thriving at the school. What more could a mother ask for? It's all you want for your child, isn't it?"

She realized her mistake at once and set her glass down. "Did you ever want children?" she asked.

"I did," Mike said, "and then I didn't. I sometimes wonder if my job hasn't made me cynical about adolescents. Not Silas, of course."

"And your wife?"

"Meg."

"It's hard to think of her as anything but Mrs. Bordwin. Silas had her for math his first year." She smiled. "Parents with well-behaved children are insufferable, aren't they?"

"Yes," Mike said, agreeing with her.

"Smug."

"Very."

"It's a dangerous attitude to have about a child. So many things can so suddenly go wrong."

"You're on solid ground with Silas."

"Let's change the subject," she said, "or I'll jinx myself."

Mike poured them both another glass. He reasoned that they had drunk the first glass too quickly because they were both a little nervous. This second glass, he vowed, he would drink slowly and truly savor.

"I shouldn't," she said of the wine. "I'll get tipsy."

Mike smiled at the old-fashioned word. "You'll be the life of the party," he said.

"I have an agenda to get through."

"You'll be great," he said. And it was then that he crossed another subtle line, equivalent to Anna's *this*. "You *are* great," he said.

Anna blushed, and Mike stared at her profile.

It took so little to move a woman, Mike had sometimes observed. Whether this spoke to the fragility or to the strength of the gender, he wasn't sure. When Anna turned back, she was trying to smile, but he could see the effort this was costing her. He was certain that had he vanished at that very moment, she would have wept in the privacy of her kitchen.

He was not sure why.

He didn't take advantage of what he was sure would have been a certain opening. Instead, he busied himself with another lemon bar while she composed herself. Her eyes had pinkened, however, and he knew that she would be unhappy when she looked in the mirror.

"Owen's looking at a particular sheep?" Mike asked, trying to steer the conversation onto more solid ground.

"Owen..." she said, and pressed her lips together. Mike knew that Anna would not say anything unkind about her husband. Another woman might have used the opportunity to complain about the lack of attention, the inability to understand, the disinclination to discuss or even to notice a wife's feelings. But not Anna.

"He'll be home soon," she said, and Mike knew it to be a warning.

Mike nodded. He pulled himself up and took a quick sip, signaling that he would leave. "I should go," he said.

Her gesture was so quick, Mike barely saw it. She covered his hand with her own.

Mike experienced that first touch not as electric but rather as a fluid movement that spread throughout his body.

He looked at their hands on the table. The gesture, he knew, was not an invitation. It was a statement, though Mike wasn't sure exactly of what.

He felt a quick pressure on his hand, and then Anna pulled her own away. "You've been so good to us," she said, allowing them that pretext.

He stood while Anna took the glasses to the sink. He noted that she was washing them with care. He knew that they would be hand dried and replaced in the cabinet as soon as he left. What she would do with the opened bottle of wine, he had no idea.

"Good luck tonight," he said, pulling on his coat.

"Thanks."

"I'll come by again."

Anna looked over through the open doorway to the dining table carefully laden with appetizers. When she turned back to Mike, she seemed to have made up her mind about something that was important to her.

"Yes," she said. "I hope you will."

Ellen

For a moment, a naked look passes between you and your son. It is a look you have never seen before, and it chills you.

"Rob, what happened?" you ask.

He shuts his eyes. He will not answer your question.

Behind you, the headmaster enters the room. "Mrs. Leicht," he says. You turn, and something in the man startles a bit when he sees your face. You have no idea what is written there.

You have met the headmaster a number of times. On each occasion, you and he talked about Rob. You accepted compliments. You chatted about the team or about the school year. Perhaps you had the same conversation with the man half a dozen times.

"Rob, I wonder if I could speak to your mother alone," the headmaster says. "You can stay here. We'll talk in my office."

Your son is happy you are leaving. He doesn't want to be in the same room with you. You can smell it.

You follow the headmaster into his office. He sits behind his desk, and you understand that you should sit in the chair in front of it. You have never really noticed before how blue the man's eyes are. He is slight, and this surprises you, too, because when you saw him before, he seemed taller. He wears glasses, and you can see, in the slanting natural light from the window, that they are smudged. You wonder why you are just noticing these details now — now, when you have so much else on your mind.

"Thank you for coming," he says.

You repeat the question that you asked of your son. "What happened?"

The headmaster asks if you would like a bottle of water, and you say yes. He reaches behind him and takes a half bottle of Poland Spring from a shelf. Your hands are shaking, and you know that he can see this. You reach up with a nervous gesture to tuck your hair behind your ears, and you note that your earring has fallen off. You check your other ear. You are wearing only one earring. You think — quickly, because there is business at hand — that it must be in the car.

"Rob and I have had a talk about the incident," the man in front of you says.

You take a quick breath. "You said on the phone only that Rob was accused of a major rule violation of a . . . sexual nature. Has he been expelled?"

"He will be," the headmaster says.

Your head jerks a bit, as if you hadn't heard correctly.

The headmaster nods.

Expelled. The word is a bullet careening in your brain. Causing serious injury.

"What did he do?" you ask.

"This is very hard, Mrs. Leicht."

"Ellen."

The headmaster studies you a moment. He shifts in his chair. You realize you are perched forward in yours.

"Your son was involved in a sexual incident with an underage girl," he announces.

It is a moment before you can respond. "What?" you ask.

The headmaster does not repeat himself.

"I don't understand," you say. And you don't. You cannot imagine.

"He was involved in an incident in which he had...sex...with a girl who is only fourteen. Rob is, I believe, eighteen?"

You nod slowly, trying to take it all in. "That's grounds for expulsion?" you ask.

The headmaster seems taken aback. "Yes, I'm afraid that it is." He appears, for a moment, to want to say more but doesn't.

"Oh God," you say.

The headmaster picks up a pen and begins to tap it lightly against a pad of paper.

"Are you positive it was Rob?" you ask.

"Yes," he says.

"How do you know that this girl, I assume she has a name, this fourteen-year-old girl and my son were...involved...as you say, in this, in this incident?"

"The incident was caught on tape," the headmaster admits reluctantly. "The tape was brought to my attention. It's how I know about it."

You put your fist to your chest and press hard. "A tape," you say.

"Yes."

"My son and this girl. You've seen it."

"Yes, I have."

"Is it...?" You begin the question, but you cannot finish it.

"Graphic?" he asks for you. "Yes, it is."

You cover your mouth, as if it were you who had been caught out. You who had been exposed.

149

The headmaster waits. There are tiny seeds of perspiration along his hairline. *This is hard for him, too,* you think. *Awful for him, probably.*

"How many have seen the tape?" you ask.

He moves in the chair, as if this were a question he didn't want to have to think about. "That's difficult to say," he answers cautiously. "Four staff members. We don't know yet to what extent it was circulated among students, but we have reason to believe some have seen it."

You are silent.

"There were a number of people involved in the incident itself," the headmaster says, adding blow upon blow to what is already hideous news. "Five, to be precise."

"Five?"

"Three boys, your son among them, and the girl. And the person behind the camera. We don't know who that is yet."

You are incredulous. "This was...it was...an orgy?" you ask, your voice faltering at the word *orgy*.

The headmaster rubs a finger under his nose, as if he might be going to sneeze. "Something like that," he says. "I would rather not get into the specifics of the tape. I don't think you need to hear details. I can't see that it would do you or your son any good. I can say, though—how shall I put this?—it appears that Rob did not have actual intercourse with the girl."

Unwanted images flood your brain. You work to erase them. You bristle at the notion of not being allowed to know everything about an event your son was involved in. Who is this man to keep facts from you? But you realize the headmaster is correct. You do not want to see any of it.

"How do you know it's Rob?"

"It's Rob," he says.

"You're positive."

"Yes. Two other staff members have identified him as well."

"Oh God," you say as another lid is sealed, another door shut. The idea that other adults have watched your son having sex with an underage girl — with any girl — makes your chest tight.

The headmaster pushes the bottle of water closer to you. You reach for it and take a long sip. "Do I need to call a lawyer?" you ask.

The headmaster looks away. "I would do that only if you wish to contest the expulsion," he explains. "Which would mean, I am bound to say, that the incident would have to be made public."

"It doesn't have to be made public now?" you ask.

"Not really. The students will know he and the other boys have been expelled, and there are bound to be rumors. But so far, the incident is contained within the school walls. I see no need to go public with this."

You shake the hair out of your face. The slanting light is in your eyes and giving you a headache. On the headmaster's desk is a framed photo of the man at a younger age with a tall dark-haired woman. You have met this woman, the headmaster's wife, once or twice, but you can't, just now, remember her name.

"What does *expulsion* mean exactly?" you ask.

"It means that Rob will have to leave the school for the remainder of the year. He may reapply in the spring for reentry next fall. I would say his chances are very good for reacceptance. Mrs. Leicht, Ellen, your son is an excellent student, an exceptional athlete, and, apart from this incident, a good kid."

The mention of the *good kid* is nearly unbearable. You

remember the Boy Scout, the skateboard rider, the baby fresh from his bath.

"It's just very, very sad that this has come to light," the headmaster says, "and believe me when I say I am just as unhappy about this as anyone."

You doubt that very much.

"I would advise, however, that you consider enrolling him in public school for the remainder of the year so that he doesn't fall behind."

"He was accepted 'early decision' to Brown." You hear the lament, inappropriate under the circumstances. A girl has been taken advantage of. Your son may be guilty of statutory rape.

The headmaster winces. "The university will have to be informed," he says softly.

You fall back against the chair. "You just never think..." you say to him.

You see the hours and hours of studying, the tests taken, the report cards proudly displayed. And for what? For this?

"My son is guilty of statutory rape?" you ask.

"Not technically," the headmaster says. "In Vermont, sex with an underage girl is called *sexual assault*. I hasten to add that your son has not been charged with any crime. But as to the question of guilt, it is assured."

"The question of guilt?" you ask. "I don't understand."

"Rob signed a written confession," the headmaster explains. "This will be presented on Friday in lieu of testimony or the need to view the tape itself."

"Rob signed a confession?"

You are aware of a certain parroting on your part, but your brain seems not to be able to process facts the way it used to.

"It's a simple document," the headmaster says in a quiet voice, as if he suspects an imminent storm.

"May I see it?" you ask.

The headmaster hesitates. "It is full of details you may not wish to read. Not at this point."

Something in you resists the withholding of a document your own son has written, but again you see that the headmaster is right. You do not, just now, want to read the details of what may have been a sexual orgy. You feel your strength dissolving.

You hear the headmaster get up from his desk and leave the room. He returns with a box of Kleenex.

You sniff, and then you shudder. "Does this girl seem willing on the tape?" you ask, blowing your nose.

"Yes," the headmaster says. "Very."

You give a small sigh of relief, which the headmaster notes.

"Unfortunately, that doesn't change the seriousness of the event," he says quickly.

Something in you stiffens as you realize that you and the man in front of you may soon have reason to become enemies. "Did the girl . . . I don't know . . . seduce the boys?"

"Your son is eighteen," the headmaster says, and you think you hear, for the first time, a note of anger in his voice.

Colm

I had stayed late at work, as I usually do. It was my beat then to monitor the small-town New England papers. We get 30 percent of our stories that way. I'm doing this online, of course, because you get the bulletins faster. So I'm scrolling through these phenomenally boring stories in the *Rutland Herald*— "Paintball Vandals Target Cemetery"; "Arson Blaze Closes School" — and I come to the police blotter for Avery. The police blotter is the most-read part of any local paper. Even more than obits. And I see these entries: *Eighteen-year-old male student charged with sexual assault. Nineteen-year-old male student charged with sexual assault. Search instigated for eighteen-year-old male student wanted in regard to sexual-assault charges.* It was the word *student* that interested me. First of all, it's slightly unusual to list a person's occupation in these blotters, and second, the word *student* in combination with the word *Avery* immediately brings to mind *Avery student*, i.e., *Avery Academy*. And I'm thinking, *If this is really Avery Academy, and there's been a sexual assault* — and already I'm guessing the victim is a student — *then this might be a good story*. I don't want to call this guy I know up in Rutland, because I don't want to tip my hand in case he hasn't noted the word *student* yet. So I call the police station in Avery. Even in these small towns, they always have someone on duty, though sometimes you have to wake him or her up at home in bed.

Officer Quinney—technically chief of police—answers the phone. I identify myself, and I ask him whether he has in custody two suspects in a sexual-assault case. He's reluctant to speak to me, and he sounds upset. He says he did, earlier in the night, and I ask who, and he says, *No comment.* I ask him if they have found the third student yet, and he says he can't tell me, which is bullshit, because if there's a search going on, the name is out there, but that's OK because I can get that another way. So I ask him the victim's name, and he says, *No comment,* again, but he's pretty ticked off now, because I should know that he can't give me the victim's name, which, of course, I do know. But you see, not all questions are asked to elicit answers. Most of them are to get the person on the other line to talk, to say words, one or two of which are going to be revealing or cause a spark that sends you in a certain direction.

I ask him if these students are from Avery Academy, and he says yes, which is a huge piece of news. I'm pretty stunned, actually, that he's given me this, but I proceed as if he's said nothing of interest. I ask him how he came to know about the case, and he says the parents of the victim of the sexual assault called him, and I ask him their names, and he gets pissed off at me all over again. But you never know when it might be worth it, because he might have said the name of a city where the parents lived or that they lived in Avery. Or anything. And he says he doesn't have any more information for me, and he hangs up.

So right away, I'm taking notes and Googling all over the place. I find out the name of the headmaster of the school—which, as we all know now, was Michael Bordwin—and I call him at home. He answers, and even though I can tell he was asleep, he's instantly alert. You can also tell that he's had a very bad day. *Who is this?* he demands. I identify myself, and he says he has no comment. I say, *No comment about what?* And he's silent a minute, and I tell him that I know that two Avery students have been arrested in regard to a sexual-assault case, and he says nothing, and there's my confirmation. I ask him if he has a comment, and I give him the standard line: it would be good for him to make a comment because the story is going to come out anyway and this is a chance for him to put his particular spin on it. I think he's going to hang up on me, and instead he says, "This has been a difficult day for the Avery community." And I say, "Why are only two boys in custody? Where's the third?" And that must be when he realizes that I know practically nothing about what's going on, and he hangs up.

But that's OK, because I'm already out the door and heading to my car. I know I'll be in Avery before dawn, and I'll go straight to the police station and demand answers. But the real reason I'm salivating is because I know I'm about to tap into the best possible source a reporter on this kind of a story could ever want. Students.

Gail

I want to make it clear that I am not commenting on this matter in a professional capacity, which is as a professor of law at the University of Vermont, but rather as a layperson who is familiar with Vermont law and who has been asked to review the case.

I have seen the tape in question. At first glance, it would appear that some degree of sexual consent on the part of the fourteen-year-old girl is present. That she has been given alcohol or has administered it to herself is partially evident as well. She does not appear to be comatose or unconscious at any time during the event. If anything, she appears to be rather competent at what she is doing.

But there were other, more important, factors present that night that should determine whether or not the law must become involved. The fact that there are three boys and one girl, not to mention the fact that all three boys are at least four years older than the girl, suggests, by its very nature, coercion. The perpetrators' assertions, after the fact, that the girl seduced them, went willingly, or even instigated the entire episode are irrelevant. The moment the boys allowed themselves to be seduced—no matter how competent or incompetent the girl was; no matter how alert or inebriated she was—they became guilty of a crime in the state of Vermont. Coercion is not a difficult principle to prove. The law is very clear on this. A situation involving three boys, eighteen years of age or older, and one girl, fourteen, is most assuredly a case of coercion. There is a tendency when viewing such a tape to say to oneself, "She asked for it." Under the law, it doesn't matter whether she asked for it or not. The boys were of an age to say no and were obliged to do so. Because they did not, they were, quite rightly, arrested and charged with sexual assault.

Other factors are of interest in this case as well and speak to a different issue. Upon viewing the tape in question, the headmaster called two of the three boys into his office and, without suggesting that they call their parents or a lawyer, demanded the boys' written confessions for a disciplinary hearing that would be held later that week. This, too, was coercion of a most egregious sort. Knowing that few eighteen-year-old boys would willingly call their parents or lawyers about such a matter—for fear their parents might have to view the humiliating tape, if nothing else—the headmaster counted on the boys' confessing, which they did. Clearly, there was an attempt here, on the part of the Avery administration, to keep the matter within the walls of the academy. Later that same day, I believe, the parents of the female victim called the school, demanding that action be taken. Before the Disciplinary Committee could be convened, the boys' statements, which were tantamount to confessing to sexual assault, were handed over to the police. At the time of two of the boys' arrests, neither had yet had access to counsel.

One of the boys, the nineteen-year-old James Robles, has sued the school, alleging that the headmaster, Michael Bordwin, treated him unlawfully and unfairly. The case alleges that the school broke its contract with Robles when he was forced to confess to a crime without benefit of parental or legal counsel. In the absence of any legal representation, the school was obliged not to accept their confessions but rather to advise them not to do or say anything without counsel. The school did not do that, the suit alleges, primarily because the interests of the school were competing with the students' best interests. While the boys, who were *students,* might not understand the necessity of having parental and legal counsel, the headmaster, not only older but more educated, most certainly did. In one of those strange cases of legal irony, the suit alleges that the boys were *coerced* into confessing. In ignoring the boys' interests in order to promote its own, the school may well have committed a crime in the state of Vermont.

Mike

For Mike, this sense of agitation, of electrical impulses disturbing thought and movement, was new to him. Had he felt this way that fateful Thanksgiving dinner when he'd looked across the table at Meg? He'd been nearly twenty years younger then, and perhaps — like an aging pitcher's — his body couldn't absorb stress as well as it used to and therefore read as spikier on the meter. When he wasn't remembering the way Anna had stood at the counter with her arms crossed under her breasts, he was thinking about the moment she had turned her head away, moved by something seemingly insignificant he had said. Or the way she had covered his hand with her own, surprising him. In his kitchen, he poured himself a glass of red, wishing to perpetuate that connection, however tenuous. He was relieved that Meg had a meeting and would not be home until nine, since conversation between them might have been impossible for Mike. Not that conversation between them hadn't become, over the last year or so, more and more strained. Sometimes Mike wondered if Meg had found someone else. He supposed it was possible. More to the point, it seemed that a narrow dismissive streak in his wife had grown to an intolerable width. She occasionally appeared to be so irritated by Mike, she could hardly speak. He wondered what it was that annoyed her so. Perhaps she had imagined a happier marriage? Had he failed to fulfill her sexually? Or was it a simple wanderlust, the yearning becoming more urgent the longer it appeared they might be stuck in Avery, Vermont—possibly until retirement, a fairly horrifying notion for Mike as well? Mike was often tempted to ask Meg what bothered her, but on the few occasions when he had done this, she had named an irritant he had given little thought to or hadn't known about—such as a series of dismal prospects for the volleyball team—or the question, to his dismay, had prompted even more exasperation, so much so that she would simply sigh or, worse, leave the room.

He opened the refrigerator but was baffled by its contents. He had little appetite. He sat down at the kitchen table but immediately stood and paced. He thought of Anna. He wished he had made some physical gesture of his own in response to hers. He wished he had touched her. Would she now be regretting that touch? Would she be embarrassed? He wished he could call her to let her know.

Know what? he wondered. *That he cared? That he, too, had been moved when she had been? That it was taking all his will to refrain from calling her on the pretext of asking how the meeting had gone?*

His thoughts were adolescent, he decided as he moved from living room to kitchen to porch. He was married. She was married. He had brought the Quinney family into Avery Academy. He had a public position that an extramarital affair might compromise. She had a son. But it amazed Mike how little weight those perfectly sound reasons had when stacked up against the paradoxical promises of warmth and excitement, of comfort and risk. As the evening wore on—at an exhilaratingly slow pace, time seemingly having stopped for examination—the afternoon visit to the Quinney household began to throb with an incandescent brightness, obliterating shadows and marital responsibilities.

Mike had never been unfaithful in his marriage. He had not even been seriously tempted. Something happened to a man, he had always thought, who was constantly around nubile teenagers: a wall went up so that the man would be quicker than most to shut off that part of himself that might normally respond to beautiful female flesh. That it had been Anna who had broken through that wall, and not an eighteen-year-old student or a twenty-three-year-old faculty member, spoke, he supposed, to a marginal sanity.

But there was Owen. And there was Silas. And there was Meg. They existed and could not be ignored.

He walked into the kitchen and poured himself another glass of wine, surprised to discover that he had drunk almost the entire bottle.

The risk for Anna was tremendous.

The risk for him was tremendous.

He opened his cell phone and dialed the Quinney number. He prayed that neither Silas nor Owen would answer the phone. If they did, he would ask for Anna in a friendly and businesslike voice. He simply wanted to know how the meeting had gone. Parental involvement was an issue any headmaster might be expected to care about.

Anna answered the phone.

"I've liked you from the first moment I saw you," Mike said at once.

There was a moment's pause. "You were upside down," Anna said with what sounded like a smile in her voice.

"You're alone?" Mike asked.

"Sort of."

"I'm..." Mike didn't know how to describe his current state of mind.

"You looked very funny," she added, "hanging upside down."

Mike smiled. He liked this lighter side of Anna. The flirting, the banter. He leaned against the counter with his eyes on the driveway. "Would it be safe for me to come over now?" he asked.

"No."

"Owen is there?" Mike looked down at his stocking feet. He had a hole in the big toe of the right foot. The sock would be thrown out. Neither he nor Meg knew how to darn.

"Yes."

"I'll come tomorrow?"

"Yes."

"Same time? To collect the bottles?"

"We drank a lot tonight," Anna said. "I drank a lot tonight," she added, and he could hear it in her voice. A certain looseness in the consonants. He wondered how his own voice sounded.

"The risk for you is tremendous," he said, turning and putting his forehead to the cabinet.

"I understand that," she said.

"It's been a long time since I've felt like this," he admitted.

Anna was silent on the other end.

"Come out now and meet me," he urged recklessly.

"I can't."

"OK, tomorrow then. Owen will be away?"

"Yes. A different trip. But yes."

Mike could see the headlights of Meg's car pulling into the driveway.

"I have to go," he said quickly. He didn't want to say the name *Meg*. "I don't want to go, but I have to."

"Tomorrow then," Anna said.

Mike shoved the cell phone into his pocket. He ought to have prepared a little something for Meg to eat. If not a meal, then a snack that might do in lieu of a meal. He hid the empty wine bottle, opened the fridge, withdrew two blocks of cheese. He unwrapped the cheeses and set them on a breadboard. He was opening the lid of a jar of olives when Meg walked through the door.

She slid her coat off and let it fall onto the floor. She set her briefcase on top of it. She flipped her shoes off.

"I need a drink," she said.

"Red? White?"

"White's good." She eyed the paltry spread on the island. "We have any good bread?" she asked, already accusing him. If one or the other was going to be late, a dinner was not expected, but a decent snack the size of, say, a French picnic was certainly not too much to ask.

Mike prayed that they did. He found a brick-hard third of a round in a drawer. He hacked off a slice and popped it into the toaster. He slid a bottle of pinot grigio from the fridge and opened it, hoping the good wine might mollify his wife. He poured Meg a large glass.

"My, we're generous tonight," she said.

"You looked whipped. Bad meeting?"

"Long, unbearable, and utterly unnecessary meeting," she said. She scrutinized her husband. "You don't look so hot your-self," she added. She cocked her head. "You've been drinking?"

164

Mike nodded slowly. "I have."

"Where?"

"Coggeshall and I went out for a few drinks."

"You hate Coggeshall," she said.

"I do. Hence the need for a large number of drinks."

"What did he want?"

"Damned if I know," Mike said. "Ostensibly we were talking about certain faculty members who aren't measuring up. Not you."

"Well, I think Larry's on thin ice," she said.

Mike nodded dumbly, condemning a man he'd hardly given any thought to. He was drunk. Or nearly there. And yet, as inebriated as he was, he had not been able to stifle those electrical impulses, all that agitation.

Meg scanned the meager meal. "This is it?"

"I just got back, too," Mike said. "I'll fix us a salad."

"No, don't," she said. "I want to talk."

A tiny fillip of fear passed through Mike's chest.

"About?"

"Sit," Meg said. She took a chair at the kitchen table. Mike leaned against the island.

"I want a baby," Meg said with characteristic abruptness.

"You hate children," Mike said too quickly.

"I hate children as a collective, not individual children."

Mike knew the difference but pretended not to. He furrowed his forehead.

"I'm forty-three," she announced. "I don't have a minute to waste."

Meg seemed determined. Would she demand that he perform right there in the kitchen? In a few minutes in the bedroom?

The little fillip of fear that had passed through Mike's heart dug in and waited.

"You must have thought about the issue," she said, exasperated by his silence.

"I thought we had decided not to," he said.

"That was five years ago." She held out her wineglass for a refill. He suddenly realized he was not drunk enough. He poured Meg another generous glass and one for himself.

"Can I think about this?" Mike asked. "For a few days?"

"It's an instinctual thing," she said. "You won't need a few days. And, as you are perfectly aware, my biological clock is ticking away over here."

"Louise had her first child when she was forty-five," he said, referring to a fellow teacher.

"And I remember thinking at the time that it was a sin because she'd be sixty-five when the boy was twenty."

"When your child is twenty, you'll be sixty-three," he calculated and said aloud, instantly regretting his unkindness.

"I'll be a very good sixty-three," she said.

This was true. Meg was nothing if not in fine physical shape.

"What made you change your mind?" he asked gingerly.

"I'm tired of always watching over someone else's kids. I think I could do a better job with our own. We'd probably be able to have only one, if even that."

"I just . . . I just don't know what to say," Mike said.

"Well, think about me when you're thinking about this: You could decide to have a kid when you're fifty — though that would certainly be a sin — but I can't. This is it for me. We might even have to go the whole fertility route if we don't get pregnant the first couple of tries."

"When exactly would..."

"The first try be? Sunday. I've been reading articles and books on this. There's a lot of new research." She paused and studied him. "Are you game?" she asked.

Mike felt as though he had no choice but to open his palms in a noncommittal gesture.

"This cheese is rancid," she said, bending over the table and sniffing it. "You got anything else? I'm starved."

Mike was tempted to point out that she was merely hungry. He wanted to be alone to think, but that would have to wait until he had fed his wife. Sunday was four days away, which was a kind of reprieve. He could not imagine how he would be able to say no to the woman standing across the island from him, now sniffing the olives as well. Did olives ever go bad?

"OK," she said, "you think about it. We'll talk tomorrow night."

Tomorrow night, Mike thought, his head spinning. Tomorrow night, he had hoped to be happy.

Ellen

After stopping at the general store to buy toothbrushes, you pull into the parking lot of the first motel you come to, a motel you normally wouldn't ever enter. Beside you is your eighteen-year-old son, wearing his maroon sweatshirt and his Red Sox baseball cap. He has not voluntarily said a word to you, though he has answered your rudimentary questions. "Do you have your books? Is that all you're bringing?" You didn't ask him if he wanted to spend the night in a motel with you. You announced it, just as you announced it to the headmaster's secretary, not waiting for permission. You would not have your son staying in his dormitory another night, even though he has not formally been expelled. You wanted him with you. It was as ferocious a desire as you have had in some time, and it surprised and pleased you that this might still be possible: this ferocity, this desire. He is your son, and you will look after him, as indeed you now think you ought to have been doing all along. You refuse to think about the irony of having sent him away from home so that he would not be in harm's way, only to have him end up in harm's way. Worse. To have allowed him to cause the harm. A notion that never occurred to you before.

No, you will not think about irony just now. You have moved past irony. You tell your son, who is looking out the window, who has been looking out the window the entire ride, who will *not* look at you, that you'll be right back. You find it remarkable that he has the wherewithal, the insolence, to wear his baseball cap backward.

A small thing, but a choice nevertheless.

There is no one in the office of the Mountain View Motel. You notice the small Formica desk, a chair in the corner, a maple table such as one might find in a doctor's office, large enough for only a magazine and a tented card listing a variety of margaritas at a bar you guess must be nearby. You look for a bell to ring.

"Hello?" you call tentatively. "Hello?"

You hear a sound, a movement from a back room. A man with a belly like a large serving bowl comes through a door. He has been eating. He has a paper napkin balled in his hand.

"I need a room," you say. "My son and I."

It occurs to you suddenly that the man may not believe you; he may think you are covering for an affair with an underage child.

"He's from the school," you say, instantly regretting that admission, too. Perhaps the locals hate the school. You don't know anything about town-and-gown relations. It never seemed important to you before.

"My son and I," you begin again, "need a room."

"For how long?" the man asks.

You don't know. Until Friday, the day of the disciplinary hearing? Is your son allowed to be away from school that long? Will you take him back to his dorm tomorrow? The news of the tape will be campus-wide, will it not? A moment of panic seizes you, and you involuntarily bring your purse to your stomach and press hard.

"Two nights," you say, though the prospect of spending two nights in a room with your son, who will not speak to you, who will not even look at you, seems an impossibility.

The man, perhaps impatient to get back to his dinner, names a sum. You mention you will need twin beds. If the man hears you, he does not acknowledge the request. You wonder if you should repeat it. He asks you for a card and you sign. He gives you a plastic key inside an envelope with the room number on it.

"Do you know of a good place to get some dinner?" you ask, and as he is answering, you think about the reality of sitting across another Formica table from your son, his eyes expertly avoiding yours. "How about pizza?" you ask. Pizza in the room might be bearable, you think, though you cannot imagine eating anything at the moment.

You return to the car and drive to the parking space meant for your room. You get out of the car with your purse and put the key in the lock. Rob, behind you, has a backpack slung over his shoulder, his hands in the pockets of his sweatshirt. He is obedient in the way a prisoner might be. Giving only what is absolutely necessary.

The room has two narrow twin beds, each covered with a dark paisley print quilt. You reach to turn on a lamp between the beds, but it doesn't work. Your son finds the switch for the overhead light and then drops his backpack on one of the beds, claiming it. He immediately walks into the bathroom. There is no closet in the room, merely a rod with coat hangers, over which one can draw a plaid curtain. You hang up your coat. You don't want to call your husband.

When your son returns from the bathroom, he sets his backpack on the floor and lies on the bed, splayed like a cadaver. He wears his chinos a little looser now. You can see several inches of his boxers. He throws an arm over his eyes, so that he cannot see you or the ceiling or the future. You walk into the bathroom and wash your hands, drying them with the thin towel hanging from a bar over the toilet. You have not spent a night alone with your son in a motel room in years. On holiday trips, Rob usually brings a friend, and they have a room adjacent to the one you share with your husband.

Arthur.

Who should be called.

You have not stayed in a motel room such as this since childhood — though it feels familiar to you. You could have described it before you entered, could even have described the texture of the thin towel. When you walk back into the room, you sit at the edge of the bed closest to your son.

"Is it true?" you ask.

After all, it might not be. It might all be an elaborate misunderstanding.

Your son turns away from you and faces the wall.

You could demand answers. You could demand he look at you. You could ask, *Why?* Could he articulate the *Why?* Could he say?

You bite the inside of your cheek. You know instinctively that to cry now is to lose it altogether.

You find your cell phone in your purse. You call your husband.

Noelle

In November, Silas and I drive to a party at which there are day students as well as boarders. Silas takes a drink, and so do I. We dance. I have never seen him dance before. Although he is as sleek and graceful as a cat on the basketball court, he is a bad dancer, and I laugh at him. He laughs, too, and we dance again. I become aware of people watching us. *Noelle and Silas,* they are thinking. We are a couple. It feels as though we have taken something precious and put it on display. Silas feels it, and I feel it. This is supposed to be normal, but I think that who we are together is in danger of being cheapened.

I remember everything. I remember the first time we stop at the Mobil station, and Silas gets out of the car to fill the gas tank. When he is done, he goes inside the store and buys me a doughnut. His aunt makes the doughnuts, he says, and they are best at about six o'clock at night, just when they are starting to go really stale. Silas smells of gasoline. I break the doughnut in half, give the rest to him. I kiss him. He tastes now of sugar and spices. Silas walks back into the Mobil station to buy more doughnuts to get more kisses. He buys all the doughnuts that are left. We drive up into the mountains, eating doughnuts and laughing. We eat until we both feel a little sick.

Silas has a heavy beard, even though he shaves every day. After we kiss, my mouth is raw.

In late November, there is a snowstorm. Boarders have school because they can walk to classes, but some of them pretend they can't. Day students are excused. Silas drives to school, even though the roads are terrible and he doesn't have his snow tires yet. The day-student parking lot is not even plowed, and Silas has to leave his car at the gym. I go to my English class, and there are only three people in it. We chat with Mr. Taylor about what we are all going to do for Thanksgiving break, but Mr. Taylor looks as though he wishes he could go home and crawl back into bed.

When I leave the classroom, Silas is standing in the hall. I am so glad to see him, I hug him right there in the doorway. A day without Silas is an empty day, good only for finishing homework or for practicing.

Silas has on a quilted parka and a maroon knit cap. His nose is reddened, and he has forgotten to shave. I know that he didn't come to school to turn in a paper or to take a test. He has come for me. I want to kiss him right there in the hallway, with the dead white light from the windows all around us. Ms. Epstein and Mr. Taylor are talking in a corner, but Mr. Taylor keeps looking over at Silas and me, as if we had signaled to him.

Silas drives me to Bennington, where I am to be in a recital. In the car, he keeps his hand on the thigh of my skirt while I picture my fingering over and over again. We do not talk. Silas knows I am nervous, so he doesn't ask me if I am nervous. In this way, I learn not to ask him questions before a game.

The road is white at either side, full of wet grit and salt that sprays all over the windshield when a truck passes. There are days when Vermont is almost unbearably grim, and it is all you can do not to get into a car and drive out of the state. I will be playing with college students, and when I picture myself up on the stage, my mouth goes dry and my breath gets shallow. Silas doesn't say, *You'll be fine,* and I like it that he doesn't lie.

During the concert, I can see Silas sitting at the back of the small auditorium. He looks nervous, the way he does at a football game when the score is too close. I think he must be like a parent watching his child perform on a stage — it's worse for the parent than for the child.

When the recital is over, Silas is jubilant, elated. He takes my face in both hands and kisses me on the mouth in full view of Ms. Irving, my music tutor, who doesn't seem too happy to see Silas. She has notes for me, she always has notes for me, but the notes can wait. Silas thinks I was wonderful.

For my birthday, just before the Christmas break, Silas asks me if he can take me to dinner. There is only one good restaurant within a thirty-mile radius of Avery. He says he has made a reservation.

I have never been on a real date before, and I am guessing Silas hasn't either. I wear a white top and a black skirt and a pair of ballet flats. I have to wear my parka over my shirt because my good coat is at home in Boston. I brush my hair and trim my bangs, and then I decide to give myself a razor cut on the sides, which turns out awful, and so I stop.

I meet Silas in the common room. He is dressed in a navy sport coat and a blue dress shirt with khakis. He has on an overcoat, like a grown man would wear, and he looks so handsome and sexy, it is all I can do not to touch the front of his shirt. There are kids in the common room watching reruns of *The Simpsons,* and they stare at us as if we might be going to a funeral.

The melting snow soaks my ballet flats before I even reach the car. My feet turn bright red with cold. Silas apologizes for the fact that the heater in the car is pathetic. He reaches around and gives me a blanket to make a nest for my feet.

When we get to the inn, a man takes our coats. Silas tugs at the cuffs of his shirt. I fix my skirt, aligning the zipper with my spine. My feet are still pink. Silas asks for a table near the fireplace, and maybe the waiter really likes the look of Silas because we are given a good table right in front of the hearth. The restaurant is small and expensive, but I can see, even in the low light, the way the curtain has been stapled to the wall, the way the electric wires run along the baseboard. To one end of the dining room is a bar that looks like an English pub. I order a Diet Coke and Silas orders water. Before we have even looked at the menu, Silas brings a small blue velvet box from the inside pocket of his sport coat. For one panicky minute, I think he is going to ask me to marry him. Maybe I gasp, because the bartender looks over. Silas puts the box on the table in front of me.

"I didn't have any wrapping paper," he says.

I am afraid when I open the box, but then I am relieved. Two tiny studs wink up at me in their white satin bed. The earrings are set with zircons, my birthstone. Some people might think it is a corny gift, but when I put the earrings on, I feel beautiful, as if my ears are twinkling.

I go away for Christmas break, and though I love my family, I am homesick for Silas. I think that must be what happens when you fall in love. The boy is home now; the family is *away*. I am so homesick, I go back to school a day early, which we are allowed to do if we are athletes or if we need the practice rooms. I text Silas to tell him I have arrived, and he comes at once. We go straight up to my dorm room, even though this is a major school violation. The RA is listening to music down the hall. I know she is resentful that she had to come back a day early because of me, and I think she is pretending to still be on vacation.

Silas and I fall onto the bed, and we kiss. We go through a lot of doors that afternoon. This door and that door and this door.

Mike

Mike sat at the desk in his glass box atop the inn. He set down his pen. He wanted to be able to do justice to the next part of his story—that of Anna and him—but he found that writing about love wasn't easy. It seemed that no matter where he headed, he was confronted with clichés or phrases so worn, they had lost their meaning. He couldn't easily describe sex. Wasn't it enough, he wondered, simply to be able to remember and not recall it in words on a piece of paper? But no, it was an important part of his story, perhaps the most important part for him personally, and to be hasty there seemed a kind of moral laziness. The cost had been very great, and if Mike was to be entirely honest with himself, which he was determined to do in this document, he had to admit that the affair, however brief, however incandescent, had been the catalyst for much that followed.

He needed a break, however. He had to move away from the writing for a few minutes or an hour and do something else. A drink might be just the thing. He must remember his sport coat. The tavern, despite its fire, or perhaps because of the fire and its resulting drafts, was always frigid.

He left his room and descended to the ground floor in the elevator. He moved through a crowd of conventioneers checking into the inn on a Sunday evening, their workweek about to begin in the morning in the Hildene Room (large mahogany conference table, open fire, Windsor chairs, fresh raspberry and peach muffins that Mike knew from experience were terrific). Mike idly calculated the average weight gain of a typical five-day stay at the inn and estimated it at somewhere between three and five pounds, though shopping clearly burned off calories, as did exercising at the inn's small weight room, a place he tended to avoid since he wasn't comfortable exposing his half-naked body to strangers (a holdover from his headmaster days, when it was a form of academic suicide to appear in the weight room at Avery). Mike preferred to walk to keep his weight at a steady 178.

The temperature outside, he had heard as he'd moved through the corridor, was seven degrees Fahrenheit, but the windchill, rumor also had it (and Mike could almost sense the shuddery gusts in the hallway), was making it feel like seven below. He thought he would have his first drink in the lounge by the fire and near the Christmas tree, set up even before Mike had arrived at the inn, but when he entered the lounge, he saw a man in a wheelchair pulled up close to the fire. Mike nodded in greeting and, though he had been planning all along to sit by the fire, moved instead to a cozy niche of upholstered sofas and chairs. He then immediately felt bad about that decision, since the man in the wheelchair was doubtless lonely and might like to chat. But Mike thought that if he were to backtrack and sit by the fire and make small talk, it would be perfectly clear to the man that he was doing this only out of pity or, to give him some credit, kindness, which Mike guessed the lonely man (or perhaps he wasn't lonely and simply wanted to escape his wife for a half hour) could do without.

The lounge had many nooks and crannies such as the one in which Mike was sitting. Until recently, these had been largely uninhabited, allowing Mike to use the lounge as a sort of adjunct living room or library. Perusing the many books on the shelves one day, he had made a bet with himself that none would be titles he would want to read—he won that handily—or that even a moderately learned man such as he would have heard of (lost that one when he came to a copy of *The Last of the Mohicans*). Lately, however, the lounge had been becoming busier as the Christmas holiday approached. Typically, Mike might see husbands there or children (or husbands with children) who had been banished from their rooms to amuse themselves while wives and mothers got dressed. Mike had noted that young couples, wishing to experience every aspect of the inn, made a point of visiting each room and sitting for a time. Mike didn't know if he would still be at the inn by Christmas, when he imagined the lounge would be mobbed. It occurred to him then that he had better ask at the front desk, because it was entirely possible that all the rooms had been booked for what he couldn't help but think of, from years of habit, as the "Christmas break." Since he had no other place to go at Christmas, except to his rented studio in New York City and to his former brother-in-law's for dinner, and since he further didn't know if he would be finished with his writing project (his current rate of production was proving remarkably slow), he decided, with just the faintest ping of alarm, that he had better check with the front desk as to how long he would be able to stay in his current room.

Until that night in September two years ago, when Meg surprised him in the kitchen with the announcement that she wanted a child, his wife had seemed aggressively not to want children. While Mike sometimes had yearnings and knew that they were sitting on a gold mine of potential babysitting, he was growing increasingly aware that even very lovely children quickly morphed into disturbing teenagers. He thought he probably knew adolescents as well as any woman or man who worked in a school setting did; that is to say, he knew them not from the point of view of a parent who loved them unconditionally but from the point of view of a somewhat judgmental, if hopeful, outsider. Thus, he was prone to notice the darker side of adolescents: the insane risks they took; the experimentation with all forms of behavior, including the obsequious and the downright cruel; a pathological procrastination that often resulted in a need for excessive sleep; a sensibility dictated by rampant hormones; and a tendency to extremes in personal hygiene (impressively long, uncut toenails on the boys; girls who changed their outfits three times a day, *not including sports uniforms*). On balance, Mike thought he probably had a somewhat jaundiced opinion of teenagers that made him hesitant about having his own. He supposed that it was possible Meg now had a child; when they separated, she'd still have been forty-three. They'd had little contact except through legal representatives since shortly after the scandal. Without children, Christmas, which in the beginning of their marriage had felt deeply romantic, had largely lost its luster for both of them and was mainly anticipated for the two-week respite it gave them from six hundred teenagers.

Mike changed his mind and decided upon an immediate drink and a meal in the tavern, where he was shown to a small booth with two upholstered wing chairs. A faint smell of potpourri filled the room, while overhead the speakers tinnily pumped out classical music that was not, as far as Mike could discern, Christmas-themed. There were behind him floor-to-ceiling windows that went absolutely to the carpet — to open them, one had to bend down and tug upward — and that were emitting frigid drafts. Mike knew the menu to be simple but reliable: Black Pepper Fettuccine, Angus Cheeseburger, Turkey Sandwich, Squash Soup. There were better restaurants in town, most of which he had tried, but he liked the ease and atmosphere of the tavern, where all the paintings were of cows, perhaps meant to remind one of the Angus Cheeseburger, which he intended to have despite an earlier resolve not to eat red meat. The resolve had been made in a vacuum, since Mike hadn't seen a doctor in more than two years, not since he stopped visiting Dr. Vaughn, a physician in Avery with a mole on his lip that was impossible to ignore and that made Mike wonder, every time he was in his office, why the man, who presumably had access to good medical care, did not have it removed. Would it take a real gouge out of his lip? Mike pressed his own lips together just thinking of the pain.

When he looked up, he saw, across the room, a woman sitting in her own booth. She was writing addresses on white envelopes, occasionally consulting a small spiral-bound notebook. She wrote, looked at the envelope, switched it for another, and then wrote again. Christmas cards? Mike tried not to stare. She had on a black sweater with sleeves that went to her knuckles, tight jeans, and hiking boots. She was blond — from an expensive bottle, if it was a bottle — and of indeterminate age. Not young, not old, and not middle-aged, either, which demanded, he thought, a short-haired woman with a thickened waist who didn't wear sweaters with sleeves to the knuckles or jeans that broke neatly over hiking boots. The woman set aside her notebook when the waitress came with her meal. She glanced up and caught Mike looking at her and didn't smile. He turned away.

He heard a small exclamation then and glanced over and saw that the blond woman had bitten into her own Angus Cheeseburger and that the beef juice — dark pink and translucent — had squirted over the back of her hand and even onto the cuff of her sweater. She laughed at herself and mopped at the spill with her napkin, and when she looked up again — a bit sheepishly this time — she once more caught Mike's eye. She gave a shallow, rueful smile and then went back to her meal.

It was unlikely, Mike thought, that she was at the inn with a husband, for it was rare for a woman to take an evening meal without a companion. Women seemed perfectly happy to eat breakfast and lunch alone, but seldom did they show up in a tavern without a man.

Mike's beer and then his own burger arrived, and he ate it with relish — and, yes, the beef juice squirted onto his thumb so that he had to lick it off. Writing seemed to be having a salutary effect on his appetite, making him extraordinarily hungry at mealtimes, as if he had been overexerting himself physically. When he finished, he thought of ordering another, but he didn't, as he already felt mild regret over eating the red meat, something he vowed not to repeat for at least the rest of the week. By the time he set his napkin on the table, the tavern was nearly raucous with large groups of coworkers celebrating their annual Christmas parties, the main feature of which seemed to be the quantities of red and white wine happily being consumed. Mike remembered such parties from his days at Hartford and at Avery, events often ending in exceptionally convivial feelings that, sadly, did not last much beyond the New Year.

After his meal, Mike went up to his room to get his gloves and scarf and hat, for he believed the bulletins about the windchill. He would walk for as long as the marble sidewalk went on, then turn up a wide street of large summerhouses, some of which had been winterized. At the top of the hill, he would walk along a more traveled road, one without sidewalks (a feature he considered essential to civilized life, not to mention safer for children; sidewalks in Vermont villages were, in fact, a rarity), and after that, he would cut back down to the main road and follow that until he reached the inn. He once estimated the walk to be nearly three miles long, which was not excessive in the way of exercise, but it seemed to be enough. When motivated, Mike would sometimes sprint up the first hill just to get the heart pumping, something he would not do after a full meal and a beer.

The cold air stung his eyes and nose, making both water, but he had not brought a tissue with him and so gave the appearance of a man in tears. His cheeks stung as well, and he had to turn broadside into some of the gusts. So great was the irritation in his eyes that there were whole stretches during which he couldn't see well and had to blink often. It was quite a broad avenue, with an assortment of dissimilar, though intriguing, homes on either side, each stately in its own way. They made Mike wonder who inhabited them and how those inhabitants made a living, a question that often perplexed him when he was in Vermont. Some were situated very close to the road so that a step or two inward would bring him flush against a doorway, while others were set back and had long driveways. All were framed by a towering mountain behind them that in summer had a road one could travel by car to reach the summit.

Once again wiping tears from his stinging cheeks, he saw in

the light from the lanterns that lined the walk the woman who'd been in the tavern just minutes earlier. She had on a black down coat with fur trim and had mail in her hand. She had wound a scarf around her neck but didn't have on a hat. He could see her only from the back, though he recognized the jeans and the hiking boots. He picked up his pace, much like a fox might investigate a vixen. He didn't think of himself as a predator, but he was aware of a male imperative when the face of a female was hidden.

She stopped in front of a mailbox belonging to one of the houses on the street and began to read, as one sometimes does, the addresses on the envelopes to make sure she had gotten them right or perhaps to check that each envelope had been properly stamped. Since there were at least a dozen envelopes, this gave Mike a few seconds to catch up to her. He tried to make the encounter seem casual.

"Oh, hello," he said, as if he had just noticed her.

She turned, and at once Mike understood his pursuit. The woman—in her face, in her smile perhaps—bore a striking resemblance to Anna. He knew why he had wanted to catch up to this stranger and why, now, he was appalled to have done so.

"I'm sorry," he stammered.

The woman looked baffled and a bit wary.

"I thought...I thought you might be someone else," he said. "I'm very sorry."

He turned abruptly and walked in the direction of the inn. His eyes watered furiously, and he could barely see where he was going. He tried to blink the tears away. Of course, he had not thought the woman was someone else; that had been a spur-of-the-moment lie. Mike would never mistake the woman in the down and fur coat for the woman who now sat in the dark in a small house at the bottom of a long hill.

Mike had believed that by writing about the scandal, he could, in some measure, put it behind him. He had thought that if he wrote his pain away—his guilt, his complicity—it would actually go away. But in confronting the woman's face and the slight fear and curiosity there, he had realized he had no right to wish away any of the guilt or the pain, or even to remember the many moments of pure joy that he and Anna had shared.

He would not write another word. Not a single word. He would, in fact, as soon as he returned to his room, the glass walls having lost their magic and seeming more like a glass booth into which one might put a prisoner, tear up all that he had written.

In the stinging cold, Mike quickened his pace.

Ellen

You sit on the bed, a thin pillow at your back, watching CNN, because not to have the television on, not to have the noise, has become unbearable. There is a pizza box, half full, on the dresser beside the television. You ate two pieces, unexpectedly ravenous. Your son said he had no appetite. You told him he had to eat, so he sat up and folded a greasy slice of pizza and stuck it into his mouth and chewed. You couldn't see his eyes. You didn't want to see his eyes.

When the policeman knocked on the door, it was an oddly gentle knock, and you thought it might be the motel owner's wife, with a spare towel and a wrapped cake of soap in her hands. You opened the door and saw the uniform, and your foot immediately slid along the threshold as if you might bar the door. You put your arms up and held each jamb before you demanded, "What do you want?"

The officer gave his name and asked if Robert Leicht was in the room. You stalled, you asked to see a badge, all the time thinking your son might run away. But where would he have gone? Out the bathroom window?

"Ma'am," the policeman said, not unkindly.

"It's OK," your son said behind you.

Still you would not give, and it was Rob who had to pry you from the door.

When they put your son in cuffs, you put your own hands to your mouth to muffle the scream you knew was coming. You kept your fingers on your son's shoulder until they made you let go. You stood in the cold and watched the policeman bend your son's head so that he could sit in the back of the cruiser. You were crying then. Your son looked up at you, and you tried to smile because you could see how frightened he was. You said, "I'll be right behind you."

Your hands shook so badly, you could hardly get the car to start. You knew where the police station was, you had seen it dozens of times on your visits to Avery. You arrived in time to watch a man fingerprint your son, and you immediately began to ask about bail. "Where do I go?" you asked. And, "How much?"

They took your son away from you into a room you couldn't see. You thought, *This is real. This is really happening.*

After the judge had made his ruling, Rob was finally released into your custody. He wouldn't let you hug him. His fingers were black with ink.

At midnight, there's another knock at the door, a fist pounding. You know who it is even before your husband calls your name. The voice is angry and demanding. For a moment, you contemplate stepping outside the door before he can get in. You are suddenly very afraid.

Arthur has come straight from work. He knows about the arrest. You called him from the police station, a cold cup of coffee in your free hand. His tie is loosened, his jacket open. Even though it is January, he never wears an overcoat. You always say to him, *What if your car breaks down?* But still he doesn't wear one. It constricts him when he drives, he says.

"Arthur," you say.

His dark eyes find your son, the boy you made together. They quickly absorb the rest of the room, sizing it up, taking its measure.

"Stand up," he says to Rob.

With a slow roll, your son sits up and puts his feet on the floor. Eventually, he stands.

Arthur asks a question you have already asked. "Is it true?"

Rob shuts his eyes. His jaw slides forward a millimeter, enough to let you know he is girding himself.

Your husband steps closer to your son. Arthur's hands are on his hips, his own jaw jutting forward.

"Is it true?" he asks again.

Instinctively, you put your hands out, wanting to prevent whatever it is that's coming.

Your son, eyes shut, nods.

Arthur's hand is so swift, the arc so blunt, you're not sure what you have just witnessed. Your son's head snaps back, and he falls onto the bed. You grab your husband's arm, and you cry, *Stop!*

With effort, your son sits up. He doesn't cry or touch his face, and for that you are inexplicably proud of him. Already there is the red imprint of the back of a hand on his jaw. You try to remember if Arthur ever cuffed your son before. You can't remember.

"What on God's earth ever made you do such a thing?" your husband demands.

It is an unanswerable question. Or perhaps there is an answer, but Rob will not give it. Not now. Not here. Not to you or your husband.

"Do you have any idea what you have done? What you have thrown away?" Arthur shouts.

Your son knows to the precise milligram the weight of all that he has thrown away. The questions are for the father's benefit only.

"You're aware that you were going to go to Brown," Arthur says, hands on his hips.

There is no mention of the assaulted girl. You wonder if your husband understands the nature of the crime.

"So what do you have to say for yourself?" your husband asks, and even he must know he will not get a satisfactory answer, if, indeed, he gets any answer at all.

Your son doesn't respond.

Your husband whips around and glares at you, as if you are responsible. And, of course, you are. You are responsible.

"I can't even be in the same room with him," your husband says to you, as if he, of the two of you, is the more offended. Is he?

You are not surprised by either your husband's strength or the flimsiness of the door, which seems to quiver in its frame even after Arthur is gone. You recognize an impulse in yourself to run after him, to call to him, to ask to talk. But right now you can't do that.

Silas

I'm up the path now, farther than even you and I have ever gone. Once, when I was a kid, my father and I hiked to the top, it took all day, but when we got there and stood on a rock, we could see the mountains all around, and I remember being amazed that there was a mountain right behind the one we were on, one you couldn't see from the ground, and it seemed like there was a taller mountain behind that one, too, so that every time you got to the top, you would see that you had another mountain to climb, but then I figured there must be a top somewhere that was the highest of all, and I wondered if I would ever get to do that one day, go to the top.

It is getting a little colder here now. I walked home and no one was there and I got my down parka and started up this path, and I have some food in my backpack. I think I can probably stay here long enough to get the courage to go back down again, and I will find out that I have been expelled and that my father wants to hit me and I won't be able to live in the house with them and I will have to find a friend to live with so I can finish out my senior year in the public school, although I don't know why I would ever want to do that because I can't go to college now, that's for sure, and so maybe I will just move away from Avery and get a job somewhere and try to find a place to live, and that will be that, and no one will know about me or anything that happened, and I can pretend I am forgetting, too, except that I can't because I will always be thinking of you and wondering where you are and knowing that you were the one and that I hurt you practically more than any person can hurt another, I can't think of anything worse I could have done to you, I just can't.

So I guess if I just think about the good times, I will warm up a bit. I forgot to look at how cold it was out, I think it must be below freezing, maybe below twenty, and I am probably going to get some frostbite, but it won't be the first time. Once when I went to your dorm, you came downstairs and you had on a short skirt with a belt around your hips, and your legs were brown from the sun, and I wondered how you had got such a good tan, and you had on a navy striped polo shirt, and your breasts were beautiful, and you had your earrings on, and I knew that you had put them on for me, and I stood up and kissed you right away, and you backed away from me and laughed that laugh you have, but you were happy I had done that even though there were people in the hallway that might have seen us.

You told me you would love me forever. I think that is not true now. And so a person can never promise to love someone forever, because you never know what might come up, what terrible thing the person you love might do. And what does that feel like, not to love someone anymore? One day you love him, and the next day you don't because you have seen him on a tape? Where does all that love go? Does it all go away at once, or does it go away in terrible bits every time you picture the tape until there is nothing left? So you cannot love me, but I know that I will always love you, even though I should never have promised you I would love you forever, because I did something that, if I had been loving you right that minute, I wouldn't have done, though I can't ever remember not loving you, and when you are not even thinking about a person, you can still be loving them, right?

My fingers are getting stiff trying to write in this notebook that I didn't take very good notes in for math. When I flip through the notes at the beginning, I can see that I wasn't paying attention the way I should, and I wonder what I was thinking about on this day or that day when I should have been paying attention. I don't even know what the notes mean. If I had to take a test on them, I would get everything wrong.

If I had to take a test on you, though, I would get everything right. I would know exactly how you smell and how you like to be kissed on the side of your neck even though it makes you laugh, and I would get everything right about how you like to make love even though I always thought there would be lots more to learn and that we would learn together. Even if you talked to me or even if you looked me in the eye one day, you would never, ever, ever, let me make love to you, and that would kill me, so it's better if I never see you again, although I think that might kill me, too.

Sometimes I think about the girl and what she is feeling now. I didn't like her before, and I don't like her now. She was twisted and she was hungry and she knew how to make us hungry, and I am amazed that we didn't have any shame. I don't know where the shame went. I guess the alcohol takes it away. I guess that's the point of drinking, to take all the feelings and thoughts and morals away until you are just a body doing what a body will do. But sometimes I think about her, she was so young, and I wonder if she feels any shame, she must, unless she cannot remember, and I hope for her sake that she cannot remember.

Gary

On Wednesday, January 25, my deputy, Bernard Herrmann, and I responded to a telephone call we received from the father of a female student at Avery Academy.

The father stated that his daughter had told him she had been raped by three students in a dormitory room at Avery Academy the previous Saturday night.

The victim was fourteen years old at the time and a freshman at Avery Academy.

Later, the girl named three of the students who had been involved in the sexual assault.

Deputy Herrmann and I immediately drove out to Avery Academy to speak to the headmaster, Michael Bordwin, to see if he could corroborate the information we had and tell us where we could find the alleged victim and the three boys who had allegedly committed this sexual assault.

The boys were Robert Leicht, eighteen; Silas Quinney, eighteen; and James Robles, nineteen.

Mr. Bordwin at that time appeared to be somewhat flustered by the accusation. He insisted on accompanying us to interview the young woman who had made the allegations to her father.

We three arrived at Upworth Dormitory at approximately twelve noon and found the alleged victim in a state of mild hysteria. Though the incident had occurred four days previously, she was sobbing uncontrollably.

She was in the presence of her roommate, Laura Stanton, age fourteen.

Despite being initially hysterical, the alleged victim stopped crying and asked to give a statement.

Mr. Bordwin advised her not to speak to us and to consult a lawyer before she went any farther with this accusation, but the girl would not listen to him.

The girl said that on the previous Saturday, January 21, at about ten o'clock in the evening, she had been taken to a dormitory room in Everett Hall by a number of male upperclassmen. There, she was given a great deal of alcohol so that she was soon in a state of mental and physical incapacitation. It was then that she was forced to perform oral sex on one of the boys and was vaginally raped by a second. One other boy, who was in the room at the time, participated in various ways in the event.

The alleged victim then stated that without her knowledge the incident had been taped by a fourth person in the room, whose name she said she did not know.

It was our understanding that both parents were en route to Avery to be with their daughter.

During these allegations, Mr. Bordwin left the room.

We then advised the alleged victim that she would need to be seen by a doctor, who would have to examine her.

The alleged victim protested, stating that the event had happened four days before and therefore there would be no evidence of the alleged rape. We informed her that this was police procedure.

Deputy Herrmann called for an ambulance to transfer the young woman to Western Vermont Regional Hospital to be examined.

She then began crying again and said she had to wait for her parents. We informed her that it was in her best interest to comply and that we would inform her parents of her whereabouts.

Deputy Herrmann and I waited in the dormitory room with the alleged victim and her roommate for the ambulance to arrive.

Deputy Herrmann and I then returned to the administration building to speak with Michael Bordwin. He invited us into his office. On his desk were two sheets of lined paper.

Mr. Bordwin informed us that he had extracted earlier that day written confessions from two of the students involved in the alleged rape. He added that he had been reluctant to hand them over to the police until he had had a chance to speak to the victim again. I examined the written confessions and took possession of them. They were from Robert Leicht and James Robles. When I asked about Silas Quinney, he said the boy could not be located.

We proceeded to Everett Hall, where James Robles was in residence. He asked what the charges were against him.

Mr. Robles's demeanor was calm and a bit aloof. I read the suspect his rights, and Deputy Herrmann cuffed Mr. Robles. The suspect was led away to the cruiser we had parked in front of the administration building. Mr. Robles went without resistance.

Deputy Herrmann and I then traveled to the Mountain View Motel. We were told by the manager in what room we would find Robert Leicht. We knocked on the door, and it was answered by his mother, revealing Robert Leicht sitting on a bed. Mrs. Leicht tried to bar the door. Mr. Leicht got up without any protest and gently moved his mother out of the doorway. We informed him that he was under arrest for the alleged sexual assault of the young woman in question. We read Robert Leicht his rights, removed him from the property in handcuffs, and put him in the cruiser with James Robles. Neither boy looked at the other.

With two boys in custody, we then returned in the cruiser to the station, where there is a lockup. It was then occupied by Johnny Bix, who had been brought in early that morning for "drunk and disorderly."

Mr. Bix was released, as there is only one room in the lockup.

It was then decided that Deputy Herrmann would remain in the station with the two suspects and that I would drive out to the Quinney farm to arrest Silas Quinney.

Silas Quinney is my nephew.

Deputy Herrmann has previously stated for the record that during the time I was away, the alleged suspects, Mr. Leicht and Mr. Robles, did not speak to each other.

When I arrived at the Quinney farm, Anna Quinney was in residence, having just returned from grocery shopping. When I told her of the nature of my visit, Mrs. Quinney seemed shocked. She stated that she had not seen her son since breakfast, at approximately seven o'clock that morning.

Mrs. Quinney went directly to her cell phone and tried to call her son. Silas Quinney did not answer the call.

I was then able to extract a promise from Mrs. Quinney that she would bring Silas into the station herself when he returned to the house.

Mrs. Quinney stated that she was certain there was some mistake, that her son was incapable of the charges. Since I knew Mrs. Quinney to be a person of her word, I then left the house and drove back to the police station.

Irene

I was the resident on duty in the ER at Western Vermont Regional Hospital on the afternoon of January 25, 2006. I examined the girl from Avery Academy for signs of rape and assault. The girl was extremely upset—crying and gesturing—and at first refused to be examined. The nurse on duty explained to her that in order to press charges, should she or her parents decide to do that, an examination by a physician would be necessary. After a time, the girl acquiesced, explaining that the rape had taken place four days earlier. She indicated that there probably wouldn't be any evidence remaining.

In the presence of the ER nurse on duty, I examined the girl, who said she was fourteen years old. Though there was scant evidence of bruising about the vaginal cavity, there was no obvious evidence of any seminal fluid in the vaginal canal. The nurse on duty nevertheless administered the rape kit.

Immediately after the examination and after the girl had dressed, I tried to speak to her about the event. I was attempting at that time to assess her emotional state to determine if medication might be needed. Although upset and at times shaking, the girl seemed lucid enough and was able to understand and answer my questions. At one point, I deliberately made a slight joke, which produced a brief smile. I did not offer any medication.

The girl said repeatedly that the events of the evening in question were "horrible, horrible" and that she didn't want to talk about them. As she herself was neither under arrest nor needed for questioning, she was allowed to use her cell phone to call a friend to come get her. It was our understanding that her parents were on their way to the school to be with her.

It was only later, shortly before the trial was scheduled to begin, that I learned that the results of a routine blood test that had been administered that afternoon showed the girl's blood alcohol level at that time to be .028. I had not smelled alcohol on the victim when examining her, but I had noted in the records the incongruity of her emotional state and the length of time since the alleged rape. In other words, though the event had happened four days earlier and though she might well have been deeply upset by it, she was reacting physically as if it had just taken place. I have not had enough experience with rape victims to know if this is a common pattern, but it is possible that the amount of alcohol in her system might have accounted for what appeared to be excessive distress.

Noelle

Silas is supposed to meet me in the dining hall. We have Saturday school tomorrow, so there will be regular study hall tonight from eight o'clock until ten. Silas and I have only until eight to be together. Two or three nights a week, we have these two hours, and they are not enough. They are never enough.

I wait in the foyer before the double doors of the dining hall. Usually Silas and I go in together and pick up our trays and slide them side by side on the metal railings. I am hungry, having had an early lunch. I even have a little headache from the hunger. I have to use the bathroom, which is off the foyer, but I don't because I don't want to miss the sight of Silas coming through the doors.

I wait until 6:45, and I know if I don't go inside right that minute, the dining hall will close, and I won't get any dinner. My headache is worse, and I am a little worried. Silas is never late. Maybe once or twice, after a long practice, he is five minutes late, bursting through the door, looking for me, short of breath from running all the way from the gym. Tonight, there is no Silas, short of breath or not.

I fill my tray with salad and soup and take it to a table. Almost everyone else has finished eating. I see the boys from the basketball team picking up their trays, which overflow with dishes and glasses and banana peels and chicken wings, and walking them to the recycling area. I want to ask them if they know where Silas is, if they know why he is late, but I am too embarrassed. I am embarrassed to be eating alone.

I call Silas's house at five minutes to eight. His father answers and says Silas didn't come home for dinner. Silas told his mother he was eating with a friend, and though I think I am that friend, I don't say anything.

From eight o'clock until ten, students cannot make or receive phone calls.

At one minute past ten, I call Silas's cell phone. He doesn't answer. I text him, but he doesn't respond to that, either. Finally, I call his house again. His father answers. Silas is in bed asleep. He had a rough practice. Do I want him to wake Silas?

No, I say. No, I don't.

The next morning I do not see Silas in the halls or on the pathways between buildings. We do not take the same classes. I am a slightly better student than he is, which I try never to talk about. I go down to the gym early to see if I can catch him before the game and ask him what happened to him the night before. I have decided that he probably wasn't feeling well and went straight home to bed. He felt so unwell, I am guessing, that he forgot to call me.

When I arrive at the gym, Silas is already on the court with the other players. He is practicing layups and three-pointers. He is running harder than the rest of the boys, as if he wants to keep going right through the tiled walls. I stand at the edge of the court, waiting for him to notice me.

He is nervous, I decide. This is a big game.

I sit in the front row, aware of other kids coming in and filling up the seats behind me. I look for Mr. Quinney at the place where he usually sits, but I can't find him. Silas comes to the players' bench right in front of me, and again he doesn't seem to see me. I know that it is bad form to distract a player while the coach is talking to the team, so I sit back. Surely, after the game, Silas will wait for me.

Silas is an animal on the court. I can't decide what kind, because nothing moves like Silas, and animals hardly ever seem angry. Stealthy, yes. Cunning, yes. But angry, no. Silas is angry. I can feel it coming off him in waves. I can see it in his eyes. I know that something is very wrong, and I try to guess what it is. Is he mad at Coach Blount? Is he angry with his father, which explains why Mr. Quinney isn't at the game? Or is Silas, in some strange way, angry at me?

From the corner of my eye, I see a basketball arc into the stands. It hits a woman on the side of her face and knocks her sideways on the bench. She puts her arms out, flailing, and another woman catches her. For one second, there is silence. Everyone is standing, looking in the direction of the woman who has been hit. People are murmuring Silas's name. The woman is being led up the aisle by Mr. Bordwin, our headmaster, who must have been sitting near her.

When I turn to the court to look for Silas, he is already gone.

Rasheed

Rasheed glanced again at the opened letter on his cluttered desk, and for a moment he'd felt a flicker of interest, a desire to say what he'd wanted to say almost two years ago. He made the impulse die quickly. It wasn't that he bore the researcher at the University of Vermont any particular animosity; it was simply that he didn't want to have to think about the scandal. He didn't want to experience the anger. He had moved on. Basketball was behind him. It had been a part of his life, like an arm he'd had once and then lost in an accident. He didn't want to be the guy walking around without an arm, everyone asking him what had happened to it.

But the memories rankled just the same: the injustice of it; the firing of the coach; the rest of the schedule canceled. Rasheed had been a junior, and without an opportunity to play, he found that even the smaller schools hadn't had a chance to scout him. In the mayhem following the scandal, Rasheed had gone home to North Carolina to talk to his father. A family practitioner in Greensboro, Rasheed's father had urged him to study the sciences in preparation for college and possibly medical school. Rasheed had good grades but not outstanding ones, primarily because he'd put so many hours into basketball. When he returned to Vermont, having to pass through locked gates, he'd had a different agenda than he'd had in the fall.

Rasheed hoisted his backpack over his arm, left his college dorm, and climbed the hill to his first class after lunch. Shakespeare was a reach for him, since most of his other classes were in the sciences. Despite the grueling labs, Rasheed was handling those well. When he reached the top of the hill, he turned and gazed over at the view of the city of Boston, which he hoped had a place for him one day. He didn't think he had a chance at Harvard Medical, but he'd been advised that Tufts University School of Medicine or Boston University School of Medicine might be within his sights.

Nearly every guy Rasheed had met in the dorm the first few weeks of college that fall had assumed that because of his height and his color, he would play basketball for Tufts. In the beginning, he'd had to fend off dozens of casual invitations for pickup games. In fact, Rasheed had played only once since arriving on campus: in the gym, by himself, practicing drills, shooting threes. The ball had felt good in his hands, but the experience had left him feeling empty and a little sorry for himself, something he'd promised his father he would guard against. When he got his medical degree, his father had said, he could allow himself a day, maybe two, of wallowing in self-pity. By then, his father had calculated, Rasheed wouldn't care anymore.

Rasheed was early to class. He stood outside the brick hall that was the English Department, even though it was November and cold and he had only a sweatshirt on. But all his height was in his legs, and they cramped up under the small desks, so that by the time class was over, Rasheed could barely straighten his knees. To avoid that, he tried not to enter the classroom until the last minute, which he knew some teachers read as a reluctance on Rasheed's part or even insolence, but that was the way it had to be.

Fuck the letter, he thought, scraping his boot back and forth against the stone step.

The team had known that Faye Academy would be tough competition, and the coach was eager to take a reading. If they could beat Faye, they might be able to beat Vermont Academy later in the season and then go all the way to the tournament. It had been a long time since Avery had had an awesome threesome like J. Dot, Rob, and Silas. Rasheed was fast becoming nearly as valuable, as was his best friend, Irwin. J. Dot elevated the game, and Rasheed, though he didn't like the guy much, watched his every move; he knew he could learn from the PG. J. Dot had all the rebounds and slashed hard to the basket. He had swagger on the court, more swagger than Rasheed had ever seen on a white boy.

Right from the get-go, though, the game with Faye hadn't gone well for Avery. They threw the ball away four times, once booting it out-of-bounds. They were nervous, and the coach told them to simmer down. Faye was playing terrific defense, trapping Avery into a half-court game. Silas was missing his threes, and Rasheed could see that the more he missed, the more frustrated he became. Once, Rob slipped to the floor and lost the ball. Then Irwin successfully blocked two consecutive Faye shots. Rasheed moved in for the rebound and sank two on successive possessions — beautiful shots, no rim — and Avery for the first time all game was up by one point. He could hear the fans going crazy in the stands. Three minutes remained in the half. If Avery could go into the locker room up by four or even five, Rasheed knew, the team would win. It took nearly the whole first half of a game for the team to settle down, to find its rhythm, but when it did, they won. It had happened so often last season and this, that it had become almost a psychological necessity for the players: Avery had to be up by the half.

After Faye finished a fast break, Rob took possession with under a minute to the half. He passed to Silas, who scored straightaway. The Avery stands went nuts. With maybe twenty seconds left, Silas got possession again and went for another three. The ball took flight but then appeared to die in the air. It fell to the floor as if filled with bird shot. Silas had choked. He almost never did that. Rasheed blocked a shot, and with seconds left, he could hear Silas shouting for the ball. Thinking Silas wanted to redeem himself before the buzzer, Rasheed passed it to him. Silas held the ball too long—the fans were screaming, *Shoot! Shoot!*—turned his back to the basket, and let it fly into the stands. Rasheed couldn't believe what he had just witnessed.

The ball hit a woman in the face. The team watched as the injured fan was taken out of the stands. The ref threw Silas out of the game and sent him to the locker room. Rasheed remembered glancing over at Irwin, and the two locking eyes, each asking the other what the hell was going on. Both knew that Silas had meant to aim that ball into the stands. Neither had ever seen anything like it. The buzzer had rung for the half, and they'd headed for the locker room, but Silas wasn't there. Rasheed wondered if Silas had just walked out of the building in January in his sleeveless jersey and basketball shorts.

The second half, without Silas—with the team just poleaxed—was all but a rout. The home team came out onto the court dead flat. Avery couldn't take care of the ball, and Faye won by an obscene margin.

Two days later, on a Monday night, Rasheed's roommate had called to him when he'd walked into his dorm room after dinner. "Take a look at this," Shawn had said. Rasheed had glanced over and had seen what looked like porn on Shawn's computer screen. "Why do you watch that shit?" Rasheed had goaded him.

"No, seriously," Shawn had said. "Isn't this an Avery dorm?"

Rasheed stood over Shawn and looked at what appeared to be a short portion of a home movie. He saw sneakers on the floor. It might be an Avery dorm. Whoever had posted it on You-Tube had blocked the faces out, though the action was apparent enough. He was about to turn away when he noticed the shirts on the floor—Silas's green flannel and J. Dot's sweatshirt with the sleeves cut just above the elbow. Rasheed looked up at the ceiling. He knew right then that basketball was all over.

He couldn't prevent the stories in the press that blamed the whole team. It was when he'd most wanted to speak out, to defend himself. But his father had counseled caution. *Move on,* he'd said. *They'll twist what you say. Be silent.* And so Rasheed had been, even when they'd fired the coach and canceled the rest of the season. Even when the newspapers wrote about the "entitlement" of the team or the "streak of lawlessness" within it. Rasheed wondered how people could get away with writing something that was completely false, but the reporters did.

Rasheed again glanced over at the city of Boston and in doing so saw his professor climbing the hill, head down against the wind that snapped at the campus in the late fall and winter. Rasheed slipped through the door and into the classroom. He sometimes wondered what had happened to J. Dot and Rob. They hadn't kept in touch. In the beginning, Rasheed had been hurt that Irwin wouldn't answer his calls. Rasheed folded himself into the small wooden desk. Under his picture in the freshman directory, it read AVERY ACADEMY. Guys still asked about the scandal. Even some of the teachers had taken him aside to get the inside scoop. Rasheed wondered if the questions would ever go away. And it wasn't just he who'd been derailed, he thought as he reached for his book in his backpack. What about Irwin and Jamail and August and Perry? No one who had been on the team that year, even the promising freshmen, would ever have an opportunity to play college ball. Four, five guys with possible futures, shut down. If the team was just now starting back up again, Jacob what's-his-name would be a senior already, and it was too late, after such a long hiatus, to attract the attention of any scout. Rasheed wondered where it was written that a school, under pressure, could do that to a team and to its coach without so much as an apology. Because Rasheed sure hadn't gotten an apology.

But he wouldn't think about that anymore, because it would just get him going. When he got back to the dorm, he would toss the letter from the researcher, get it out of his room. Whatever the letter was about, it no longer concerned him. He had other things in life to think about now. He had work to do.

Anna

I saw the letter. You left it on the table. Why did you do that, leave something that would remind me? That is not like you. I saw it when I went down for water. I saw some words and knew. More people wanting to talk about Silas.

Will you call her, the researcher named Jacqueline?

I lie in my bed and stare at the ceiling. I wish that I had not seen the letter. How can you have been so careless — you, who are usually so careful? Were you interrupted by the telephone? Were you rushing out the door?

I try to think about the ceiling, about the structure of the house behind the wallboard and the plaster, about how the unseen rafters and boards rise to a peak. I lie on the blue quilt, the one I made after our wedding. I cannot remember making the quilt. I do not want to remember the wedding.

Some days all I do is remember.

■

We never talk, you and I. We say small bits of sentences once or twice a week. Questions, mostly, or statements. *I made a meat loaf for dinner. Have you seen my brown boots?*

I stand up and draw back the quilt and the top sheet and crawl into the bed. I punch the soft pillow into a mound and mold it around my hair and face. Will you tell the researcher from the University of Vermont, as you never said to the press, as you have never even said to me, *It all happened because of my wife?*

You will not. I cannot imagine you saying such a thing.

But it is true, and you are entitled to say it. It all happened because of me.

It all happened because I wanted.

How much easier to have no memories of the crime. Of the crimes, repeated. I have stopped asking why. It isn't a question that can be answered.

I was lonely and I wanted.

No, that's not true. I wasn't lonely. I had you and Silas. But still I wanted.

It was obscene, that wanting.

■

I watched as the EMTs took him from the car, that sturdy Volvo that refused to buckle, even with the tremendous force of its tumble. He tried to stand, but they wouldn't let him. I watched them hoist him onto a stretcher and slide him into the ambulance. I minded that I didn't even know his name. Later, in the newspaper, I saw his name. It was Gary who told me he was with the school.

If he hadn't come back to the house to apologize and to offer to pay for the damages, would I have forgotten all about him? Would the reaching out to hold his arm have become one of those small things in life that seem sweet or meaningful in the moment but are forgotten before you've even reentered the house?

I knew the day he came to the house to pay for the damage that I wanted to see him again. It was not a real desire. It was a series of questions and answers that seemed to be moving in a certain direction. I asked to visit the school.

I am responsible for Silas going to the school. You didn't want that. You didn't want him to go.

For months, I thought I was doing it for Silas.

It wasn't true. I did it for myself.

I remember his visits. I remember the blue oxford shirt and his tie. The jacket always taken off and carefully laid over the kitchen chair, even when it was chilly. He smelled of lime and sometimes of sweat as we sat together, looking over the applications and then later talking about the parent-teacher association. Later still, he came to dinner.

Once, after we had been to bed together, I picked up his shirt from the floor and inhaled the scent. Just touching that shirt had been, for years, my only concrete fantasy.

He came with wine. I reached across the kitchen table and covered his hand. He was shocked. I could see that. His eyes met mine and then slipped away. We were drunk, or I was drunk. I wouldn't have had the courage to touch him otherwise. But I was glad I had done it. I can feel it still, the rough skin of his hand, the knuckles knobby, the fingers warm. I pulled away.

He called, and I knew that it would happen.

Was I afraid? Was I at any point afraid of the consequences?

That afternoon, I waited for him, watching the low sun turn the fields pink, making a sharp silhouette of the mountains against the navy sky. I was happy then. I opened the door as soon as he set foot on the back porch. I had worn a gray sweater and a black skirt. He did not immediately embrace me, and I knew that he was nervous, too. I took his coat, and, as always, he shrugged off his sport jacket and laid it on the back of the kitchen chair. He seemed to be calm and waiting. The way he had in the tumbled car. The box with the leftover wine was on the floor near the table.

■

"Can you stay?" I asked.

I saw confusion on his face. He put his hands on his hips and looked in the direction of his car, as if he might have important places to go. But I knew that he would stay.

"A cup of tea?" I asked. "A glass of wine?"

"I never say no to a glass of good red."

It was a relief to both of us to have that over with.

He took the bottle from my hands as I went to get the corkscrew. I reached for two glasses from the cupboard. "You knew I'd say yes," he said.

I moved toward the table. I sat down.

He poured the wine, and his hand was steady. I took a sip. When I glanced up at him, I saw that he was smiling at me. It had been a long time since I'd seen such a fond look on any man's face.

"Tell me about the evening," he said.

I could not imagine you, my husband, being interested in the doings of the parent-teacher association. But that is not why I did it. Not at all. I didn't care that you didn't care. It was only that I wanted.

■

My voice quavered when I spoke, and I tried to bring it under control. I had a sudden and frightening impulse to cry. I pressed my lips together to stem the urge. He stood and moved in my direction.

He lifted me up from my chair. I put my hands flat against the front of his shirt. Not to push him away but simply to touch him. He kissed me. I leaned against him.

"The risk for you is tremendous," he said.

"You said that last night."

"I'm saying it again."

"Don't."

"Don't what?"

"Don't talk me out of this."

He kissed me again.

"Are we safe here?" he asked.

"Owen's away, and Silas has practice," I said.

I know now that those six words were the most treacherous of my life. The implied forethought. The planning. The imagining. All confessed. All revealed.

■

He put his hands in my hair and lifted it away from my scalp, surprised by its weight. He held one of my breasts in his hand. I tilted my head, and he kissed my neck.

I pushed away from him. I brought my hair to the front of my sweater and combed it with my fingers. I was thinking: *I can stop this now.*

There, that was the moment I made it happen.

I climbed the stairs, and my skirt swayed against my bare legs. I had shut the door to the bedroom that you and I shared then, but I had forgotten to shut Silas's door. He might have seen Silas's unmade bed, the poster of LeBron James on the wall. I led him to the guest room. I watched him take it in, the double bed covered with the floral-printed quilt, the dresser with the doily my mother had crocheted. I caught a brief glimpse of myself in the mirror over the dresser and straightened my shoulders. I turned and walked behind him and shut the door.

I removed my skirt and sweater. I had on a white slip. I saw for the first time the same want on his face that I knew was on mine. As I moved toward the bed, he took off his clothes.

"I've liked you from the first moment I saw you," he had said on the telephone.

Under the quilt and between the sheets, we moved toward each other. I was still in my slip, and he was in his boxers. I

215

burrowed into his shoulder, glad that he could not see my face. Our legs found their fold, as if we had been long married. We moved slowly at first. He slid the strap of my slip over my shoulder and played with my nipple. The thing that rose up in me was quick and sharp. He touched me between my legs. He moved over me, still touching me, and I reached for him. He may have gasped. Or it might have been on another afternoon that he gasped. Sometimes he would startle me when he entered me, and I would be the one to gasp. He was easy. I was easy.

Afterward, when he lay in a state between waking and sleeping, his arms around my half-clothed body, I would draw the covers up over his shoulders. Sometimes it would be cold in the room. It was September, October, November, before Thanksgiving, and then it was December and then it was January. Through the dormer window, I could see the forest of tree branches, later of limbs with snow on them. In the corner was a sewing machine that had belonged to my mother. I was conscious of time. I was a wife and a mother, acutely aware of when you and Silas would arrive home. Each afternoon that I took him into the guest room, I made sure he was gone before either of you drove into the driveway. I needed time to make the bed, to bathe. I was careful not to get my hair wet lest you wonder why I had felt it necessary to shower in the late afternoon.

There was no end to my treachery. No end. I was aware of want and deception, want always winning out. Though I sometimes thought about his wife, I never asked him a single question. I didn't want him to say her name. Eventually, we would have had to talk about you and his wife, but we ran out of time. Or time ran out on us. Time tripped us up and punished us.

I hear your truck in the driveway. You will come in and see the opened letter on the kitchen table and quickly put it away. I hear your footsteps on the back stoop. I open my mouth and bite down hard on the pillow. I stuff my mouth with the pillow so that you won't hear my scream.

Mike

Later, he thought that he had probably dozed off. He had made well over a dozen visits to Anna's house since the first time they had made love. Sometimes he thought they were the most important days of his life. Yes, he had dozed off, because he remembered being startled awake, as if jolted, by an odd sound.

"Mike," Anna said beside him.

The sound itself had been only a clink, as of keys falling into an ashtray in a distant room, but it had stiffened Anna in his arms. He heard then the suction and resistance of a refrigerator door.

Mike thought that anyone who had ever had a teenager might be familiar with the scene. The boy, having barely noted the presence of the headmaster's car in the driveway, barrels through the kitchen door, drops his keys into the same glass dish he always leaves them in. He opens the fridge, looking for a carton of milk or juice to drink. He is always thirsty right after practice. And although practice was today cut short due to a meeting the coach had to attend, the thirst is still there. Maybe the boy intends to have a shower and then head out to find his girlfriend. Maybe he will have dinner in the dining hall with his friends. With hardly a thought as to where his mother and the headmaster might be—in the living room possibly, going over papers—the boy rounds the corner with an athletic swing and takes the steep stairs two at a time.

Mike listened with dread as Silas peed in the bathroom. He heard the boy run the water in the sink, perhaps to wash the sweat off his face. Mike pictured him in silky basketball shorts and a cotton T-shirt and wondered if he'd hop into the shower. If so, Mike could make his move then. Or possibly this was but a pit stop on Silas's part, and he would be headed out soon.

He didn't know what had given them away. Perhaps it was that the door to the guest room was closed.

"Mom?" Silas called in a tentative voice.

Anna had already pulled her slip over her head. She had tugged on her sweater and wrestled herself into her skirt. Mike saw that she'd forgotten her shoes.

She opened the door to the guest room, stepped out, and shut the door fast, but not before Mike caught the anxious sliver of a face.

Silas's voice was loud. Anna's sought to defuse. Silas asked questions. Anna answered them as best she could. Silas started yelling. Anna tried to stand her ground.

"You're fucking that asshole?" Mike heard Silas cry. *"You're fucking that asshole?"*

A door slammed. Almost immediately, it opened again, its knob cracking against a wall.

"Fuck it! Fuck it! Fuck it!" Silas shouted repeatedly, the sound spiraling down the stairs and out the door until Mike could hear it only through the thin glass of the guest-room window. He listened to the low growl of Silas's engine, the spit of gravel as he sped away.

Mike dressed quickly and stepped onto the landing. The door

to the Quinneys' bedroom was closed. Maybe Mike only imagined the sound of Anna crying, because now he pictured her sitting at the edge of the marital bed with her palms pressed hard against a crocheted coverlet. She is as still as she can make herself. She is hardly breathing.

Owen

Owen sat there, thinking. That girl of his, that Noelle, she called. Owen could hear the worry in her voice. He sat there and he thought, *Maybe they had a row. Silas not eating at home. Going straight up to his room. Maybe they had a tiff.*

After the second call, Owen went up the stairs and knocked on Silas's door. You had to respect their privacy.

Silas didn't answer.

Owen opened the door a crack. Even though it was dark, he could see that his son's eyes were open. Owen said his name. *Silas.*

He didn't answer. Owen stepped inside.

That girl of yours, he said. *She called.*

Silas didn't say anything.

You sick? Owen asked.

Silas said no, but Owen could hear in the word, that one word, that he'd been crying.

Owen let the door open a little to let in some light.

The snot was all over Silas's upper lip, and his eyelids were swollen. Owen said, *I don't understand. Did you have a fight with that girl?*

Owen didn't know why he hadn't said her name. He knew her name. Noelle. He could have said it aloud.

Silas shook his head. He shook it violently, but he was spent, too. He was tired from the crying.

What is it, son? Owen asked. No, he didn't say the word *son*. He wished he had, though.

What is it? Owen asked.

Silas clenched his face, and his mouth wrinkled up into a hole. His eyes went into slits.

Owen watched this happen until Silas's face relaxed. Silas looked over at Owen. *Go away, Dad,* he said. *Just go away.*

Owen knew enough not to interfere with whatever a boy had to get out of his system. If that girl Noelle had broken up with him, he was hurting, and there wasn't anything Owen could do about it. He wasn't any good with advice the way Anna was. Not that any words could have fixed Silas's hurt.

Owen stood too long at the door. He couldn't help, but he wanted to help.

Go away, Silas said again.

The words were still in Owen's ears. Even now.

He shut the door and stood outside it, listening. For what, he didn't know. For something.

Behind Owen, Anna opened the door of their bedroom. He'd thought she was taking a bath, but she was still dressed in the clothes she'd had on at dinner.

Owen, she said.

You know what's wrong? Owen asked, pointing a thumb over his shoulder.

Anna put her hands over her eyes. She started to cry. Owen felt like the only man in the world who didn't understand his family.

We have to talk, Anna said.

Silas

It is getting cold, it is getting so cold. Pretty soon it will be completely dark, but I can make my way down to the barn and sleep there if I have to — if I'm not ready to go into the house. When I wake up in the morning, I will write to you some more, because that is all I can do now — write to you to tell you how much I loved you and still do. It's all I want to say, and if I had not done that terrible thing, you would have heard me say it a thousand times, and probably even more than that because I would have tried very hard to get you to marry me after you got out of college or wherever you went. And I think now that you will play beautiful music and I will never hear it, and that is almost the saddest thing of all, though not really. Maybe one day, I will read about a concert you are giving, and I will sneak in and sit at the back and watch you play, and you won't have to see me or look at my face, I will be so far away. I will just be able to hear the music.

I'm so sorry I didn't answer your calls. Really, really sorry. I know you must have been frantic. But I was just so upset with my mother and that horrible man. I know she told my father, because I could hear the kitchen door slam and the car spin out, and then I could hear her crying in her bedroom, and I thought that the family was all over then, that she had ruined us, that the horrible man had ruined us because he had come into our family like a snake and poisoned everything we had. Now we can never be a family, never, because of what he did and what I did.

If my father ever sees the tape, I can never go home again anyway. There's no way I could ever look him in the eye, or he look me in the eye. I would have to leave the house.

It is getting cold and it is getting dark, and I was stupid because I forgot my gloves, I don't know how I did that, yes I do, I was upset, but I can keep my hands warm in my parka, it's just that I can't write with this pencil for very long without my fingers getting too stiff to write, so I have to keep warming up my hands in my pockets in order to write another sentence. I just ate a PowerBar, so I am not hungry, but I am a little thirsty, and that is another stupid thing I did, I forgot to bring a bottle of water, though if I get thirsty I can just eat some snow.

I wonder what you are doing right now, right this minute, and I hope you are not lying in your bed and crying because I have hurt you so much, and now I have just gotten afraid that you will think that you have to leave school, that the pain and the humiliation will be too much for you, and I just want to tell you—oh God, if I could just tell you this because I just thought of it—please, please don't leave school because of this. Because you have to go to Juilliard or wherever you get in so that you can continue with your music. And this had nothing to do with you, you were not involved, it was something stupid and shameful that I did when I was not thinking, and though I deserve all the punishment I will get, you shouldn't get any punishment at all, even though my hurting you is probably worse than any punishment they will hand out to me. And I will go down the mountain and get the punishment, because I am not afraid of it,

I just wanted to talk to you before I did it, before I had to leave or whatever I have to do, and so I wanted to write this because it feels like I am talking to you. And, oh God, I so wish you were here with me, and I would tell you I was sorry a hundred thousand times, and I would not ask you to look at me or let me touch you or even let me say I love you, I would just tell you how sorry I am that this had to happen to you. And then, I think, maybe you would forgive me, you would look at me, and even though you would be sad, you would believe me when I say how much I love you, and maybe someday you would even lean over and kiss me, just to let me know you forgive me, and stranger things have happened, maybe one day we would even be walking on a street together or walking into a store or sitting across a table from each other and talking, and the thing that tore us apart would be so far in the past that we could hardly remember it, and then one day you would take me into your house and into your bedroom and you would lie down on the bed and I would lie down with you and you would let me make love to you, and I would savor every moment, and it would be nothing like what was on the tape, it would be slow and sacred and everything there was, and I would be so happy.

Noelle

I do not call Silas again. I think that if he wants to talk, he will call me. But I know that something is wrong. His flinging the ball into the stands means either he was so angry he simply couldn't help himself or that he wanted to hurt someone. Silas is too good with the ball not to put it where he wants to. It is not possible that he meant to hurt that woman, so I am confused.

People ask me, in the afternoon: *What happened with Silas?* I shrug. I cannot answer them.

I go to the practice room and try to play the violin. Inside, I am nervous, and the nerves come out in the playing. Fits and stops. Frustration. Impatience. Even the notes themselves sound off, as if there are spaces inside the music.

From time to time, I worry. *Is it all over?* That it is a Saturday and he hasn't called or texted frightens me. But I can't call his home again. I just can't.

No one goes to dinner on a Saturday night, though I am hungry and want to.

We are seniors and no longer go to the dances. I sit in my room and try to read, but the reading is like the music, irritated and full of blank spaces. I read the same page over and over and then I look out the window. The snow is thick and hard-crusted, sparkling where the lights shine on it. My roommate has a boyfriend and has gone to Burlington for the night. I am alone in my room, but I keep the door open because it feels too alone with it shut. From time to time, I check and recheck my cell phone. I plug it into the charger, just to be on the safe side. I check my computer every five minutes. *I could call his home,* I think. *What if he is only sick, with a fever, say, and I'll have worried all this time for nothing?* Maybe that's why he behaved so strangely on the court. Yes, that's it. He is sick, which explains why he went to bed early. I find this explanation so convincing that I start to relax. If Silas is sick, there is no need to worry. Calling will only disturb him.

But then I think: *If I were sick, I would call him. Just to let him know. Wouldn't I?*

A shape with long dark hair moves quickly past my open door. Within seconds, it returns, back-stepping.

"Noelle?" Sherry asks.

"Hey."

"What are you doing here?"

"Reading," I say, holding up the book.

"I thought you'd be with Silas."

"He's sick," I say.

"Really." Sherry bites the inside of her lip.

"Why?" I ask.

227.

"It's just that, I thought I just saw him." I can see that she is regretting having stopped by my room.

"Where?" I ask, sitting up a little straighter.

"I *think* I saw him at the dance, but it might not have been him," she says, trying to backpedal now.

"Silas, at the dance?" I ask. "The dance at the student center?"

"Yeah. I think. But it might not have been him."

I know that she is lying.

"There are a lot of seniors there tonight," she says.

"Why?" I ask.

"Nothing to do. The roads are terrible."

"Weird," I say.

"I gotta go," she says.

I sit like a stone on my bed, the book never moving from my hand. Silas is not sick. He has gone to a dance without me. A dance he normally wouldn't give a second thought to.

Maybe Silas has a new girlfriend.

No, that can't possibly be true.

I stand up and take a quick look at myself in the mirror on the inside of my closet door. There is no time for a shower. I have on an Avery sweatshirt and a pair of jeans I've been wearing for two days. I run a brush through my hair, which immediately stands up as if electrified. Probably it is. The air is dry, and the temperature outside is no higher than twenty degrees. I throw my parka over my sweatshirt and leave my room.

The paths are lit with lantern light, and if I weren't so anxious, I would say it is beautiful outside, the cones of light on the crust, the black sky awash with stars. In the distance, I can see the student center, which can be tricked out to resemble a club, with multiple levels and booths and a dance floor. For a dance, the lighting is dimmed to manufacture an atmosphere, and I am always amazed at the way lighting can transform a place so completely. In the daytime, with the light through the large windows, with the tables covered with books and baseball hats and sugar from powdered doughnuts, the blue and red of the walls and the diamond pattern of the stained carpeting is not just ordinary but ugly, as if a student had been let loose to decorate it. But at night, with the overheads dimmed and tea lights on the tables, it is just possible to believe in romance.

I can hear the music as I approach. The steady beat of the bass. There will be freshman girls at the dance who will think they are at a rave or a Manhattan club and who will be dancing with their hands in the air, some with drinks — Diet Cokes in plastic glasses — to imitate the girls they have seen in the movies.

I wish there was a way to look in but not be seen myself. I want only to know if Silas is there. I make my way past a crowd of underclassmen on the stairs who are running out to smoke or find a real drink or simply pretend to. They move in pods of threes and fours. No freshman girl is ever alone. I feel oddly like a parent checking out a school event — underdressed, older, and worried.

J. Dot and Rob, I spot at once. They are at least a head taller than the other boys, even Silas, who I don't see right away. I am a little surprised to see J. Dot and Rob in the student center. Is it a joke? Were they so bored, it actually seemed like a good idea? Does J. Dot or Rob have a new girlfriend, a sophomore or a junior, and the others have come along for the ride? I push into the crowd. My feet encounter a sticky substance on the carpet I don't want to think about. I look down and then I look up, and that is when I see Silas—dancing, which is odd enough since Silas never dances; and wild, which is nothing but strange. I cock my head this way and that, and then I have a clearer view. He is dancing with a small girl, a pretty, lithe girl who is blond and amazingly agile despite her spike heels. I wonder briefly, in a practical kind of way, how she made it to the student center in shoes I am not sure I could stand up in. Silas is moving against the beat, and the wildness is in his arms and in his low spins. He is a terrible dancer, and if I weren't so startled, I would be mortified for him. He seems half crazed, but I notice that no one is laughing.

I move closer. His skin is glistening with sweat. He swirls, and as he does his eyes skate over mine with no sign of recognition. He has on a green flannel shirt over a T-shirt, a pair of jeans that are wet in the hems. His Timberland boots are muddy. It seems the crowd has parted just to watch Silas, but they haven't really. It is only my own spotlight that shines down upon him. He and the blonde in the high heels never touch, never even look at each other, as far as I can tell. But the girl is in her element, the expression on her face alternating between a sexy dance pout and a flashing white smile. The smile is for show, to impress her friends, who now are standing on the sidelines, cups in hand, taking small sips. Envious. Who wouldn't be? She moves like a dancer in her own universe, her own orbit, only occasionally intersecting with Silas's. Did he ask this girl to dance? Why is he here? Clearly, he is not sick. And if he did come here, why didn't he ask me to join him?

This seems to be a Silas I do not know, just as I didn't know the Silas on the basketball court today. I am afraid of this Silas, this Silas moving like a dervish on the dance floor, no longer in tune with the beat now, a Silas who might become a laughingstock were it not for the ferocity of his movements, the gleam in his eye. Perhaps everyone is fascinated by this new Silas. Perhaps they are waiting for him to fling a ball.

I watch until I can't any longer. Some people have noticed me on the sidelines in my Avery sweatshirt, and I know that within minutes, rumors will begin to circulate. That Silas and I have had a fight. That Silas and I have broken up. That Silas has a new girlfriend, a lithe blonde in impossibly high heels.

I turn and push my way through the crowd. As I do, I wonder: *Did we? Does he?*

Colm

I will agree that the press created a monster. Or the public did. Or, really, the school itself did. One can argue blame indefinitely on this one — though one fact I can't argue with: the press did fan the flames.

I filed my story on Thursday, January 26, so that it would make the Friday morning edition in Boston. My instincts were right about the piece. The editors put it just below the fold on the front page. It was only the second time I'd had a piece on the front page, but that's beside the point. I think I got the description of the tape more or less right, though really, until you actually see the thing, you just can't imagine it. Of course I had to water the hell out of it so that it could be digested over morning toast and coffee. While in Avery, I'd gotten ahold of a copy of the student directory and I'd called students randomly. Amazing how many kids at that point were willing to talk to the press. And the thing about students? They rarely lie. They always exaggerate, and you have to listen carefully for that. But they seldom lie. Not to a reporter, anyway.

I hadn't talked to any of the participating students at that point. I couldn't get near the Quinney family. Rob Leicht wouldn't talk, either. But James Robles later had a lot to say — against the advice of his lawyer, I might add. And I did have one extraordinary, though short, phone conversation with the girl who'd been assaulted. I'd obtained her cell phone number from a classmate, and I called her and got some unusual and rather contradictory quotes from her. I believe I was the only one ever to speak to her directly.

The story dominated the *Globe* for five days running. After that, there were frequent pieces, right up until the first anniversary of the incident. And every time there's a story of a similar nature anywhere, the Avery story is trotted out. There were a lot of editorials as well, particularly about risk and entitlement and alcohol abuse. Bordwin's resignation was a big story. Also the Robleses' civil suit.

I would say that within an hour of my filing the piece, which went online before it hit the streets, every local news affiliate and every Vermont paper was on its way to Avery. By late morning, the big guns were there—CNN, NBC, ABC, CBS, FOX, the *New York Times,* the *Washington Post*—you name it. Everyone wanted a piece of this.

CNN got the first raw footage of the tape, and though they couldn't show much—the faces and all the body parts had to be grayed out—they made a big deal about the ethics of airing the clip in that nauseating, self-congratulatory way that the cables and the networks do. "We're going to show this, even though we've spent all day debating the ethics of doing so, because we feel it's in the best interest of our viewing audience." What a load of bull. Then, trying to take the high ground, they bring out all the ethics experts and a million other experts, who debate everything from alcohol on campus to the definition of *sexual assault* in Vermont to the way the school tried to cover up the crime. Every night, you'd tune in, and there would be the Anderson Coopers and the Brian Williamses camped out in front of the

Avery gates. And if you pay attention to these things, you can see they're all wearing North Face jackets to be like the students.

I held on to the story at the *Globe* for as long as it lasted. I received a Pulitzer for my work on it. I could go on and on about the ethics of accepting a prize for a sordid tale about alcohol abuse, sexual assault, and privilege, but you take a look at any story that's won a prize in the last ten years, and you'll see that a lot of them are built on greed or lust or sex or murder. You tell yourself you're trying to go for a fair and responsible take — unlike the tabloids — but the truth is, we're all tabloids.

In Avery, you could only watch with wonder. Eventually, they had to lock down the school, but during those first couple of days, when the networks were interviewing the students, some of the kids let everyone know what was going on (same thing, by the way, that's going on in the public schools). Can you imagine being a parent and watching the news on national TV and seeing your "Julie" or your "Joshua" going on at length about beer pong or blow jobs?

I had found a place to stay at the Mountain View Motel — same motel, as it happened, that Rob Leicht and his mother were at when Rob was arrested. I don't think Avery had ever seen an onslaught like this before. There were hundreds — and I do mean hundreds — of reporters, newsreaders, cameramen, and tech support looking for rooms. The owner of the motel said later that he'd done the best business of his life that first week (I think I was the only one he didn't jack up the price on). People started renting out rooms in their houses — hell, they rented out whole houses in some cases and went to stay with Aunt Sally or whomever while they raked in the money. More power to them. I know for a fact that one of the female newscasters got a room with a bathroom down the hall that first night and had a fit and had to have a trailer hauled up from New York with a dressing room and a bedroom.

Avery couldn't handle it. There were only two guys on the police force, and their entire job became directing traffic and policing the press. Eventually, when the townspeople realized how the school and the town were being portrayed, they clammed up. Silas Quinney was a local, and a lot of people had feelings for Anna and Owen Quinney. Gary Quinney was Silas's uncle. Richard Sommers and his wife, Sally, who was Owen's sister, ran the only diner in town, a Qwik Stop attached to the Mobil station, and they shut down. Everyone had to send over to the next town for takeout. Some takeout. Pizza, tacos, really bad Chinese. Good cheeses, though. Excellent cheeses.

By the third day, the press was banned from setting foot on the Avery campus, and if you go back to the tapes and look, you'll see that all the shots from then on are done in front of the courthouse across the street, and the Anderson Coopers and the Brian Williamses are dressed in suits and ties. Periodically, someone from the school—at first Geoff Coggeshall, who was asked to be acting headmaster and then finally got the job as headmaster—would come out and issue a statement and take no questions. They were trying for damage control—they had future enrollment, alumni, and the current student body to think about—but the damage had already been done. Eventually, they hired a PR firm from New York, and that firm handled all the queries from then on.

I still have all my notes and a lot of footage. I've been approached by a number of publishers to write a book about the Avery case, and frankly I'm surprised someone else hasn't done it.

Natalie

The town exploded. There's no other word for it. We were in the news ten days running, and even after that there were articles. It was like one of those stories you see about miners who've been trapped and all the town folk are waiting to find out what happened. Or like the story of a bus going over a bridge, taking children with it. We were a town under siege.

Parents swarmed the place, not necessarily to get their kids but to be here, to protect them. You have to serve anyone who enters the dining hall, that's school policy. It's so the parents will feel welcome on parents' weekend or when there are special events, or even if they've just come for a game or a tour. So, during the scandal, there were dozens of parents in the dining halls for meals, and you couldn't charge them. We had no setup for that. We don't even have a cashier. The cooks had to order more beef and pasta and vegetables and milk, and some of the parents, if you can believe it, began to complain about the salad bar, so we had to order more of that stuff. And then, you see, you couldn't tell the parents from the reporters, they were sneaking in, too, before the gates got locked and you had to have a pass to get through. I'd say for three days anyway, we must have served an additional fifty meals at a time to the press.

But that was the least of it. This town hasn't been the same since. George and Jill Marsh moved away for good. They went to stay with Jill's mother up to Ludlow while they rented out their twelve-room house, which happened to be ideally located between the Avery gates and Peet's store. They rented it to CNN and asked a thousand a night, and, God love 'em, they got it, even though the house has seen better days and only had two bathrooms, neither of which I would care to spend any time in. George and Jill raised $20,000 that way, and then one of the CNN technicians took a shine to the house and offered them $150,000 in cash "as is," which they realized was enough to buy themselves a condo in Florida. So they're in Tampa now for good. I thought about renting out our double-wide, but Ebbett wouldn't hear of moving in with my sister, Lily, so that was that. I could've got four hundred a night easy, even if it was a double-wide. The bathrooms are excellent. I make only four hundred a week, and that's before taxes. But no, as I say, Ebbett wouldn't hear of it, so I ask him once in a while, just to get his goat, *Where's my condo?* Which neither of us is ever going to have. But Ebbett, I will say this for him, he had a loyalty to the school, and when they shut the gates, he started calling anyone who was helping the press—even if only renting out to them—a collaborator, like in World War II. And he wasn't the only one. And it's odd, but that kind of split the town in two. It was a division that stuck. It started out, either you were helping the press or you weren't, and even today, Ebbett won't set foot in Bobby Peet's store or speak to Fred Greason, who made a bundle in rentals he couldn't load off on a tourist in October.

People were desperate for beds and meals. The population of Avery—not counting the school—was, last time I looked, just over a thousand souls. At the height of the scandal, Samuel over at the post office reckoned that number had doubled, what with the press and the gawkers and the parents who had come to see what was what. I got no head for math, but I wish someone would've calculated the gross domestic product of Avery for that month.

Greason had it great. He made three sales I'm aware of that were a direct result of the influx of folks. Maybe more, for all I know. As I say, Ebbett and me, we don't socialize with Fred anymore, though I don't hold a grudge like Ebbett does. If I see Fred and his wife in church, I'll say hello like any good Christian.

But even that's the least of it. People took sides. The boys were guilty. The boys were just being boys. The girl was the victim. The girl was asking for it. But nobody, *nobody*, didn't feel sick about Silas. He was one of us, you see, not some rich kid from New York. His family was just making it, like we all were. We were all proud of him. A lot of us would go to the games just to watch him. It was Jill Marsh, by the way, who got hit with the ball.

What Silas was doing there that night, I can't say. And if it wasn't for that cursed tape to prove it, I'd never believe it. Never. It just ripped this town apart. Anna, I haven't seen Anna in town in, oh, more than a year at least. I see Owen, but it isn't the same Owen as before. He's a shell, he is, hollowed out. Big scoops out of his face. Reminds you every time. You'll go days, weeks, forgetting all about the scandal, and then you'll drive by the Quinney farm—well, it ain't no more a farm now than my double-wide—or you'll see Owen at the Mobil station, and you'll remember, and it'll catch you up, and you'll realize how fast, how fast, a life can get all twisted around.

■

Enrollment at the school is down. I got less work at mealtimes. They haven't cut my salary yet, but every once in a while, there's a rumor that it's coming. The cutbacks. They cracked down on the drinking big-time. There's ten chaperones at every dance now, and they've got security cameras mounted on trees — not to keep the kids safe, mind you, but to catch anyone not on the up-and-up. Michael Bordwin, he's long gone, and Mr. Coggeshall, he runs a tight ship. They're always having initiatives. Initiative This and Initiative That. I do think the kids are probably drinking less, though, because it's so damned hard to get the booze anymore. Anyway, attendance at Sunday breakfast is way up, if that's any indication.

J. Dot

Yeah, sometimes I think about Rob and Silas. I wonder why they were there that night. I know I was thinking, *What's Silas doing this for?* Because he had Noelle. But I was thinking that with only half my brain, obviously, because I should have been asking myself the same question. *Why am I doing this?* And the answer is . . . the answer is . . . it was pure sex. No one will say that, but that girl, she was *on fire*. It was a kick. A kick and a thrill. And we were hammered. It was mad fun. It was wild. What can I say?

Why was Silas there? He was in a terrible mood, a dangerous mood all day, I know that. Something had happened at home or with a teacher, I never learned what it was. But he was ripped. I remember him, right in the middle of the game, slinging the ball as hard as he could at the stands. It hit a woman in the face and shocked everybody. The ref threw him out of the game. You probably heard about that. They reported it in the press, like one thing was the cause of the other. Silas left the court, wouldn't talk. Then later that day, when we found him in his car, he was already on his way to oblivion, you could tell. So something happened. And it wasn't about Noelle, because she was just as shocked as the rest of us.

Yeah, we should have talked to him. We should have done

a lot of things. But when you're seventeen, eighteen, you don't think. You're just letting go for a few hours.

Yeah, I was nineteen. Big deal.

She came right for us. She had a plan all along.

What do I think of students and drinking? This is a serious question?

You turn eighteen, you're a grown man. I'm sorry, but you are. If you can get drafted and go to war and kill people, then you ought to be able to drink a goddamn beer. Six beers, if you want to.

Well, I realize the girl shouldn't have been drinking. I don't know where she got it.

Do I think the kids are drinking at Avery, even after all this? Are you shitting me? I mean, you realize we were all already in AA.

That's a joke.

Avery Academy?

Matthew

That Shakespeare shit. Just thinking about it made Matthew furious. "Entitlement." "Pride of Avery." "The flower of youth." "The fortunate son, about to inherit the mantle." Where did they come up with that crap?

It wasn't entitlement, for Christ's sake. It was pride. A sense of invulnerability. Who didn't want that for his son? Obviously, James came from a privileged, educated background. Matthew and Michelle, both working at a college, had shaped the household. They'd never had the television on, for example. James had read voraciously as a boy. His mother might say differently, that she'd had to goad him to read, but once you put a book in his hands, you couldn't tear it away. Homework seemed to be an issue, and Michelle had been a saint about that. James had organizational problems, and Matthew was sorry now that they hadn't had him diagnosed. It was possible that all along James had suffered from a constellation of mild learning disorders.

James owed a great deal to his mother, but Matthew could see that he was aching to escape her, too.

They said James was the ringleader. The press presented him in that light simply because he was the oldest. But that wasn't the way Matthew understood it had happened. Matthew hadn't viewed the tape. He didn't want to. That was private and should have remained private.

Those boys, they felt alive, that's all. You combine that with rampant hormones and a vixen and alcohol, and, Matthew guessed, you had a potent soup that he'd dare any seventeen-year-old boy to resist. Nineteen-year-old boy.

Sienna

I'm wondering if you, like, pay for interviews? It's OK if you don't, except that I felt I had to ask since maybe you do, and I have, like, expenses. Not huge expenses, but my parents wouldn't let me get a job over the summer, they sent me to a camp for the performing arts, which was pretty funny and a whole long story all by itself, but I don't have any, what's the word, petty cash, to buy, you know, stuff I need. So, but that's OK. I understand. You're a student, too, right, even though you're, like, what, a graduate student? I'm kind of curious how you knew my name and where to write to, since my name was never given to the press, but I guess anyone with half a brain could have figured it out just by looking at the class directory the year after and seeing who wasn't there anymore. But you'll just use Sienna, right, because even though this is academic and all, the rule about protecting the victim must still apply, no?

Yeah, I think about Rob and J. Dot and Silas. I try not to, not that I shouldn't. It's just that it's all part of putting this behind me. I think we should probably leave. I've got a class in ten minutes. I wish Silas hadn't been there, hadn't been part of it, but they were all together, and he was just kind of there, and maybe he didn't exactly know what was going down, not that I knew what was going down, either. I thought probably he and Noelle had broken up or something, and he was way out of line and really acting out. Maybe she broke up with him and he was messed up, and I never did find out. So I feel bad, even though he did it, he definitely did it. But it was, like, I have to say, it wasn't Silas. I know it was him, and it was his body, but he was long gone, really wasted, and I wouldn't be at all surprised if when he woke up the next morning, he didn't even remember what happened. I've had blackouts, I know what they're like. You can remember bits and pieces, but you can't put it all together, you know what I mean? And if it hadn't been for the tape, well.

Do you have, like, extensions or something? Because your hair is really thick and pretty. I guess that's a rude question. But everyone's getting them now. I've been thinking about it. I think I could talk my mother into it. I could use a water right now. A bottled water. Are you going right back to Vermont tonight? You just came all this way to interview me in person? 'Cause, you know, we could have done this through e-mail. I'm amazed they gave you the money for the plane fare here. It must be a big study you're doing. Or the University of Vermont must have a lot of money. I won't be applying to college there. I'll never set foot in Vermont again, and besides, UVM has, no offense, a terrible reputation as a party school.

Noelle

On Sunday, I call Silas. His mother says he is sick and can't come to the phone. She says he came home late and he was drunk, and do I know anything about it? There is no scolding in her voice, which surprises me a little bit. Wouldn't she be mad that Silas came home drunk? Instead, she seems almost sad, and if I knew her better, I would ask her why.

He's been throwing up, she says, and I think, *Good.*

Silas doesn't come to school on Monday, which I attribute to a monster hangover and a nice mother.

On Monday night, I pass an open door in my dorm. Three girls I know are sitting around a computer. The one standing girl has her hand covering her mouth, as if she wants to shout out but doesn't. One girl is sitting in front of the computer, and another is crouched beside her. The crouching girl sees me and nearly slams her fist into the arm of the girl in front of the computer, and whatever was on the screen goes off. A home movie, I am almost positive.

The crouching girl looks at me and in an exaggerated manner slowly stands and stretches. She yawns. Her name is Krystal.

"What's up?" I ask.

Krystal says nothing, as if stretching makes her deaf. She

seems to be stretching to the moon. The girl in the desk chair turns to look at me in the door. I have come from the practice room and am carrying my violin. I have my flannel pajama bottoms on, a knit hat on my head.

"Hey, Noelle," the girl says. The girl who had her hand over her mouth puts it in her pocket, but she doesn't turn around. No one answers my question.

There is a long silence while I try to think of another question to ask.

"You guys watching a movie?"

"Just something stupid on the Internet," Krystal says too quickly. "You've been practicing?"

I am suddenly wet with heat under my parka. I pull off my knit hat.

"Yes," I say.

When I see Silas on Tuesday, he is across the quad and he doesn't even acknowledge me. I leave five messages on his phone and text him twice. Even though he is at school, he must be skipping classes, because both Cynthia and Molly say Silas wasn't in class. I wonder if he is going to go to practice, even though he has been suspended for four games. The coach must be beside himself, because no one can get to the basket like Silas, and no one is better at threes.

Early Wednesday morning, I hear that Silas is at the gym. I skip my eight o'clock class and head down there. When I see Silas emerge from the boys' locker room, I stop him.

"We have to talk," I say.

His face is pasty white, and his eyes are red-rimmed. There is an odd smell coming off him, though maybe it's just the smell of unwashed gym clothes.

"I can't," he says.

"I have to do this now," I say.

"I have to get to class. I'm already late."

I stand my ground. I study him.

He moves around the corner. I follow him down a corridor and into a stairwell that almost no one ever uses.

"What's going on?" I ask.

Silas's eyes begin to fill. I am gutted and afraid. I have never seen Silas cry, and it is a terrible thing. He turns away from me.

I know right then that it is all over.

He knows it, too, which is why he is crying.

I wind my arms around my stomach. I want to sit down, but I'm afraid to move. Everything—everything—inside me is praying that I am wrong. That Silas, idiotically, is somehow worried about his basketball career. That maybe someone died that he was close to. I can't believe I am wishing for that, but I am.

Silas takes hold of the metal stair railings and bends his head. He wipes his nose and eyes on his arm. He still has his back to me.

"Are we over?" I ask, begging him to whip around and say no, no, it's not that. And I will take him in my arms and help him. But he doesn't do that. He doesn't move.

"Silas?" I ask.

He raises his head and stares at the ceiling.

A teacher opens the door above us and skirts us on the steps. He's maybe a squash coach, I think.

"Everything OK?" he asks.

I nod, needing him to leave.

He must think we are having a lovers' quarrel. But it is more than that. Much more.

"We have to be," Silas says when the coach is gone.

"We have to be what?" I ask. He still has his back to me.

"Over," he says.

"Over?" I ask.

He doesn't answer me.

"This is it?" I ask, panic closing my throat.

Again, Silas is silent.

"Silas, look at me."

He turns. He doesn't need to say a word. It is all in his face.

"Did I do something?" I ask, my whole body shaking.

"No," he says. "I did something."

"What?" I ask.

What could he have done that means it is all over? I think about the blond girl he was dancing with.

"You've met someone else?"

He pounds his fists against his thighs. He does this again and again. I reach out to stop him from hurting himself, but he jerks away from my touch.

He grits his teeth. His face is a stone mask. He starts to speak and then closes his mouth.

"You will never..." he says.

"I'll never what?" I ask. I am all panic and nothing else.

He wipes his hands over his face. He turns and takes the stairs two at a time. Before I can even call his name, Silas is out the door.

Gary

On the evening of Wednesday, January 25, I returned to the
Quinney household to speak to both Owen and Anna Quinney
about where their son might possibly be. I gave them to understand that my need to speak with Silas was urgent.

Mrs. Quinney was extremely confused and upset but tried hard
to think of where Silas might be. The boy was not answering his
cell phone. His car was not in the driveway. Owen Quinney got
into the cruiser with me, and we made a quick tour of the town
and then drove through the Avery gates. It was in a school parking lot near the gym that Silas's car was located. By this time, it
had begun to snow lightly. It had been snowing off and on for
days. Owen did not have a key, but I was able to gain entry to the
car. In it we found various items of clothing, including a pair of
gym shorts and a practice jersey. We also found his cell phone.

Mr. Quinney suggested that we contact Silas's girlfriend, Noelle,
since she was, in his opinion, closest to Silas. She might know
where he was. Owen Quinney waited in the cruiser while I
entered Foster Hall, where Noelle resides. I was directed to her
room, where I found her in a distraught state. She was with a

friend who was trying to calm her. She said that the last time she had seen Silas was at approximately eight o'clock that morning, and that he had left the gym by the side entrance near the parking lot. He was wearing his gym clothes, she said. I asked her why she was so distressed, and her roommate answered that Silas had broken up with Noelle that morning. I asked Noelle to let me know as soon as she heard from or saw Silas again.

I returned to the cruiser and informed Mr. Quinney of what I had learned. He tried to think of another place Silas might have gone. Using the numbers logged in Silas's cell phone, we called several of his friends on the team, one of whom gave the same answer as Noelle: Silas had been in the gym early in the morning. No one seemed to have seen him after that.

Mr. Quinney and I returned to his house. Although Anna Quinney understood that Silas would be arrested if located, she appeared to be as eager to find him as we were. The snow was thickening, and we knew that the temperature would be below freezing that night. Mrs. Quinney was concerned that without a vehicle, Silas might try to walk home from wherever he was. I then left the Quinney residence with assurances that they would contact me as soon as they had any word from their son.

I made the rounds of the town, stopping at the general store and the Qwik Stop to ascertain if Silas had been seen anywhere near there that afternoon. I drove to Avery Academy and asked security to conduct a thorough search of the school to find the boy. Following that, I returned to the station, where Rob Leicht and

James Robles were in lockup. At 8:30 p.m., Mrs. Ellen Leicht posted bail, and her son was released to her custody. At 9:10 p.m., Matthew Robles appeared at the station and posted bail for his son, and James was released to his custody pending further review of the case. Matthew Robles was particularly upset that a confession had been signed without benefit of legal counsel.

Before I went home for the night, Avery Academy security called to say that a thorough search had been conducted, and they had not found Silas Quinney.

At approximately three o'clock in the morning of Thursday, January 26, Anna Quinney called my house in a state of mild hysteria. She still had not heard from Silas, she said. She had made an inventory of his clothing and had noted that he had taken his parka with him to school that day. He had, however, left his gloves at home. I told her that I would organize a search party at first light.

At 6:30 a.m. I was able to assemble ten men and women from the town who were willing to aid in the search for Silas Quinney. Because Silas had left his car in the gymnasium parking lot, we initiated the search on the grounds immediately adjacent to the gymnasium and spread eastward from there. During the night, we had had nearly four inches of snow. The snow would continue through that day and into the evening.

By three o'clock, we had had no success with our search for Silas. I received a phone call from Owen Quinney saying that he thought we should look around the Quinney farm, in case

Silas was on the property somewhere. I selected four volunteers, and we headed over to the Quinney farm. Anna had to be forcibly detained from joining us on the search party. Owen told her she had to stay by the phone in case Silas called. I think it was at this point that Owen, out of the hearing of his wife, asked me about the possibility of foul play. I told him I thought it highly unlikely.

Using snowshoes for the job, since there were now nearly ten inches of new snow on the ground, we fanned out from the house, trying to locate the boy. After about half an hour, one of the Quinneys' dogs bounded up a hill approximately nine hundred yards from the house and started barking. Owen and I set up the hill, following the dog's tracks.

Owen

This was a path that Owen knew well. He and Silas had often hiked it together — when Silas was a little boy, carrying a branch for a rifle, and then later with a real gun when Owen had taught the boy how to shoot. Owen couldn't see that there was much of a reason for hiking the path otherwise, unless it was to take the dogs for a walk. He was trying to puzzle out why Silas would have come this way. Yes, there had been that barking, but that might have been just dog memory. Owen hated the idea that he and Gary might be losing valuable time looking in the wrong place.

Why would Silas, who knew better, have come up this path while it was snowing? Owen understood his son's desire to get away, but wouldn't he have taken his car instead? Gary had told Owen and Anna that Silas, if found, would be arrested for sexual assault. Owen had been struck dumb when Gary had said that, and he thought that Silas had done the awful thing he had done because of what his mother had done. He wondered if Anna understood that, too. He glanced in her direction, and one look at her told Owen everything he needed to know about that.

He explained to Gary as they trudged up the hill that Silas would know how to survive a snowstorm. He reminded Gary about the Eagle Scouts, and Gary had nodded, keeping to himself. Who knew what Gary was thinking? Over the years, Gary had described some awful scenes that he'd had to come upon, and Owen didn't know if Gary was picturing one of them right now.

The dog turned and bounded back down the hill, leaving Gary and Owen a good quarter mile up the path. Why had the mutt gone down? Could he no longer find a scent? Had he seen a squirrel and started to chase it? Owen knelt and gently brushed away the day's accumulation of snow. He felt something and asked Gary to feel with him. Owen took his gloves off. He could detect the faint outline of a bootprint that had been made in a previous snowfall — maybe yesterday's snowfall — and had crusted over. Gary felt it, too. And Owen knew exactly what the man was thinking when he asked Owen if he would like him to go on alone while Owen waited back at the house. Owen told him no. That's all. No.

Owen estimated that they had probably an hour before it would be too dark to see their way down. Gary said they would go one half hour longer and then turn around. Owen pretended to agree. He had no intention of leaving that path until he had found his boy.

The urgency Owen had felt before increased the farther up the hill they went. He knew the temperature the night before had gone no higher than seventeen degrees Fahrenheit. Though he and Gary didn't speak about it, Owen guessed that Gary had that in mind, too. While Silas could have survived those temperatures overnight by burying himself in whatever he could find, the fact that he hadn't come down made Owen think his son might be injured. Or impaired in some way. Not right in the head.

Owen didn't know how much longer they climbed. He

couldn't remember if they'd passed the half-hour limit they'd agreed upon earlier.

Owen understood at once that the blot of orange against the forest floor was a piece of Silas's parka. As he started his dead run up the hill, Owen prayed that Silas had simply left his jacket in the woods but had gone elsewhere. Or that Silas was there, but he was sleeping. Or that even if Silas was freezing, Owen and Gary could immediately make him warm. Owen didn't like the fact that only a patch of the parka was visible, but when he got closer, he was certain he would see the rest of the jacket and Silas, alive, in it. Owen had all these thoughts in an instant. When he reached the patch of orange, he fell forward, as if that might help him to get to his son faster.

He whipped the snow from Silas's face and from all the stiff crevices of Silas's jacket. Owen had seen frozen things in the woods before—birds and foxes and squirrels—and the stiffness was always a shock. He cried Silas's name and held him to his chest to keep him warm. He rocked back and forth. By the time Gary reached him, Owen was kissing his son's face and weeping. Gary, radio in his hand, knelt beside the body.

Owen's son. His only child, gone. Just yesterday morning, Silas had been alive, eating his breakfast at the kitchen table. If only Owen had thought to look for bootprints yesterday when Gary first came over, Owen would have found Silas and brought him down.

"*Why?*" Owen bellowed into the woods.

Slung between Owen and Gary, Silas weighed a thousand pounds. Owen had lost the strength in his legs. It was as though they walked in slow motion. Even the slipping and sliding seemed strange and unreal. *This can't be happening,* Owen kept saying to himself. Over and over. *This just can't be happening.*

Owen and Gary went down the path carrying Silas. Owen's eyes went to the window in the kitchen, and he could see Anna. Her hands were over her mouth, but the scream was leaking out anyway. Owen had hold of his son, so he couldn't go to his wife. But she came running out in her stocking feet in the snow, her arms outstretched, and she was pumping in the snow to get to them, and Owen and Gary were still slipping and sliding down the steep part of the path at the end. Owen was praying to God to strike him dead right there, because he was only seconds away from seeing his wife's face when she looked at her son.

Gary and Owen brought Silas into the house and put him on the dining room table, and Anna tried to breathe the life back into her boy. Owen knew she believed she could do that, but all the men standing around, you could see on their faces that they knew Silas had been dead for some time and that no amount of breathing, even from a mother, was ever going to bring him back.

Owen thought when Anna finally gave up, she would collapse onto the floor and probably stay there forever, but she did something he would never forget. She kissed Silas's face and then she unzipped his parka, as if he might be uncomfortable in it in the overheated dining room. Owen was standing there, wailing inside, for her and for Silas and for himself, and when she unzipped the jacket, that was when she found the sheaf of papers Silas had been writing while he was up the path. At first, Owen thought they might be Silas's letters to his mother, and he wished so much for that, even though he had every reason in the world to hate Anna. But he knew the letters would help her afterward. But those were letters to Noelle. They weren't so much letters as ramblings. Later, Owen read a page, but then he had to put them aside. They weren't for him, and Silas would not have wanted Owen to see them.

Someone came and took Silas to the funeral home. There had to be an autopsy, they said, because he had died under unnatural circumstances, even though everyone knew he had frozen to death up there on the path. Owen believed that Silas could have gotten down that path, even in the dark, he knew his son well and knew that he could do that. So Owen thought that there had to be some part of Silas that wouldn't walk down that path, that didn't want to come back to his life. And this was the thing that hurt Owen the worst, and he knew the hurt would probably never go away, because Anna and Owen would have forgiven Silas, they would have embraced him, they would have loved him no matter what happened to him after that. And Owen thought that maybe this was something you learned only after the thing you loved most in the world had been taken away from you. What Silas did was nothing compared to the love Anna and Owen would have given him. Owen knew that Silas had hurt a girl, and Silas would have paid dearly for that, but Anna and Owen would always have loved him and held him and breathed life into him until he could stand on his own. They would have done that for their son.

Anna, though, Anna was ruined. She wouldn't leave the house now because she was afraid she would see teenage boys. She had wanted to go to Canada, but Owen couldn't do that. The TV was never on. Anna wouldn't answer the telephone. Owen had

had to tell the newspaper boy not to come around anymore. Owen didn't know exactly what his wife did all day. Sometimes she cried.

Silas died hating his mother. And Anna, she knew that. And there was nothing she could ever do about that.

Anna

Freeze the soil. Kill all the pigs. Let the rafters collapse in the barn.

Slaughter the birthing sheep. Why did we take their lambs?

Where is Silas? Where is my beautiful boy?

Is he in the wind ripping at the corner of the house? In the panes of glass making a soft, bumping sound? Is he trying to come back to me?

How can mail come to the door? How can the telephone ring? Why have the walls not tumbled down?

Why have you stayed with me? Do you owe it to Silas to keep me alive?

How long has it been since one of us said his name aloud?

Sienna

That was really sad about Silas, and I didn't go to the funeral, but I know practically the whole school did, and the town, too, but my parents said it would be a horror show, and you know there were people from town who didn't think I was the victim, especially after Silas, and my mom was worried I might get harassed, so it was no way. But I kind of felt like I should've been there. I did feel it that morning, the morning of the funeral, and I know there were pictures in the paper of the coffin and of people coming out of the church and all. He was Catholic, right? Yeah, he was, and so I felt like I should have been there. To pray or something. I'm not religious, but I could have gone to pay my respects and think about Silas in silence, about how he was a victim, too, even though, like I said, he was there.

I really have to go now, I've kind of missed my class already, but that's OK because I can get my notes from my roommate, and the teacher is pretty lame anyway. So if you need anything else, you could call me, and instead of flying all the way down here, they could maybe use some of the money to pay for the interviews because I feel that I'm giving you good material here, and you've pretty much got an exclusive. But, you know, it's not a big deal or anything. I'm just saying.

Noelle

Ms. Gorzynski comes to get me while I am in my dorm room. She says that I am needed in the administration building. When I walk out into the corridor, fear twists my stomach. I know that Silas has been missing, that there has been a search party. All day, I walked around the campus, visiting all the places we'd ever been together. Ms. Gorzynski says that Mr. Bordwin wants to see me. Get my jacket and boots, she says, and she will walk me across the quad.

I ask her what this is about, and she says that I am not in trouble but that he just wants to talk to me about what has been happening the last several days. I know that she is lying. We walk together, and she keeps up a steady chatter, asking me how I like my classes this semester, what my plans are for next year, have I had any recent concerts, the one she went to was like a dream, and by then we are in the administration building, which I have hardly ever been inside, and we are standing in the doorway of the headmaster's office. Mr. Bordwin stands up. He tries to smile at me, to put me at ease, even knowing that after what he is going to tell me, ease might not be possible for a long, long time. Ms. Gorzynski squeezes my hand as she leaves, and that alone, I think, tells me all I need to know.

■

"Please sit down," Mr. Bordwin says. And I do.

"You're aware that Silas has been missing," he says.

Tears flood my eyes. "Oh God," I say quietly to myself.

"I'm sorry to say that he was found an hour ago. He was..." Mr. Bordwin takes a breath. "Silas has passed away."

"Nooooo," I cry.

Not possible, I am thinking. *Not possible. Not possible.*

"He walked up a path near the back of his house. He may have lost his way in the dark. He spent the night in the woods and froze to death," Mr. Bordwin says.

A series of violent spasms seizes my stomach and chest. I turn and vomit onto the floor. Mr. Bordwin calls for Ms. Gorzynski, who comes running back in with tissues in one hand and a paper towel in the other. She slams the door behind her so that no one else can see.

I can't get my breath. I think that maybe I will die, too.

It is not possible. This is not possible.

Mr. Bordwin holds my shoulders tightly. I bend my head and sob. My body shakes, and Mr. Bordwin tries to hold me upright. "I am so sorry," he says.

He hands me a wad of tissues. I wipe my mouth and blow my nose.

"I wanted to tell you before the news became public," he says, making a tentative move away from me and back to his seat. "I didn't want you finding out from someone else in your dorm tonight. Or seeing it on TV."

I wrap my arms around my head. I want the world to stop, back up. Give me time to enter it yesterday when Silas was walking up the path. Let me go find him and bring him down. Let me go with him and fall asleep, nestled in his arms.

"Where is he?" I ask.

Mr. Bordwin names the funeral home. He says that there will have to be an autopsy.

I open my mouth wide. The image of Silas being cut open is a horror.

"You don't need to know any of this," he says quickly.

"Why will there be an autopsy?" I ask.

"To determine cause of death."

"I thought you said..." But I can't say the words aloud. *Frozen* and *death*.

"That's what they think. But because he died in unusual circumstances... Do you want me to call your parents? To come get you?"

"I need to see Silas's mother," I say.
  "Silas's mother?" Mr. Bordwin asks.

I nod.

"I don't think that's going to be possible... at least not tonight. As you can imagine, she is not doing well."

I imagine. I don't want to imagine.

A picture slips in sideways. Of Silas running away from me up the stairs and out the door. It was the last time I ever saw him. "Oh God," I cry again.

"I'm going to call your parents. You can remain here until they come. I think it would be best for you if you left the campus for the time being. You will need a rest."

"No," I say quite firmly. "I need to be here, near Silas. You don't have to call my parents. I'm fine."

Mr. Bordwin looks skeptical.

"Why did Silas go up the path?" I ask.

"We don't know," Mr. Bordwin says, though it is the only time he looks away from me. "We can only imagine. The last several days would have been extremely difficult for him."

"Silas was in trouble?" I ask.

"Yes, Silas was in trouble," he says.

"What did he do?"

"Now is not the time or the place to go into that," Mr. Bordwin says, and I can see determination on his face, and something else. Bafflement. Fear, maybe. He is surprised that I don't know about Silas and the tape. Which I don't. Not then. Not yet. That will come later, when I am back in the dorm, when my roommate locks our door and comes over to my bed and gets into bed with me and holds me and tells me in what is almost a whisper about Silas and the girl and the tape, and she holds me for hours, during which I discover that it is possible to be angry with someone who has died. It is possible to hate yourself for being angry with someone who has died. It is possible to believe that you will die from grief, that somehow your breathing will catch itself up and simply stop. It is possible to believe that you could have stopped the terrible thing that happened at any time, if only you had known. It is possible to wonder how it is that Silas, who loved you, could have done this to you, could have left you and not said good-bye. It is possible to know, even though you are only seventeen, that your life will never be the same again. Never. No matter what anyone tells you.

I don't want my mother and my father to come to the school. I don't want them to know the terrible thing that Silas did, because they will never understand how good he was and how much I loved him.

Because of the press, there is no wake. But the Quinneys are Catholics, and there must be a funeral. If you have an Avery student ID card, you are allowed into the service. My roommate goes with me, holding tightly on to my hand as we climb the steps to the Catholic church, which I have never been in. All around us are people from the newspapers and the television stations, taking our pictures and calling out to us. When we enter the church, I see the casket at the front. It is closed. I cannot see, but I can hear, Silas's mother crying in the front. My roommate and I sit in the middle of the church, though I insist on being at the aisle end of the pew. I want to be near Silas when they take him out.

I don't remember the service. I don't remember what the priest says. It seems irrelevant. Later I will read bits and pieces in the newspaper. The priest does not mention the scandal in any way. Silas is remembered the way a parent would want to remember him.

At the end of the service, the pallbearers lift the casket, and I know that this is the last time I will ever be close to Silas. They begin their journey down the worn carpet. When they come past my pew, I reach out and touch the wooden casket.

I leave my pew right then and follow him. I see Silas's father behind me. We walk together out the door of the church, Silas leading us.

At the bottom of the steps, Mr. Quinney gives me a sheaf of papers he had tucked inside his overcoat. He gives them to me at the funeral because he says he doesn't imagine that our paths will ever cross again. The papers are folded into quarters and have ruffled edges on them, as if they had been ripped from a notebook. Mr. Quinney is not the sort of man you hug, and so I don't.

I think a lot about whether it is possible to keep a person alive in your thoughts and imaginings. All I have is what I can remember. What I remember is all the doors that Silas and I went through together. This door and that door and this door. The only way I can have them now is to flip through the pages of this diary, and in that way, I suppose, Silas and I can go through doors forever.

Colm

In the days following the death of Silas Quinney due to exposure, the focus of the story made a subtle shift from the guilt of the individual boys to the mismanagement of the case right from the get-go by Avery Academy. A great deal of pressure was brought to bear on the administration of Avery and particularly on Michael Bordwin, who had extracted confessions from two of the boys without benefit of legal counsel.

As for the boys, Robert Leicht and James Robles were charged in Avery District Court with one count each of sexual assault. If convicted, the boys would have been required to register as sex offenders and could have faced up to three years in prison. The parents and their legal counsel wisely chose to have the boys plead guilty to lewd behavior instead. They were ordered by Judge Wycliff to seek counseling and to perform two hundred hours of community service in addition to serving two years' probation. They were not required to register as sex offenders.

I think Robles, as much as I came to dislike him as a human being, has a strong case against Avery regarding the forcing of the confession and his legal rights. The school would be wise to settle before it goes to court. An interesting argument, which was not part of the criminal case but is an integral part of the civil case, is that Robles believes he ought not to have been charged in the first place since he never actually touched the girl. Though he was present in the room, he says he was simply "minding his own business." It's clear from the tape that a *part* of James Robles touched the girl. Depending upon your point of view, either the footage exonerates James Robles or it doesn't. Frankly, I think this particular part of his case is hooey. Though I must say, I would love to be in the courtroom when the Robleses' lawyer presents his case.

Ellen

It is 5:30 in the morning, and you survey the kitchen. It is considerably smaller than the one you used to have and therefore looks more cluttered, or maybe there is actually more clutter than there used to be. You have lost the habit of washing the dishes at night because it seems that after a long day of commuting and working, tidying the sink is more than you can handle. Sometimes Rob, who always goes to bed later than you do, will clean up, and that is a nice surprise in the morning. You can usually tell what your son did the night before by his leavings on the counter and on the kitchen table. There might be an empty Coke can next to a crumpled package of Smartfood Popcorn, or the previous day's newspaper might be folded in such a way as to reveal the TV schedule. Or possibly he will have left the light on in the living room, where his current reading book is splayed open on the hassock. Rob has a part-time job in the library across the street, and three or four times a week he will come home with an armful of books he reads in his generous spare time.

You think that you and he might as well live in different time zones for all the hours that you see each other. When you leave the house to go to work, he is still in bed and will stay there until noon. His job begins at one, on the days he does work, and he is home by eight. You will have left supper for him in the fridge

271

or in the oven, and occasionally he will eat it with you in front of the television or at the kitchen table. You ask him questions, and he answers as best he can, but always you are aware of his impatience with the questions. Sometimes, however, curiosity or simply your own frustration gets the better of you, and you ask if he has met anyone at the library or if he has thought about going back to school or what he plans to do over the weekend.

He doesn't seem ever to meet anyone at the library, he has no concrete plans to go back to school, and he doesn't think far enough ahead to say what he will or won't do on the weekend. It is not that he is impolite or disrespectful. He is over that now, and older, aware that if you and he are to live together, a truce of sorts must be respected. You will go to bed at nine or nine thirty and will read for half an hour before falling asleep. For Rob, his day, his true day, is just beginning. Once in a while, you will hear him leave, taking the car you share out of the driveway, and you will wonder, *Where exactly is he going?* You are not aware of any particular friends he has. Rob comes home, he says, about 4:30 in the morning, an hour before you wake up to begin your day.

There are coffee cups and cereal bowls and plates in the sink. The yellow sponge has something black on it that will have to be investigated. There is a vase of flowers, bought in a flower shop near a place where you work. Several days ago, over the weekend, you carefully cut these flowers and placed them in a short square vase with a flower frog at the bottom. You were happy with the arrangement. It seemed unpretentious and cheerful. Now, however, the water is brown and the flowers need to be thrown out, which you will do in a minute when you have had your second cup of coffee. On the kitchen table is a pile of mail from yesterday and the day before, several magazines that have already shed their ad cards, two discarded wrappers from Weight Watchers Fudge Bars. Three days' worth of newspapers have taken up residence on chairs and at the end of the table. One has been left on a burner on the stove. When you get up, you will remove it.

Arthur left you shortly after Rob was expelled from Avery. It was and wasn't a surprise. You had known it was coming, or you had felt that it might come. What surprised you was the speed with which he did it. As if he blamed you for the scandal itself. You knew that it might be impossible for Arthur and Rob to share the same living space; what you didn't know was that Arthur might not be able to share it with you. The house you had all lived in was sold in the divorce, and you found this apartment in a different town near Boston, a town in which most of the people do not know that you and Rob are in any way connected to the Avery events of two years ago. You have a new job now, in the shoe department of Macy's. Apart from the artificial light, it is not a terrible job, though the commute by public transportation, mainly subway, is arduous and time-consuming. You try to read on the trains, but if the air is stuffy, the jerky movement brings on a mild case of motion sickness. On those days, you just close your eyes and rest.

Arthur has moved to a condo in the South End of Boston. You have never been there, but you gather from Rob, who visits on a regular schedule suggested by the court, that it is fairly spiffy, with exposed brick walls and a balcony. You wonder how it is, if all the moneys were equally divided, that Arthur could afford a condo after the divorce. You thought about having your lawyer look into that, but since you count on Arthur to send child-support payments monthly, which he doesn't really have to do since Rob is twenty now, you thought it best to let things be. You can manage; you can even save a bit each week. You chose to live in this particular town because it is not far from your sisters, who live in adjacent towns, and they have been a help to you. They have adored Rob all his life, and you think, despite the scandal, they still do. They have put the scandal away somewhere, compartmentalized it. The Rob they see when they visit — if they happen to visit when Rob is at home — is the Rob they always knew, though less ambitious. They worry about that, they say. He had so much promise, they add.

You walk over to the fridge, trying to decide what to make for dinner tonight, taking inventory of what is there so that you will know what to shop for, if anything. Sometimes you leave a note on the table for Rob, and he will do the shopping, and maybe today you will do that. You feel more tired than usual, but perhaps it is just the time of year. It is dark out now and will be when you get home from work. You close the fridge and stand over the pile of mail that has been accumulating. You may as well tackle it now, or the pile will simply grow taller and taller, eventually falling over onto the floor.

You separate the envelopes into three piles: junk, bills, and personal. There is always more of the first than the second, much more of the second than the third. Personal letters are rare, though you suppose that is true for everybody. You come to an envelope from the University of Vermont that has been addressed, in ink, to you. For a moment you are confused, thinking that Rob has applied to the university and has neglected to tell you, and they are already asking for money, which would be absolutely fine with you, you would be so happy if he was

274

returning to school, though you are enormously surprised that he would pick a school in the state of Vermont.

You tear open the letter and read it. A researcher wishes to interview you about the events of January 2006. The letter is respectful and assures confidentiality. The interview is for a study of alcohol and male behaviors in secondary schools. The letter is signed *Jacqueline Barnard*. You read the letter a second time to make sure you have not missed anything. When you have finished, you methodically tear the letter up into small pieces and carry the mess to the wastebasket. You will not speak about the scandal. You will not answer anyone's questions. You wonder if your son has received his own letter. You go through the rest of the envelopes and can find nothing addressed to your son from the University of Vermont.

For nearly a year after Rob left Avery, it was a torment to find, in the mail, forwarded brochures from colleges and universities trying to capture Rob's interest. You imagined that his SATs had put him on a list of high-school students to receive such literature. You further imagined that no one had ever looked closely at these lists. If they had, you wonder, would they have sent a brochure to a student who had been expelled from high school, who had pleaded guilty to lewd behavior, and who was nearing the end of the two years of probation he had to serve?

And that is another worry you have. That when Rob is through with his probation and with the necessity to live in the same place and to report regularly to his probation officer, he will leave you and go off. He has never mentioned such a thing, but you worry about it nevertheless. On good days, you imagine he will go to school somewhere. Arthur would pay for it, you are sure of this. On bad days, you are simply afraid you might never see him again.

You walk to the window and look out over the street. Your car is parked in the driveway in its usual spot. You think about your lifelong fantasy to get into the car and drive. You have been thinking about this a lot lately, and you know precisely in what direction northwest is from the window at which you are standing. You have even gone so far as to imagine the journey in detail. You would write Rob a letter, explaining that this is something you have wanted to do for years, that it has nothing to do with him, and that you will be in touch soon. You will withdraw your savings from the bank, pack a small bag, and put it in the backseat of the car. It seems important that you bring as little as possible from your current life with you, though there are mementos that are important to you that might have to go into another suitcase. Or perhaps you will leave these behind to be collected later. You will back the car out of the driveway and turn left and you will take back roads until you are in Upstate New York or Canada. You might, if the urge has not been satisfied, keep on driving. And it is then that your fantasy begins to lose its momentum. You cannot picture the place where you will stop, the motel in which you will stay, the diner at which you will eat. You cannot go so far in this fantasy as to wish upon yourself another job, other commitments. But the urge to get into the car and drive is very great. It is sometimes amazing to you that you have not done this yet.

You turn and glance back at the kitchen. You decide that you will shift into high gear and whip the kitchen into shape before you have to leave for work. You have your shower and dressing timed to the minute and know how long you can remain in the kitchen in order to make it to the subway stop. You take hold of the sponge and turn on the hot water, waiting for it to actually get hot. You stare at the cabinet in front of you, the one that holds the cereal boxes and the salt and pepper and the toothpicks and the can of Pam and the bottle of Extra Strength Tylenol, and wonder how it is that the events of one single night, which might have been lewd or shameful or simply bacchanalian, can change the lives of so many people forever. You can't say for sure about Arthur, but you are pretty certain that you and Rob will never be the same, even if everything works out for him and he does go to school. A single action can cause a life to veer off in a direction it was never meant to go. Falling in love can do that, you think. And so can a wild party. You marvel at the way each has the power to forever alter an individual's compass. And it is the *knowing* that such a thing can so easily happen, as you did not know before, not really, that has fundamentally changed you and your son.

The water is hot and is scalding your fingers. You pour dish soap onto the sponge and try to get the black stuff off.

Mike

He stood with his coat over his arm and his suitcase at his feet, and surveyed the glass box in which he had been living. It was snowing just beyond the windows, the views illuminated by street lanterns, the front lamp of the church across the way, and small squares of interior light shed from the windows of adjacent houses. It looked a bucolic scene, about as close to perfection as Mother Nature and human beings could combine to make. He might have stayed simply for that—to be able to sit and look out and imagine the lives of the people who passed in and out of those cones of light—but he had returned from his truncated walk determined to leave. He had stopped by the front desk to ask if they would make up his bill, and the concierge had been surprised; Mike had booked ahead for another ten days. But Mike knew he had to leave the place where he had come to write: he would no longer be writing anything having to do with the events of January 2006. He had wanted to shed his meager manuscript as soon as he had reentered his room, but then he had worried that one of the staff might take it out and read it, and so he had it in his suitcase, its weight seemingly greater than the suitcase and the rest of its contents.

What was it that he had hoped to find in this room? A letter from a researcher at the University of Vermont had triggered a desire to write about the scandal. Was it possible Mike had sought redemption, simply by writing out a chronology of events? Or had he wished, in some small way, to reconnect with the story, to discover its meaning? Large and terrible things had happened to many people as a result of Mike's affair with Anna. Had it not been for that affair (or had Silas not caught them at it, though Mike thought it unrealistic to imagine it could have gone on without someone catching them), Silas would not have been drinking that Saturday morning, he would not have thrown the ball at Mike during the game, nor would he have gone to J. Dot's that evening. Instead, Silas would have been with Noelle.

Mike had once calculated the carnage. One boy dead. Two boys expelled. Two college opportunities missed. One girl brokenhearted. One girl gone to ground, reinventing herself (or trying to, he had heard). Two divorces. One marriage hollowed out, empty. Two mothers devastated. Another mother numb. A father who had lost both his son and his wife. A school saddled with a bad reputation. A school in its death throes. A town ripped apart. Families not speaking. Townspeople moving away. Had any good come of this? Any at all? And how about the many other students who had been turned down from prestigious schools that year simply because they had come from Avery Academy? There was no way to tell, but Mike guessed the Avery name to be a factor in some of those decisions. He thought, too, of all the students who had been enrolled at the time of the scandal and all the questions they would have had to answer, both to parents and to friends. Their diplomas were foxed at the corners. One couldn't calculate the carnage; it might be endless.

Mike shut the door to his room, checked out at the front desk.

He tipped the relevant staff and made his way to his car, parked in the lot around back. Despite diligent shoveling by the hotel staff and plowing by the town, the snow was coming down faster than they could get rid of it. It occurred to Mike that this might not be the best time to drive to New York City. He would give it a go, he decided. If worst came to worst, he could find another hotel or motel in which to stay until the roads had been cleared. But right now, he had to leave this tourist town.

He made his way through the village and came to an intersection. To the right was New York City. To the left was a road that would take him north, farther into Vermont. He lingered at the intersection until a truck driver behind him honked his horn. Not having consciously planned to do this, Mike quickly made a left turn.

The roads immediately grew worse, less diligently plowed, less traveled upon. Mike knew how to drive in snow; he'd had decades of experience with it, and he'd had his snow tires put on precisely for this journey. If he traveled slowly and didn't brake fast, he would be OK. With any luck, he might find a sander and remain some distance behind that truck. It would take considerably longer to reach his destination, but he had time. His only obligation was to show up for Christmas dinner, nearly two weeks away. Paul, his ex-brother-in-law, who had shown himself to be an unusually decent man, had hinted at a job. He had need of a fund-raiser. Paul was aware of Mike's excellent reputation in that capacity and had suggested they might talk after the Christmas meal. Mike wondered if he would have the courage then to ask about Meg. Despite the half-dozen conversations he and Paul had had, neither had ever mentioned Meg. Mike guessed that Paul had not wanted to open up that hurt for Mike, but

Mike thought that perhaps it was time to discuss his ex-wife. He would like to hear that she was settled, even with another man, even with a child. To know that she was happy and had a child would in some way mitigate his guilt. For he had wronged her nearly as badly as he had wronged Anna and her family. Oddly, Meg had never learned of Mike's affair with Anna. At least he thought she hadn't.

Meg, hearing that Mike had been asked to leave the school because of his alleged complicity in what may have been a cover-up of the scandal, was both appalled and furious. She had been shamed, she said. (Had he remembered to add that particular shame into his calculations of the carnage?) She had left the headmaster's house within hours, not saying good-bye and not informing him of her future whereabouts. Mike had had the distinct impression that she was more than ready to bolt, that she'd been waiting for the right moment, which had handed itself to her and which had provided her with a delicious view from the moral high ground. Mike had not been able to ask Meg not to go. If anything, it spared him from having to tell her about Anna, which would have produced the same result in the end but would have left Meg wounded (he doubted that Meg would have been heartbroken) and further shamed. And what would have been the good of that?

In due time, Mike had left the headmaster's house as well. He, too, was ready to go. What he hadn't liked was the way Coggeshall and his wife had been in the driveway with a car full of clothes and household items. Couldn't the man have waited a decent interval after Mike left to claim the headmaster's house as his own?

So Mike would go to New York City, where he rented a modest

studio apartment on the West Side (its anonymity near perfect), have his Christmas meal with Paul, who now remained his only friend, and perhaps be offered a job, settling the matter of the immediate future. Since the scandal, Mike had been living on his savings, half of which had gone almost immediately to Meg. He still had enough remaining that he might have stayed at that expensive hotel for another month. But then he would have been penniless.

As to the Robleses' civil suit, the accusations had been made against the school as an institution (prudent on the Robleses' part, since the school, despite its troubles, still had deeper pockets than Mike did) and not Mike personally. Still, Mike had been forced to hire a lawyer to protect his own interests. There was that expense to think about, a bill that would come due soon enough. If Paul had a job to offer, Mike would take it.

As Mike neared the village of Avery, his grip on the wheel tightened. The roads were worse, but the real cause of his anxiety was his increasing proximity to a town that had expelled him. He was glad for the snow, for its cover, though some might wonder about the idiot who was out there in the treacherous weather. Others might recognize the maroon Volvo. Mike inched slowly by Peet's grocery store, by Greason's real estate agency, and by the old mill housing, all of which were decorated with Christmas lights, bulbs that would have been strung since Halloween. He passed the courthouse, deliberately avoiding looking at Avery Academy as he went by. He drove past the Mobil station, not wanting to stop there, either.

He made his way along a dark road, the snow a thickening wall before him. When he got to the small farmhouse, he pulled to the opposite side of the street and turned off his lights. He guessed he was sufficiently off the road so as not to scare any car coming at him. He thought of his fateful skid across the black ice. There was no black ice this night, but the unplowed snow could cause a decent skid, albeit a softer and slower one. Rattling just the same. Through the passenger-side window, Mike could just make out a light on in the kitchen, another in an upstairs bedroom. Was anyplace on earth as desolate, as empty, as this wooden shell? Mike felt queasy in his stomach but forced himself once again to take it in. He had made this happen. Silas had contributed, but it was Mike who was to blame. But for him, husband and wife might have tried to make a life together after Silas, even with their terrible loss. But for him, there might not have been that terrible loss at all.

Mike saw a shape in the upstairs window, impossible to make out in the snow. A man? A woman? Mike couldn't tell. Could he or she see the Volvo? There were no streetlights this far from town, nothing to illuminate the car. He studied the shape as one studies a star, trying to identify it. The more he focused, the harder it was to see whoever it was in the window. Once, he blinked, and the shape no longer seemed to be there. He peered but could see nothing. Snow was mounting on the base of the Volvo's side window, making a mountain landscape all its own. In a minute, two minutes, Mike might not be able to see the house at all. In three minutes, he would have to get out and brush the snow off or lower the window to clear it.

I've come to make reparations, Mike wanted to call out.

But who could make reparations for a lost son?

Four times, Mike had wronged Owen. First, by skidding upside down across his land, demolishing his mailbox and fence. Second, by drawing Silas toward Avery, where the behavior on the tape had been made possible. Third, by stealing his wife. And finally, worst of all, by causing a chain of events that took Owen's son from him.

Many times since that fatal moment when Silas had run up the stairs, Mike had wanted to speak to Anna. He hadn't formulated exactly what he would say, but he had wanted, in some way, to express his sorrow, his confusion, his certainty that he had loved her more during those short visits than he had ever loved anyone. He guessed that she might spit at him or claw his eyes out. In his mind, her sorrow had made her powerful. He imagined her wrath more easily than he could remember her face as they moved toward the bed. And it seemed a kind of sin to think about those visits now. He should not be allowed to remember them with any fondness. All visions, all pictures, should have been expelled from his mind.

Mike made a quick U-turn on the road, skidding out only a little. He felt himself hunch his back as he drove toward town. Not out of fear of being hurt but out of cowardice. He might have climbed those steps and sat with Owen. Anna would not have come down, he was certain of that. But perhaps Mike would have been able to offer the most sincere of apologies and laments. Would Owen have cared? Would he have been murderously angry? Or was he unbearably lonely, too?

With trembling hands, Mike made his way along a worsening road. He guessed that another six inches had come down since he had gone into the tavern for his evening meal. There was no evidence that any sanders or plows had yet been out. Perhaps, to save money, they were waiting for the snow to stop before they set out on their runs.

When Mike reached Avery Academy, he stopped his car again,

and this time he got out. The snow immediately grasped at his calves. He did not have boots on, and he felt the ice under his trousers. He drew his gloves out of the pockets of his coat and walked to the locked gates. He had left his hat in the car. The snow fluttered into his eyes and on his face. He peered through the gates to see if he could make out any lights at all. He hoped he wasn't triggering some new security alarm, installed after he left. He hoped he wouldn't see, at any minute, a dozen men running toward him from inside.

Mike turned away from the wrought-iron fence and leaned his back against the solid stone gatepost. When had it been built? He didn't know. The death of Silas was on his shoulders. That is what he would have said to Owen, who would not have denied it. *I caused your son's death.*

He closed his eyes.

He thought about the tape itself, a tape that had been converted hundreds of times now into digital film and stills. He imagined the pixels still out there somewhere, floating in the universe, pixels that had combined in such a way as to cause irrevocable havoc. Sometimes he wondered if what he had witnessed on that tape had been simply rapture or abandon, no more dangerous, in the long view, than a film of kits frolicking or of animals mating. That the tape had horrified him had been true, but he wondered if his horror derived simply from embarrassment mixed with an uncertain knowledge of the consequences (and a certain knowledge that he would be at the center of those consequences). Had he viewed the tape as a private citizen, would his reaction have been as severe? *Possibly,* he thought. There were children on that tape. The girl was only fourteen.

Still, though.

When Mike opened his eyes, he walked back to his car. He would not return to Avery again. Of this, he was certain. He would drive south now to New York City and the small studio that awaited him. When he reached his car, he turned slightly so that he could take in, at a glance, the entirety of the gates of Avery—dark and shuttered and waiting for youth.

Rob

Rob wrote:

Dear Ms. Barnard,

I hope I can add to your knowledge and understanding of the events of 2006. This will be my sole academic contribution of the past two years. I hope one day to make more contributions, but in what area is unclear to me at this time.

I began my senior year in an optimistic frame of mind. Apart from the perks that go with being top dog at any private school, I was anticipating a leading role on an outstanding basketball team. I was also looking forward to taking advanced classes with the best teachers at Avery. Though trying to decide upon and complete the paperwork for the various colleges I would apply to would take a great deal of my time, I was excited about that process as well. I knew I had an unusual academic record that included both highs and lows (the highs marginally more exceptional than the lows), and I was fairly certain I would receive at least one outstanding recommendation. My test scores were also very good. I was hoping to apply "early decision" to Brown University. I had visited the college in the spring and once again in the summer, and I felt that immediate sense of a good fit that my teachers and counselors had spoken of. I particularly liked Brown's lack of a core curriculum. For the first time in my life, I would be able to focus on those areas that were of most interest to me. The day I got the letter from Brown was undeniably an exhilarating one for me and my family.

I was looking forward to my senior year for another reason as well. With each successive year at Avery, students had more freedom. If that meant simply the freedom to get into a day student's car and take a drive to buy a pizza, even that was welcome. There is a tremendous sense of confinement in any private school, and by necessity the rules are strict. But if one has a good reputation and is trusted, the rules can be bent to accommodate. On some days, I felt an almost desperate need to get away. Because I was a boarder, I couldn't have a car, so I would take long walks — through town, along the back roads, and occasionally, on a Sunday, on a hike up the mountains. All my life, I have liked to walk. It seems to be the only time I can really think.

I had known Silas Quinney since junior year, but I met James Robles (J. Dot) the first day of my senior year. I had heard from the coach earlier in the summer that a PG who'd been recruited by Gonzaga was coming. I worried a little bit about being overshadowed, because in general PGs ruled. They set the tone for the social life, and they were usually the stars of the various teams. I know why schools like getting PGs, but in essence these older students ruin it for the students who have been at the school for four years. For one thing, a lesser player who was just on the cusp of making the team as a senior will be, after having put in years on the basketball court in school and town leagues, shut out his final year because a PG has usurped a place that ought to have been his. For another, the PGs, having already been seniors and most having graduated, tended to be cynical about school. They put a damper on school events. They wouldn't, for example, go to school dances or allow themselves to be seen at pep rallies for the football team. School spirit was beneath them. More to the point — or at least more to your point — they tended to have a lot of experience with alcohol and drugs. They knew exactly where to get them. I can't say that without PGs there would have been less alcohol on campus, but the PGs made it more glamorous. They were celebrities of a sort, and it was hard to resist their appeal.

It was particularly hard to resist J. Dot. He was tall and good-looking in a slightly goofy way, and he had an entertaining if vicious sense of humor. He could skewer anyone, especially the faculty, and he did an amazing impression of Bordwin and of Coach Blount. It bordered on heresy to make fun of your own coach, but somehow J. Dot got away with it. The flip side of enjoying that entertainment was the knowledge that as soon as you walked away, you were undoubtedly the target of his two-faced asides. Sometimes, as I was leaving his dorm room, I could feel my shoulders hunch against what felt like tiny darts at the center of my back. And the odd thing is, I truly think J. Dot regarded me as one of his closest friends at Avery. I don't believe he had any understanding of what friendship or trust or loyalty really meant. They didn't register on his radar screen.

Still, I tended to hang out with him. The whole team did, even off-season. There was a definite bond among us.

I liked Silas a lot, though I saw less of him at the end of his junior year and the beginning of his senior, since he was involved with a girl named Noelle. Silas was a good kid. The younger players looked up to him. They feared J. Dot, but they genuinely liked Silas. I'm thinking of guys like Rasheed and Irwin and Jamail and August and Perry, the juniors and sophomores on the team. They watched J. Dot and all his moves, but it was Silas they listened to. I always thought Silas would make a great coach someday. He used to say he wanted to teach high school. I don't think he had a clue what he really wanted to do, only that he *didn't* want to take over his father's farm. He loved the farm, and you could see his pride in it and in his father. But Silas had seen the farm up close, and he didn't want the burden.

On the morning of January 21, I was in the locker room before the Faye game. I'd come in early to tape up my knee, because it had been giving me trouble the day before. I thought I was alone in the locker room, apart from the trainer, whom I'd seen earlier, until I heard, from a corner, what I thought was a beating sound, like someone kicking a locker. I let it go; kids kick lockers all the time. But then I heard what sounded like crying. Angry crying: snorting and cursing under the breath.

I found Silas in the corner, stabbing the bottom of his locker with his foot. His eyes were shut and his head was bent, and he'd been crying. Or he was still crying. His face was wet. After half a minute, I said, "Hey, man, you OK?" He looked up at me, and I'll never forget that look.

It seemed like, for a second or two, he didn't recognize me. And then he said, "Fuck off, Leicht."

That was it. "Fuck off, Leicht."

I left, but I felt confused. I don't think Silas had ever spoken to me like that. He was one of my closest friends. I tried to imagine what could have happened to put him in such a state. Either he had been kicked off the team for reasons I wasn't aware of or his girlfriend had broken up with him. He was usually a pretty steady guy. It took a lot to rattle Silas. Not like J. Dot, who could be placid, almost comatose, one minute, and then frighteningly ramped up the next. I was worried about Silas that morning, and in retrospect, I should have said something to the coach. If I had, the coach might have talked to Silas and helped to calm him down. Everything that happened afterward might not have taken place.

You have undoubtedly heard about what occurred at the game that day. It was reported dozens of times in the press. I'm not sure anyone ever got a satisfactory explanation as to why Silas threw that ball into the stands. I have to believe it had everything to do with why he was crying that morning in the locker room.

I do know one thing, though. When we went out onto the court to warm up before the game, Silas had liquor on his breath. I thought it might have been from the night before, that he'd gotten drunk late into the night and it was still on his breath, but I wasn't sure. I suppose that's another thing I could have alerted the coach about, but that felt, in a way the other hadn't, disloyal to Silas. He'd have been benched. I was counting on the alcohol and whatever else was poisoning him to have worn off by game time. As you know, it didn't.

The locker room was silent after the game. J. Dot came up to me at one point and just looked at me, and I could see the question on his face, and I shrugged, and he said, "I think we should find him." And that surprised me, because J. Dot wasn't the type to care about another person's troubles. I guess what had happened on the court had impressed him.

Though we had dinner first (because we were starving), we bolted our food down and then went on a search. We were fairly certain that whatever had happened involved Noelle, but we didn't want to approach her directly, in case she was in bad shape, too. Neither one of us could remember if she'd been at the game or not. J. Dot put in a cell phone call to her roommate, but she didn't pick up. I called Silas's house, and his father said he hadn't come home yet. I asked him if he'd seen what happened at the game, and he said no, he hadn't been there. And, oddly, he didn't ask me what had happened at the game. He didn't even want to know the score. I began to wonder if what was bothering Silas had happened at home.

We found Silas in the gym parking lot, in his car. He was a mess. It was freezing outside, and he didn't have the car running, because he hadn't wanted to attract attention to himself. J. Dot opened the door, and Silas just stared. He was drunk. Seriously hammered. As soon as he saw J. Dot, he started laughing maniacally at a joke he wasn't going to let us in on. J. Dot pulled him from the vehicle, got the keys from Silas, and locked the car. J. Dot put the keys in his own pocket because obviously he didn't want Silas driving in that condition. "Let's get you inside," J. Dot said.

And that's kind of when the party started.

By eight o'clock, J. Dot's room was filled with guys already getting sloshed. J. Dot had bought the booze earlier in the week in anticipation of a party at a day student's house that had not materialized, and had stashed it in Jamail's Jeep under some old blankets. We'd all gone out to the parking lot one by one with our book bags and had surreptitiously brought the beer in. You would think that any teacher with a brain in his head could have spotted us in a second and known what we were doing, but apparently no one was monitoring the day-student parking lot that night. By early in the evening, we must have had the equivalent of three cases in the room, plus half a dozen bottles of Bacardi. J. Dot had the music pounding, and no one was complaining. Not too many guys had the nerve to knock on J. Dot's door and complain, and I think there was a sense, even among the resident teachers, that something pretty terrible had happened on that court in the afternoon, and maybe we all needed to let off a little steam. Jamail was in the room, and August and Irwin and some other guys.

Naturally, in the way these things go, as soon as everyone had a good buzz on, girls were wanted. Since there weren't any girls in the boys' dorms, that meant finding them elsewhere. Because it was below freezing outside and no one had heard of an off-campus party, that left us with the school dance. The school dances were generally pretty lame, but it was the only place we were ever going to find girls.

I keep thinking: *If it hadn't been cold that night... If a teacher had walked into J. Dot's room... If Silas hadn't thrown the ball into the stands... If the girl hadn't gone straight for J. Dot the minute he walked in the door of the student center . . .*

In the past two years, I have been through every "what if" there could conceivably be.

I feel reluctant saying the girl's real name here, even after two years and even though this is for research purposes only, so I will call her "Sienna," which I understand is the name she goes by now.

We all knew who Sienna was. We'd all known who she was ten minutes after she'd arrived on campus in September. You check out the freshman girls early, you take stock, you talk about them that first week of school, and you form opinions. They were easy to make about her: hot and a little nuts. To be honest, I was surprised J. Dot hadn't gone right for her that first week. You could see she was all about the PGs. But for some reason, and he never said what it was, he didn't. And I can tell you this: I don't believe it was because of the age difference. You might find this incredible, given what happened and the seriousness of the crime, but I don't believe any of us—not J. Dot, not Silas, and certainly not I—gave a single thought to the age difference. We knew there was a disparity, of course, but I think because we were all part of the same community, allowed to attend the same dances, even *encouraged* to attend the same dances, it never occurred to us that one girl might be off-limits while another wasn't. No one slapped our hands if we were dating freshman girls. And, as everyone knows, in most dating relationships of any duration, some form of sex will occur. I once knew of a senior girl who dated a freshman boy. Truthfully, that was a little sad, but again, there was no rule against it.

I don't offer this as an excuse, because there is no excuse for what transpired later that night. None. I have no desire to make excuses for myself or for anyone else. We did what we did. It's just that I find it odd that no one at the school thought to mention to any student that it was actually illegal in the state of Vermont for a senior boy to have intercourse with a freshman girl. It seems that someone might have mentioned that.

At the dance, Sienna went right for J. Dot. J. Dot had been drunk on a Saturday night many times since arriving at Avery, so I can't say exactly what it was that caused him to take her hand, almost as soon as he walked in the door, and lead her out to the center of the dance floor. Was he more drunk than usual? Was he desperate to get laid? Did he find her attractive that night in a way that had eluded him before? There is no denying that she was attractive. She was the definition of *hot*. Pure *hot*. I don't know how else to say this. She had a round face with a pretty smile. Beautiful green eyes. She had thick blond hair that she'd pulled off her face, and it made her look older, more sophisticated that particular night. She was petite and wore high heels, which set her apart from the other girls. Not too many girls in Vermont in January wear heels. She had a great body. Sometimes, even now, I wake up and I find I've been dreaming about her, but the dream is always a nightmare, and I'm always drenched in sweat.

Next to me, I became aware of Silas making his way toward the center of the dance floor. As he went, he was doing this weird dance move, as if he were going to just segue into J. Dot's and Sienna's dance. Though he was quick on his feet, he walked a bit like a bear in a lumbering sort of way, and he wasn't, by any stretch of the word, a good dancer. I started laughing at him. I was pretty drunk myself by that time. I'd been drinking straight Bacardi in J. Dot's room. I'd done Bacardi before, so I knew how fast it could get you sloshed, but I'd just felt like doing it. I'd felt reckless that night. There was something all out about that night in J. Dot's room, and it was starting to show at the student center. There was Silas, and he and J. Dot were dancing with Sienna, and Sienna was really turning it on. She was on cloud nine, because now she had both a senior and a PG falling all over her, or so she thought. J. Dot had this small smile on his face, and you could tell that he was half putting her on, or he was playing some private game and she wasn't getting it. She thought it was all about her. You could tell in the way she was moving. A little wilder. A little wilder still. It was very sexy. And you just knew, you just knew, that if she were in a private room, she'd have been taking her clothes off. This might sound like pure "guy" fantasy, but I don't think so. It's exactly the way it was.

As for Silas, I don't believe he knew whom he was dancing with or where he was. He'd gone over the edge. You had the sense that it wouldn't take much for Silas, laughing his head off, to lose it completely.

I found myself moving toward the center of the room. Overhead there was a strobe, and there were candles on the tables, and it was fairly dark. I was dancing without too many inhibitions, either, and I was loving it. It was like driving very fast away from the school. We were doing this and getting away with it. It was incredible for those few minutes. And had it just been those few minutes, we'd have laughed about it the next morning, and that would have been that. I'm a terrible dancer, and God knows what I looked like that night. But I didn't care. You get to that point, and you know you're making a public ass of yourself, but everyone is laughing, and somehow that seems OK. More than OK. It seems like the greatest time you've ever had in your life.

I do remember being kind of amazed that Mr. Coggeshall, who was chaperoning that night, didn't break it up, or tone it down, or change the music or something, because it was becoming a little too *Lord of the Flies* at one point. There were now five guys dancing with one girl, and it felt tribal. Guttural and tribal. I'm sure there were other girls from time to time, but I don't remember much about them. We were all on the basketball team, we'd spent hours and hours together, and we were letting off steam in a big way. I was expecting Mr. Coggeshall to come over and break it up, even though I knew it was all innocent fun, or some part of me thought it was innocent fun. I had a sense that maybe we were crossing a line somewhere, but since no one came over to us, the line just kept moving farther and farther away. Sometimes there were five of us dancing with her, sometimes two, sometimes one, while the rest of us caught our breath. Sienna never stopped. I don't think she had ever been happier in her life. Seriously. I mean that.

So when was it that we did cross the line? There on the dance floor?

Or when we made our way across the quad to J. Dot's room, laughing and calling out and falling all over one another? Or when we crowded into his room and started tucking into the beer and the Bacardi again? Or when J. Dot put on the music with the slow bass?

The beat was mesmerizing.

I remember that Sienna started moving to the beat, a beer in her hand, as if she were in a world of her own, just slowly turning this way and that, and moving her hips to the music, and little by little the raucous laughter started to die down, and we were all just watching her. She was the music, she was the beat. Her whole little body had become this pure animal thing. She might have been dancing alone in her room. She didn't look at any of us, even as she seemed to be looking at all of us. There was no smile on her face. If it was a performance, it was an incredible one. I don't think anyone in the room had ever seen anything like it. She was in this light-blue halter top with these tight jeans. The heels and her little jacket were gone already. And you just knew. Looking at her, you just knew.

It grew quieter in the room, so that after a while there was only the low bass and this girl, this utterly beautiful female creature, seemingly unaware of us all, moving slowly with the music.

I could hear the door open and close. Jamail and August left.

I have asked myself a hundred thousand times why I didn't leave the room with them. But I already know the answer. Nothing—nothing—could have induced me to leave that room right then. That room was where it was happening. Everything you had ever read about or dreamed about or heard about was in that room. To walk away from that was to never have it again. Ever. Your life would pick up where you'd left off, but you would never even come close to an experience like this one. The stars were aligned. Circumstances had conspired.

J. Dot picked up a movie camera.

It was a secondhand camera from his parents, and he used it from time to time, usually to put movies of himself on YouTube. Everyone, it seemed, was photographing themselves that year. I'm not sure why. To beef up their Facebook pages? To get their fifteen seconds of fame? To document every exploit, legal or not? I don't know that it was J. Dot who posted the tape on the Internet, but I'm guessing that it was. He'd already learned how to do that, and he might have known how to blur the faces. I can imagine him thinking it would be a kick. He was like that. Pushing everything to the edge. Taking risks.

I was aware that he had the camera in his hand. At the time, though, it all seemed like just one more piece of this outrageous and extraordinary experience. I wasn't thinking about the consequences. Obviously.

The section of tape, the one that apparently no one ever saw, and I can't say what happened to it, was just of Sienna. Dancing. We watched as she untied her halter top at the neck. The blue cloth fell to reveal her breasts. They were beautiful and firm and rounded like her face. You knew at that moment that you were in it for good; there was no leaving the room then. We watched, all of us, in fascination as she did a striptease. No, it wasn't a striptease, because that implies she was trying to tease us. It was actually something quite beautiful—something you might witness through an open window, the girl having no awareness of anyone around her, just moving a little bit to the music and undressing herself. It was lovely. It was very lovely. This small lithe girl who had something inside her none of us had ever seen: elegance and poise and beauty. Real beauty, not just the surface kind. I have never seen anyone more beautiful than she was in those moments. I'm not sure I ever will again.

We were all seduced, rooted to the spot. It was group seduction of the most powerful kind. I don't believe any one of us could have left the room. Not J. Dot, with his cynicism. Not Silas, with his girlfriend waiting. And not Irwin, to whom J. Dot had given the camera.

I don't know why J. Dot gave the camera to Irwin. Did he guess that Irwin, because he was black, would not participate? Did he not *want* Irwin to participate? Or was it because Irwin happened to be standing right beside J. Dot at the moment J. Dot decided he wanted to enter the tableau? I don't know. I do know, however, that no one ever gave up Irwin's name. We didn't give up Irwin's name *because* he was black, and we knew instinctively that if any one of us had said Irwin's name, all the shit would have rained down on his head. The media would have distorted the entire event. "Black Student Forces White Girl to Dance Naked." If we didn't have those precise thoughts, we felt them in our bones. It's the only thing we did right during that whole putrid scandal. We didn't give up Irwin. Even Sienna, amazingly, given the lies she told afterward, never said his name.

And it was right that Irwin didn't come forward. I never begrudged him that. Why should he have? It would have ruined his life, too, and what would have been the point of that?

J. Dot took off his clothes. Silas also took off his clothes. Later, I took off my clothes. I am guessing that you have seen the tape. I am guessing that I don't have to describe to you what happened next.

Afterward, for about two or three minutes, we all just lay on the floor. And then reality came screaming in. I remember that J. Dot went back over to his bed and lay down and pulled the covers up. Irwin put the camera down, opened the door, and quietly walked out. Sienna put her clothes on real quick, stood, and slipped on her shoes. I remember that as she left the room, she turned and blew us a kiss. It seemed so wrong, so hideously wrong of her to do that. This wasn't an event that you walk away from and just blow a kiss. Walk away from and shut the door and never speak of it? OK, I understand that. But blow a kiss? As if we might meet up next Saturday and do the whole thing again?

By then, Silas was puking into the wastebasket. Terrible heaving, choking puking. I got dressed and went over to him and put my hand on his back, and he flailed his arm around and said, "Get the fuck outta here."

"Silas," I said.

He turned around and squinted his eyes into an expression of pure hatred. It was a terrifying expression. And then he started heaving again into the bucket. J. Dot had passed out. I later thought he must have been pretending, because he would have had to check in with his dorm parent at curfew.

I left the room.

It was both the stupidest and the worst thing I've ever done in my life. Worse than what I had just done minutes earlier. I'd left one guy on a bed who might be, for all I knew, comatose, and he might not wake up. I'd left Silas, my good friend, heaving into a bucket. For all I knew, he could pass out and choke on his vomit. And as for stupid, I'd left the camera on the bureau, where Irwin had set it down.

I was already in my dorm, in my bed, before I realized that the camera was still on top of the bureau. I tried to call J. Dot on his cell phone. He didn't answer. I was feeling nauseated by then, and I didn't think I could make it across the quad back to J. Dot's room. I figured I would call him in the morning, or he would wake up, find the camera, and destroy the tape. The room was spinning, and I was feeling sick to my stomach, and suddenly I had this tight feeling at the back of my throat, and I knew that I was going to hurl. I couldn't make it to the bathroom in time, so I let go over the side of the bed. My roommate woke up, and he just freaked out. "What are you doing?" he cried. He made me get up and find a mop and a bucket right there and clean it up. I spent the rest of the night huddled on the floor of the bathroom with my quilt wrapped around me. I don't think I slept a single hour that night.

And as bad as that was, it was nothing compared to what

lay ahead. The worst moment of my life was not when I discovered there was footage from that night on the Internet. It was not when Headmaster Bordwin called me in and told me he had the original tape. It was not the moment my mother walked into the conference room and I was sitting in the corner, and I had to look up at her. It was not even the knock on the motel door with the police outside, ready to arrest me. No, the worst moment of my life was the moment Mr. Taylor came to the motel and knocked on the door and had me sit down and told me that Silas had been found.

Nothing will ever erase that moment.

I have thought long and hard about why we did it, but I think the *why* was in the act itself. It was an act without a why.

That isn't an excuse, either. It is simply what I believe.

Though I don't believe there was a why, I know that it was wrong. It was immoral. It may even have been criminal. And the consequences of that one night have been catastrophic. In the beginning, when I had thoughts of Silas and his parents and Noelle, I wanted to climb that path myself and stay there until I, too, froze to death.

My parents got divorced shortly after the scandal. I knew they did not have a good marriage, but I thought that perhaps it was getting better my last year of school. Or at least I hoped it was. When my mother visited in the fall, she had seemed happier. But maybe it was only because she was with me.

I see the concern on her face every day. She worries about me constantly, and I hate that. I just hate it that she has to worry so much. I know that it would be better for us both if we could live separately, and shortly we will be able to do that. I spend a lot of time on the Internet looking for programs that do community service. Not fake community service, like the two-week programs kids do just to write about on their college essays or the Mickey Mouse community service I had to do for my probation: teach basketball clinics in surrounding towns. Some punishment. No, I am speaking of a longtime commitment. I have found one program in Uganda that is focused on building a medical clinic, and I have been in touch with Doctors Without Borders about a vaccination program in Thailand. I need to get away. Although this isn't literally true, it is as though I have spent the last two years in a locked building, unable to take a walk. If it were the old days and young men did such things, I would probably ship out with the merchant marines. I have been reading a lot of Eugene O'Neill lately. The day after my probation is finished, I will talk to my mother and I will leave.

I don't believe I have ruined my mother's life. If I did, I wouldn't leave her. She wants to go, too. I can feel it.

Though many people might assume this, I do not believe I have ruined my own life, either. I have had a great deal of time to think in the two years since I was expelled from Avery. I have read a lot as well. I think that though I will never be the same, my life is not destroyed. Perhaps it is better that I was pushed off the track or that I stepped off the track—and possibly it was a desire to do just that that prompted me to remain in that room—because I am a different person now. I cannot go along the path that everyone else in my generation will go on. I will have to find my own.

Truthfully, I don't think anyone's life was ruined. Not J. Dot's and I hope not Sienna's. Maybe Mr. and Mrs. Quinney's. Yes, I think their lives were ruined. But as for the rest of us, we'll get by.

To answer your last question, I believe that alcohol made it happen, but the "it" was inside of us.

I hope this helps you with your research.

Sincerely,
Robert Leicht